GHOST MOB

Lock Down Publications and Ca$h
Presents
Ghost Mob
A Novel by *Stilloan Robinson*

Ghost Mob

Lock Down Publications
P.O. Box 944
Stockbridge, Ga 30281
www.lockdownpublications.com

Copyright 2021 by Stilloan Robinson
Ghost Mob

First Edition January 2021
Printed in the United States of America

This is a work of fiction. Names, characters, places, and incidents either are products of the author's imagination or are used fictitiously. Any similarity to actual events or locales or persons, living or dead, is entirely coincidental.

Lock Down Publications
Like our page on Facebook: Lock Down Publications @
www.facebook.com/lockdownpublications.ldp
Cover design and layout by: **Dynasty Cover Me**
Book interior design by: **Shawn Walker**
Edited by: **Lashonda Johnson**

Stay Connected with Us!

Text **LOCKDOWN** to 22828 to stay up-to-date with new releases, sneak peaks, contests and more…

Thank you!

Submission Guideline.

Submit the first three chapters of your completed manuscript to ldpsubmissions@gmail.com, subject line: Your book's title. The manuscript must be in a .doc file and sent as an attachment. Document should be in Times New Roman, double spaced and in size 12 font. Also, provide your synopsis and full contact information. If sending multiple submissions, they must each be in a separate email.

Have a story but no way to send it electronically? You can still submit to LDP/Ca$h Presents. Send in the first three chapters, written or typed, of your completed manuscript to:

LDP: Submissions Dept
P.O. Box 944
Stockbridge, Ga 30281

DO NOT send original manuscript. Must be a duplicate.

Provide your synopsis and a cover letter containing your full contact information.

Thanks for considering LDP and Ca$h Presents.

Stilloan Robinson

Chapter 1

Charlotte, North Carolina: 1995

Blood was everywhere in the living room, ten-year-old Kasper stood over the dying body of Ishmad Mudina, immolated for falsifying prophecies in the Vodou cult. He gripped the floor like he was trying to climb it, as blood flowed freely from the knife wounds to his chest and stomach. The man was not going to make it.

"Uy tanon a tefarp," Kasper hissed. The man's death was ordered sanctioned by the Amudakies.

"Os uan uyid," the boy was speaking the Krepesk language, pretty much telling the false prophet that he was not at all a prophet and had to die for claiming to be so.

Outside breaks squeaked, Kasper craned his neck to look out of the open blinds. A dark-colored Sedan was parking in the driveway. Kasper thought it may have been his wife.

Kasper dashed out the back door, though the night provided an additional layer of disguise, Kasper vanished into the darkness for home. The boy entered his home through the back door, turning immediately to lock it. When he turned around his great-aunt Jean was right there with her hands on her hips and long dreads wrapped in a Kerchief. Kasper looked at the women he called his 'Grammy' and slowly pulled off his hood revealing cold, grey eyes that glinted against the contrast of his dark brown-skinned complexion, and two long braids poured down to his chest.

Aunt Jean put a hand out for the bloody knife. When Kasper gave it up, she threw her head to the side telling Kasper in their French vernacular to go shower. Before she let him move past her Aunt Jean grabbed Kasper by the arm. "Take your clothes off so I can burn them."

Kasper got naked without protest. The basement at the bottom of the two-story home served as Kasper's bedroom. His necessities consisted of a big-screen TV, a desk, a collection of remote-control cars and air pistols. There was a heap of Michael Jordan posters, an

autographed home Jersey of the icon hung there in a frame above the boys King size bed that only sat on its box spring.

"Turn my radio on," Kasper said to himself and played a *Bone Thugs N Harmony* tape, '*Thuggish Ruggish Bone*' was the choice song. He stood in his full-length mirror, with a towel around his body, and braided two braids back into his hair before going to bed. He had taken them out earlier to wash his hair.

The next night Kasper wandered through the woods. He waved away a cloud of mosquitos that bumped into his face. Kasper was looking around as if he was in search of something. "May-Day, that's my word dog I ain't set you up!"

Kasper stopped in a quick jerk. That's when he noticed May-Day and Dreon talking to Rico in the path twenty yards away. He snuck closer so he could get a better view, hanging in the shadows like comfortable old coats.

"Nigga soon as I pulled up the niggaz rushed me and whipped out," May-Day was saying, "And told me to give the fo' ounce up!"

Kasper lowered his eyes to a gun in Dreon's hand. His grip on it expressed the primal urgency of possession. The boy's thin lips pushed his cheeks back into deep wrinkles as a smile took shape on his face.

"How da fuck dey know I had fo eggs on me and I was comin' to serve you?"

"Dreon, you know me bra," Rico stated his voice full and resonant.

Dreon said, "Tha hell you talkin' to me fo?"

Then Rico said to May-Day, "Bra, that's some bullshit,"

"Yeah, it is, Dreon pop this nigga."

"Nah, man, com' on." Rico thrust out his hands like a cartoon sleepwalker, as Dreon pulled up his gun and the bullet penetrated Rico's head. Kasper watched as both Dreon and May-Day ran down the path, Dreon was holding up his sagging pants. The boy extended from the shadows and moved over to Rico's body. Right then Rico's naked soul sat up, pressing his hands to the ground, and stood to its full height, with its eyes snagging on what was once his body. The soul then looked to Kasper who was watching Rico's reaction.

"Lil' Kasper, you can see me?"

"Yeah, I can see you," Kasper replied before squatting to inventory Rico's pockets.

"Go get me some help lil' cuz please!" Rico's soul pleaded. Kasper ignored Rico's soul's request for relief as he pulled the money. The boy secreted that into his own pocket.

"You gon' steal from me, Lil' Kasper?"

Going into the other pocket Kasper said, "What choo gon' do widdit?" Kasper found some weed but dropped it deciding that he didn't want it.

"Man go get me some help, lil cuz, please. Goddamn!"

While lifting Rico's shirt, Kasper said, "You awready rose out cho boy, it's too late." He looked up at Rico's soul and his eyebrows took the graceful arch of a raptor's wing in flight. "You had a gun on you, yet you let Dreon kill you?"

"Lil cuz go get me some help please!"

Kasper took the gun, stood and said, "You dead." Then he walked off.

Rico's soul followed Kasper. "Please call the ambulance!"

"You done rose up out cho body," The boy replied again while moving ahead of Rico's soul. Then thinking about it, he stopped and turned around. "Dreon shot choo and you had a gun." He turned and continued.

"Tell my people who shot me, so they will know and get me some help!"

"I ain't no snitch dog."

"Please," the soul begged.

Kasper stopped and turned to the soul again. "Stop following me, man. Tha Shrac Klupenjnx 'bout to come get choo anyway." The boy moved on.

"Tha who?"

"Man," was all Kasper could say.

"Don't do me—" Rico's words were cut short when the Shrac Klupenjnx, pronounced Shrack cloo-penz, appeared from nowhere, it was 7'9", Ebony complexion, with long dreads that hung freely at the waist, curly goatee that was a foot long, glistening slits like

gleaming diamonds for its eyes, the Shrac Klupenjnx was the gate-keeper for Empyreon, the place where the souls of black people went. The Shrac Klupenjnx wore a full-length black fur coat, gloves and long pointed slippers of emeralds. It grabbed Rico's soul by the arm as it cried out with subtle resistance and vanished. Gone. Kasper paid this visit no mind, he'd seen it before and didn't care.

Down in his room, Kasper held his image at gunpoint in the full-length mirror sayin'. "Want meda shoot cho ass nigga?" Then he imitated a gunshot and the gun recoiled saying, "Pow!" He looked at his gun and said, "Yeah, I got me a real gun now." Then Kasper remembered something because he said, "Oh my money." The boy pulled out the money he had gotten off Rico, went and plopped down on the bed laying the gun beside him and looked at his prize. The money was in tens, twenties, fifties and hundreds. He peeled off a fifty and a hundred for himself.

Mother Eba, who was Kasper's grandmother, and Aunt Jean, her sister were up in the living room watching a recording of a ceremony ritual that had taken place in Port Novo, Benin West Africa. The two sisters were from high ranks in the Vodou worship. Their disciples were so vast in numbers that they had to issue invitations to different ceremonies as active high-ranking members. Not only were the two sisters high ranked they had their own Vodou line called Kiejkle Douve, which uses the practice of magic.

The Port Novo Ceremony was a ceremony aligned to them. In the 1930s the two along with three brothers, their mother and father fled Conakry, Guinea West Africa and landed in Belle Ansa, Haiti where they picked up the voodoo worship. Their brothers later passed, followed by their parents, Mother Eda and Aunt Jean had run out of Haiti along with their children and husbands. Aunt Jean's husband had been killed in the process by the Tonton Maecoutes where they ended up in America.

Kasper laid the money on the coffee table. He made it back to the threshold where it led back down to his room. "Where you get this money?" Aunt Jean asked in French this was the dialect she chose to speak to family in though she knew English. She still had her eyes glued to the TV when she asked.

"I was in the woods when a nigga got kilt," was what the young boy said never turning around. "And went into his pockets, I found that and a gun." Kasper waited for a comment. When none came he said, "I'm keepin' the gun." Then he moved down the steps.

Stilloan Robinson

Chapter 2

Stacey was a hustler who would sit on her platform in the uptown Piedmont Courts projects all day selling weed. She'd moved to the projects only recently. After four years of boxing in the Golden Gloves Division Stacey took a much-needed hiatus. It was ironic because people told her she was a *Laila Ali* triplet. That's was because she had a twin named Kacey who was attending Military School in West Point Virginia. Stacey was average in body shape she wasn't too thick she was just right, she has a pretty, caramel complexion, hazel brown eyes, long hair she keeps strangled into a bun, she stands 5'6 and a half, and was only nineteen-years-old waiting on a birthday to come.

"Sup Big, Susta?"

Kasper came in through Stacey's screen door. She looked up from filing her nails while sitting on the couch. The TV was on her favorite show *Beverly Hills 90210*.

"You," Stacey replied and went back to filing. "Lock that do fo' me, Phat-Man," she said calling Kasper by a nickname she had given him when he was a toddler. Kasper was a plump boy back then but somehow he lost it when he turned three. The name was just something that always stuck.

"And who dropped you off?"

"Aunt Yazette," Kasper said. "Aye look." He showed the gun with his tongue out, smiling like a dog in a cartoon.

"Thess not real."

Kasper steered the gun to the ceiling. "Wan me da shoot it?"

"Yeah, so I can whoop yo' lil' ass," Stacey said, and Kasper chuckled. "Let me see it."

"Iss mine," Kasper said before he gave it up.

"Nigga shut up fo' I make it mine." Stacey sized the gun up. "P97" she read then turned the gun this way and that.

"What choo want fo' this gun?"

"I keepenit,"

"I'll give you a few dollaz fo' it."

"I said I'm keepenit!"

"Nigga, who tha hell you talkin' to?" Stacey said and Kasper chuckled. "You, betta sit cho' ass down or I'll keep this shit."

"Man, gid back." Kasper reached for it.

Stacey sucked her teeth, drew the gun back and said, "You ain't gon' take it," she teased.

"You on't giv' it back—"

"Wha?" Stacey smiled showing pretty white teeth like Kasper was her dentist. "Huh?"

"Come on man gid here."

"Here." Stacey thrust it toward her baby brother. "How you get that gun?"

Kasper told his sister the story.

She said, "He tried to follow you?"

"Yeah."

"He went out like a sucka," Stacey said

"I soulda kept his weed for ya."

"Nigga, I. Did. Not. Need. His. Weed. I got my own shit, and boy you took that gun to school?"

"It was in my bookbag."

Stacey shook her head and went back to filing her nails. "You bet not let Kandy know you got that gun. She gon' beat choo ova tha head for it."

"She ain't gon' do nut'n."

"Don't make me tell ha you talkin' shit," Stacey said, then Kasper went and sat down quietly. "I thought so."

Mike-Shine had picked his son up from Starmount elementary school in his '94 Cadillac Eldorado the following day.

"Sup lil' Man?" Mike-Shine asked when his boy Kasper got in. Mike-Shine was a hustler from Philadelphia whose drug ring was slowly crumbling because people were getting killed or locked up.

"You do good up in there today?" he asked as he pulled off.

"Man, my teacher said she gon' make me do extra work cuz I be talkin' during class."

"Well, son you gotta stop talking and listen. But check this out, young boy—I gotta run over here to get wit' Cam right quick. I'ma just pull up and holla et 'im. I ain't gonna be long et all."

Mike-Shine pulled into his homeboy's driveway in the Westside community called Clanton Park.

"Hold on, baby boy," Mike-Shine said as he threw the car in park and got out. Cam was looking under the hood of his Buick Roadmaster looking at the engine.

"Okay, Sup Mike-Shine?"

"What's goin' on?"

"You tell me." They slapped five.

"Yo' I gotta go up DC to pick up some work, so I need you to roll wit' me and hold me down."

"Oh, yeah?" Cam's thoughts began rioting. He was not directly Mike-Shine's inner circle, he was only just around it.

"Where Skip?"

"Skip? He had other business."

"A'ight yeah, yes I'll roll witcha," Cam said.

"Yo, I'ma pull up at eight sharp."

"That'll work, I'll be ready." Cam looked down at his motor and said, "I don't know what's wrong wit' him."

Mike-Shine tapped the side of the car and said, "We'll get that taken care of. I got my boy in the car, eight sharp."

Cam was outside waiting on Mike-Shine to pull up, and as he said eight sharp, he turned his explorer into the driveway. The two men were on the road to D.C. It was 2:19 a.m. when they arrived. Mike-Shine pulled up to a dilapidated house on K Street after he called his connect. A tall, burly man came out of the house with a rucksack as somebody else stood on the porch.

Cam said, "That's yo' people?"

Mike-Shine didn't answer. He got out with a mesh bag stuffed with cash in the amount of two hundred and twenty-two thousand dollars.

"Mike-Shine what's up?"

"Sup, Yah-Yah?"

"Nothing much, Champ." Yah-Yah gave over the rucksack as Mike-Shine gave up the Mesh bag, both men were participating in the market of the drug-trade.

"Seven kilos," Yah-Yah said.

"Everything everything."

"A'ight." Yah-Yah slapped five with Mike-Shine before he got back to the car. When Mike-Shine got in he slung the sack into the back seat. He'd gotten him and Cam back to Charlotte.

Cam said, "Swing by this chick's spot right fast so I can try da get tha car."

Mike-Shine had pulled into the driveway Cam led him to.

"Don't even look like nobody stay here homie," Mike-Shine said.

Cam fired his gun over at Mike-Shine shooting him seven times, killing him. He went around to the driver's side, pulled Mike's body out and got in, then took off with the drugs.

Michael's death was devastating to his family. No one had seen Kasper. He had not been in front of the school when his aunt Yazette arrived to pick him up. It was night and the family was worried sick.

Kasper traversed through the immaculate forest that smelled of licorice. The foliage looked as though it was from a brilliant Michael Angelo painting. Trees stood at two thousand plus feet. The trunks were as big and round as an elephant's body, with coils of vines that had bundles of small yellow berries draped on them. You could see the mountain island of the trouge in the far-off distance to the left. Bushes of sweet fruit that resembled peaches were the source of the sweet licorice smell. The shinnig sun gave off a reddish color.

His hair was down making Kasper look like he had a thick mane. He was distressed by the death of his father. The boy had not been home in days. A sound behind Kasper drew his attention. Fifteen yards away was Golden Bluse and its young eating on the sweet contuse.

The Golden Bluse was a buck like animal that was albino in color, with antlers and real gold tips on them. Kasper did not see or hear a figure appear out of thin air before him.

"My child," an accented voice spoke.

Kasper turned to a beautiful, woman wearing a white cloak, lavished in gold. She wore two flesh-colored ribbons crossed which symbolizes latent spiritual powers. A triple, papal tiara with green gems sat on top of her head.

The woman was barefoot, she stood smiling down at Kasper before moving to kneel before him. She took his face into her delicate hands, then tilted her head slightly, as she looked deep into the boy's eyes, maybe looking beneath his soul.

"You have beeyouteeful eyes," she told him still smiling. "Why child?" The women asked. "Why must you put worry in your pupil?" Her smile was like a magnificent glory dazzling the hebrewa. "Hmm?"

Kasper's eyes downcast from the woman's gaze. A tear rolled out of his eye. The beautiful woman lifted Kasper's chin, then softly kissed his lips. "You go, home child," she said. "Yo' family worry about shoo. Yooz ah a special boy," said the women strumming Kasper's cheek with a thumb. "Yoo mus go!" She smiled but was serious. She loved this child with every bit of her heart and soul. "Cipherdeen anhchoo special? Di first son? Yoo come from a good family, hm? My grit grandson. Ya peepool went through a lot behind dees beeyouteeful eyes you have no?" The woman asked her great-grandson. "What saddens you, my child? Eaze it yoo fadda?"

Kasper's grey eyes leveled toward the ground and another tear nose-dived. When it landed it turned into a diamond.

The beautiful woman picked it up, showing it to Kasper and said, "Yo' see how special yoo ah?" Then she curled her fingers around it into a fist. "Yoo no special?" The woman kissed her fist and opened it releasing a monarch butterfly.

Kasper watched as it landed on his shoulder, soft hands brought the boy's eyes back to the woman's. "I love yoo' so mush." She nodded in her truth. "Yo' ah my child no matter what. Buh you need to go home." The beautiful Goddess took the butterfly back into a fist. "Please my beeyoouteeful son." Opening her hand, the diamond was restored. "Tek it, my child," she insisted.

17

Kasper slowly took the gift. His great grandmother kissed his lips once again. "Naww go home." The woman stood with lightning speed and swung the cape of her cloak around Kasper.

Chapter 3

Kasper stood there in his own backyard, darkness had been replaced with all that brilliance. "Go home my child," the wind had said in a passing gust.

The small boy looked into his left hand at the diamond. When he moved through the backdoor his aunt Jean took him into her arms with all the love denied to her.

Cam had told one of his homeboys turned government inform- ant about the murder of Michael Gadez and got himself indicted. He blew trial and had gotten a life sentence. But Michael's death wasn't the only death the family had to deal with. Right after he had gotten killed, some people had run up in his house, robbed Kasper's mother and shot her ten-year-old niece Blusha in the mouth.

3 Years Later:1998

Dressed in a black Chicago Bulls hoodie and a black bandanna around the bottom half of his face, Kasper trekked through the woods. He was now a boy designed of his own living and cold- blooded was how it was now. The P97 he still owned was in the vice hold of his grip ready to avenge violence, wrath, and ruin on a world of the cut-throat and corrupt. This was going to be a way of life for the boy.

Sticks snapped under the footfalls of Michael Jordan sneakers as they walked over the leaf litter that announced fall's clarity. Some trees were toward naked looking tall like towering observers. Strong wind caused high grasses to bow before the thirteen-year- old reminding him of devout supplicants before the Messiah. Tree branches reached out like talons ready to snatch prey.

Kasper's eyes swept the area in quick jerks. He stopped, some- one was in their back yard going through the trunk of an '89 Caprice Classic.

"That's Quincy," Kasper said in a soft whisper. He knew Quincy, Quincy was a dope-boy. The dope-boy heard nothing be- hind him then a voice said, "Gid up!"

"Hoh!" Quincy spun around in a quick response. He sucked his teeth and said, "Kasper take yo' lil' badass home and put that air gun up."

"Gid to me alive or I'll take it from you dead!"

"Lil' Kasper go 'head on and find you somebody to play wit' boy."

A shot cracked open and a bullet crashed into the top right of Quincy's chest, spinning him around and almost sending him into the trunk. Four more bullets snapped following in their tragedies as they found Quincy's backside. He sort of heaved back then he fell to his left side as if that leg had given out on him.

Kasper hurried over and kneeled down, setting aside his gun as he rolled Quincy over onto his back. His left leg was up under his right. Quincy's eyes were open in breathless bewilderment. He was coughing up blood as it ran down the side of his mouth, his arms were bent at the elbows and he was working his hands as though he was practicing trying to make perfect fists.

"I told you to gid it to me," Kasper said as he went into his pockets. He pulled out a chunk of tan stuff that was in a sandwich bag. "Dope," Kasper said and smelled the bag.

He gave it a questioning look and threw it back behind him. Quincy coughed violently. Kasper ignored that and went for the other pocket. He pulled out a mass wad of cash.

"Yes!" the boy whispered as his eyes lit up with elation. Quincy's body relaxed, he was done.

"Siryon," was the word Kasper spoke as this would summons the Shrac Klupenjnx quicker than usual. At the same time, he lifted Quincy's shirt. "No gun." Then his eye went to the left for a listening look. Voices—Kasper grabbed up his gun then vanished. Gone!

Kasper came hustling through the back door. Mother Eba and Aunt Jean sat cleaning fish at the table. They looked at the boy in an asserted pause.

"Sup?" Kasper threw his head up as he locked the door.

The grey-eyed sisters gave a nod. Before passing through the kitchen Kasper sat the money on the table, gave a nod himself and

20

proceeded about as if nothing had occurred. Four eyes tailed the boy as he turned the corner.

'*He's been into something,*' the two sister's thought.

"I don't believe that," Stacey said to Kasper the next day sitting on the platform.

Young boys out in the parking lot were running a game of two-hand touch football. A stereo system somewhere had a speaker in the window playing Master P's '*Make 'Em Say Unh.*'

Kasper had told his sister of last night's event.

"A'ight then," came Kasper's reply.

"Well, why you ain't keep the damn dope then nigga?" Stacey stated from her chair looking down at Kasper who sat on the ledge. "I coulda sold it, shit. Next time you run across some work take it and bring it to me please."

Twiddling with one of his two braids Kasper only responded by throwing up his head.

"And, Phat-Man don't be jackin' nobody where you stay either. Please I'm beggin' ya. Jackin' people and then shootin' nem. You crazy!" Stacey shook her head and looked off to the left. "I'll get a junky to steal you a car so you can move around." Stacey looked back down to her wayward brother. "I know you know howda drive. Got 'bout a hunnit go-karts," Then Stacey said, "Go on out there and play football wit' them."

"Yeah, right,"

Stacey laughed and Kasper shook his head. The boy never grew up playing with friends. Anything Kasper wanted he would get it and didn't need help playing with his things. Mainly mothers in the neighborhood made their sons stay away from the boy, saying he was a craft of some type of satanic cult. But not only him, his family had been criticized of being the family of an infernal damnation. Residents avoided Kasper's family all together.

"You need to do some 'em," Stacey said, "Fo' yo' ass catch a case. I'ma get Kandy on yo' lil' ass. You know how she be doin' you."

Kasper could only smile.

"Yeah, she be bullyin' you, don't she?"

"Hell no."

"Quit lyin' boy, you need it." Stacey looked at her toes that were exposed by Adidas flip flops. "She don't play 'bout choo tho."

That night, for twenty dollars, Stacey had gotten a fiend to render a stolen car for her baby brother. The two siblings were out on the back stoop, sitting on the ledge.

The Nations Bank which would later change to Bank of America building threatened the heavens with its towering height. Highway 277 that wrapped around the city with a delicate embrace was to the left. Straight ahead across the walking bridge that ran over a brooke was a parking lot, then an outreach center that sat on a hill. Then it was the C.A.T.S *Charlotte Area Transportation System* city bus garage and lot. Off to the right was a field, a basketball court and then a bridge for the train that had collapsed a few years back.

"Kebo Green," Stacey said then pulled on the blunt she was smoking.

Kasper said, "What about 'em?"

After blowing out some smoke Stacey said, "Got that money Phat-Man. He drives that sour apple Caprice wit' the gold spokes. Got the numbers and gambling spot Miss Fanny run up there. You can follow his ass home. He'll leave tha hood 'bout two-somethin' in the morning."

"A'ight." Kasper grinned.

He had gotten a rush of ecstasy when he got the drop on Quincy. The boy had relished the moment living in that glory.

"Fa real lil' nigga," Stacey said, "Uncle Juda wazza stick up kid. Les' see if this shit in your blood or if you fakin'." She put her arms around her young brother.

"You gon' get high wit', Big Susta?"

"I ain't know howda smoke."

22

"Don't worry, here." Stacey put the blunt to Kasper's lips. "Puff and I'ma let cho know what else to do."

Kasper sat in the stolen Honda Civic across the parking lot from where Kebo Greens Caprice was parked. He sat up on the steering wheel, gripping it with one hand watching. Seeing Mrs. Fanny's apartment. His intoxication sustained him, ingratiating his conscience.

The boy was ready to get money.

The time 2:27 a.m. had shown up on the dash and Kebo Green still had made no attempt at coming out – leaving. Another thirty minutes had come and gone.

"I hope that's his bitch ass," Kasper said as he saw someone come stumbling out the door. Anxiety bellowed through Kasper's body with rapid virtue.

Kasper took the screwdriver and stuck it into the gutted ignition. He was going to let Kebo Green get up to the entrance before he began to follow. Then someone else came out and stopped Kebo Green before he could get in his car.

'*Da fuck is that?*' Kasper thought.

He became angry, this shit was taking too long.

The man gave Kebo Green something. They dapped and parted. Kasper turned over the ignition and let Kebo Green get to the entrance before he put the car in drive and followed. The boy made it to the Southside with his tail on Kebo Green.

Stilloan Robinson

Chapter 4

Kebo Green was a little drunk and had been popping quaalude pills. He was very tired and ready to get home and go to bed. On nights like this, he did not ride with weapons or drugs. He'd much rather get locked up for a DUI then additional charges. Making a right onto the Foxboro community, Kebo Green was home now. He pulled into his driveway beside a champagne-colored Honda passport. The pills were the cause of his sluggishness as he got out of the car. A red-hooded figure appeared before him at his car door out of nowhere.

As he pointed the gun at Kebo, the assailant spoke menacingly. "You know what's sup!"

"What the fuck!" Kebo fell back into his car. "Don't shoot."

"Get me up in that house where the money at."

"I got a few grand on me."

"If I gotta ask me one mo' time," the stickup kid snarled.

Kebo huffed and go back out of the car. He had even forgot to close his car door. The stickup kid followed behind Kebo Green who was mumbling something.

Kasper said, "Man shut the fuck up. And if you try anything I'ma pop yo' ass." Kebo had a time fitting his key in the door. "Hurry yo' punk ass up."

The door finally opened after threatening words gave him encouraged effort. Kebo led the boy back to his room.

"Where yo' girl?"

"Sleep."

"Wake her up when you get in there, and she bet' not panic."

They entered quietly. The boy stood by the door, closing it, while Kebo shook his girl awake.

"Hmm?" She turned over.

"Don't yell man!"

"Why—what's goin' on?" Her voice was groggy and scratchy.

Kebo looked over toward Kasper who had his pistol up. His girl brought up the rear of his gaze. Quickly she pressed both hands to

the bed and sat up with a gasp that sounded like seeing this masked man decremented breath.

"What he want?" The woman exclaimed

"He wants da money."

Slapping both hands down on her thighs, the woman said, "Well, just give it to him, shit!" She huffed loudly. The light came on and the women sucked her teeth, flinched at the light and covered her eyes with both hands.

Kebo went into the drawer and sat a cigar box on top of it. "Dere you go."

"That money in yo' pocket, too," Kasper ordered.

"Hohhh boy!" The woman was agitated and upset.

Kebo went into his pocket, got the money and tossed it at Kasper's feet. Three shots opened the silence. The woman screamed when she saw her fiancé flare back into the nightstand, with his arms splayed open like that of a drunkard being thrown through saloon doors. He had been shot in his chest. Kasper gained on her and shot her in the face twice.

Kasper pointed the gun back down at Kebo. He shot him in the head to assure his death, then Kasper took the money and left.

The Next Day

"So, what—you just gon' kill people?" Stacey asked her brother from where she sat in the chair on the platform.

Kasper was sitting on the ledge, as usual, he twiddled with his braids and shrugged his shoulders, then replied, "Fuck them."

Stacey said, "Lil' Cold Blooded thirteen-year-old killer. How much you get, boy?"

"It was like fourteen, fifteen thousand."

Stacey got up and went inside when she came back out, she gave Kasper some keys. "You can get that Caprice in Aunt Ponda's back yard. All it needs is a transmission and a power steering pump. Everythang else is good."

"A'ight."
"Be careful out here."

Several Days Later

Kasper was backed into a parking space in his sister Stacey's parking lot in his car. The doors were open, he was wearing Xlll Jordan's as his foot hung out of the door, while he flipped through his CD book. *Jay-Z's 'Money, Cash, Hoes'* was on the radio. It was a very hot day in October. The boy had his shirt off. He wore black Karl Kani shorts and a black bandana was tied around his head like he was a Los Angeles gang member, one gold nugget earring was in each ear. Kasper also had a mouth full of gold teeth and on his neck was a gold Cuban link chain and the Rolex watch was an item his father passed on to him.

"Stacey in there?" A sweet voice asked.

Kasper looked up and saw a female in a turquoise colored Lexus 97 LS 300 taking the space beside Kasper.

"Nah." He closed the CD book and laid it in the seat as he got out of the car. "Why what's up?" Kasper went up to the window.

"I wanted some weed," the female said with beautiful innocent eyes.

"I got some weed." Kasper plunged a hand into his jean shorts inducing a sack of weed mobbed in small buds. "You ain't gotta buy," Kasper said.

"Well, okay."

The female looked into Kasper's eyes and for some reason or another, they made her smile. His own smile curled the corners of his lips, he blushed and then grabbed at the few buds.

The female was pretty, with dark eyes and her dark skin was a flawless layer on her body. She stood at 5'10, with a Halle Berry styled haircut, she looked to have weighed 158 pounds, she wore rings on every finger. Her nails were unpainted but well-manicured. Her ears were laced with diamond studs.

"Why you smilin'?"

"You da one smilin'," Kasper said as he gave the woman her prize.

"You a sweetheart, huh?"

"Nah."

She ripped off a piece of a grocery bag. "You seem like it, baby." The female wrapped the weed up and stuck it down into her console.

Kasper jammed the weed back into his shorts. "What's yo' name?"

"Lacey."

Kasper bit his bottom lip and smiled. Lacey laughed, she thought this boy was smooth and adorable especially with his two long braids and the way he wore his bandana.

"How you know my big susta?"

"Who, Stacey?" Lacey pointed to Stacey's apartment.

"Yeah."

She seemed surprised. "Oh, that's your sister?"

"Dess my susta, yeah."

"Ohh okay—well actually, I met her through your other sister the twin." Lacey stuck her index into her chest. "I work at the county jail with your sister and cousin. I'm a nurse."

"Okay."

"Yeah, so—I know your older sister, the lieutenant"

"Sheba?"

"That's her, I like her. She's always smiling, just like you," Lacey said

"Yeah, I do det sometime."

"You seem like a sweet person,"

"*Man, I'm a goddamn killa,*' Kasper thought. "How old you is?"

Lacey said, "Twenty-nine and you?"

"Thirteen!"

"You don't seem like it." Lacey's facial expressions took on a more serious tone. "You seem to have an old soul. Like you've been here before." Then she said, "Are you mix with some type of

Indian?" Laceys squinted. Before Kasper could answer Lacey was already speaking, "You look a little wild in the features. I know you have Guinean and Dominican in your blood—"

"My daddy was aboriginal and African American."

"Okay, Indigenous tribe of Australia"

Kasper said, "Yep."

"You favor, Sheba, she's all in your face." Then Lacey took one of Kasper's braids into hand. "You have some long hair." She tested the texture of Kasper's hair. "Sure, I don't owe you for the weed?"

"Nah, I charged it to the game." Kasper smiled and Lacey laughed. She let Kasper's hair go. He said, "I can give you my page number."

"Awe baby—you're only thirteen. Then on top of that—your people the sheriff."

"My people come from a country where age is oblivion." Kasper had enchanted Lacey. She had become a customer enthralled by the boy's personality. He had a polished elegance that manifested in him. He said, "Get da numba and call me later if I'm on yo' mind. I ain't say I was tryna be yo' man." Kasper smiled yellow gold and Lacey laughed again.

Stilloan Robinson

Chapter 5

Ten minutes had passed since Lacey left and Stacey took up the parking space. "Lil' nigga, sup?" she said to Kasper then rolled up her windows.

Kasper shut his car down and got out. Stacey got out of hers. "Hey, baby."

"Sup, big susta?"

Stacey could only give her brother a half-hug because she had four dozen roses covered by a trash bag in the other arm. "How long you been here?"

"'Bout two hours chillin'. I check your mailbox and put the mail on yo' bed." As she walked up to the apartment Stacey took a white rose from the dozen, kissed it, placed it down on the grass and went into her apartment to change the roses, replacing the old ones with new ones from the bag. The old ones she would give a woman a few rows up. This was Stacey's every Tuesday ritual.

Kasper had sat down on the ledge.

"You do yo' homework, Phat Man?" Stacey asked when she came back outside.

"Yeah."

"Yeah, you, betta had. Or I'll whoop yo' ass." Stacey sat in her chair and did a special whistle.

"You cannot beat me," Kasper countered.

Stacey begged to differ saying, "Nigga I will knock yo' ass out boy. Den again I'll get Kandy on yo' small ass." Kasper sucked his teeth.

"Oh, don't you act like she won't. Kandy gotcha ass in check, Phat Man, and you know it. If she pull up right now and hop out, first thing you gon say," Stacey imitated Kasper in a mock tone, "*Kandy quit playin'*. She won't even be on yo' ass yet."

Kasper smiled. "Yeah, right."

"Phat Man please don't act like I'm lying. Eh' time you used to see Kandy you holla." Stacey imitated again. "*Kandy leave me alone man. Why you always gotta play so much?*"

"Kandy do play too much." Kasper smiled again.

"She be on yo' ass cuz she don't want choo bein' no punk,"
Stacey admitted. "You grew up around all females. Don't nobody
want choo being soft." Then the ear-piercing call of birds sounded
through the thick air with a sharp force. Up to the right, a large eagle
sized bird was declining altitude.

"Here comes my sweet-sweet." The bird which was a Vadancre
white as snow with gold flakes. It resembled a Falcon but the bird
was the same shape and size of an eagle. It landed by that white rose
Stacey has placed down. It looked to Stacey and she blew it a kiss.
The Vadancre collected the rose and lifted itself into gravity, gliding
up, vanishing into the sky. The flowers went to a godmother, who
did not abide life on earth.

Night had taken its sister's place and Lacey had put a blunt out
in an ashtray. A pair of booty shorts were lined around Lacey's body
and a spaghetti stringed top squeezed her upper body. A recorded
TV show of *New York Undercover* was on.

Kasper had been on Lacey's mind and for some strange reason,
he had a scent that she could still smell. Lacey picked up the phone.

Kasper had gotten out of the shower when his pager went off
on his bed. He grabbed it, looked at the digits and dialed out on the
cordless phone.

"Hello?" Came that sweet voice.

"Sup?"

Lacey said, "Well, I paged you so what's good?"

"You is. Where you et, Lacey?"

"I'm at home. Do you have a curfew?"

"Nah."

Lacey was silent a moment. "Okay, uh—can you get to me or—
of course, you can't."

"Yeah, I could. Why?"

"I was gonna ask you over."

"I can come, but I want choo to come pick me up."

"Okay, tell me where you stay, and I'll come get you then."

Lacey went to pick up Kasper as he requested. He and Lacey
were sitting on her couch in Lacey Eastside English Hill apartments.

"Yo' accent kinda proppa."

"I'm from the suburbs of St. Louis. I've been here in Charlotte twelve years," Lacey stated. She was sitting on her legs facing Kasper, her elbow was on the back of the couch, and her hand was messing with her hair. Lacey's eyes snagged onto Kasper's crouch. "You go to school?"

"Management school," Kasper replied. "Nigga et da school I went to before I went to McClintock snatched my chain offa my neck. I beat his got damn ass for it right in front of da girls, he was tryna showoff. Nah." Kasper shook his head. "I'll beat cho' ass."

Lacey said, "You have a girlfriend?"

"Nah, hell no. When I do dey get jealous of girls det be whisperin' my name and suspecting me of cheatin' so dey dump me." Kasper smiled.

Lacey said, "Aww."

"I get happy whe'ney do. It allows my transition."

Lacey laughed and laughed. When she subsided, she said, "You usin' big words aren't choo?" She stole another glance at Kasper's groin. "Det word ain't det big. I just use it in context, and it comes out big."

Lacey smiled. "Oh, yeah?"

Kasper took a whiff of the air. "Yo' place smell good don't it?" He asked and took another sniff. "Smell like peaches." The boy smiled yellow gold.

"Carpet freshener," Lacey said, and her eyes took that glance for the last time.

One cheek pushed back into a smile, the boy said, "Man I see you keep takin' a glimpse et my dick." Lacey laughed out and Kasper chuckled. "Want meda take it out?"

Lacey put a hand up to her mouth. She was shocked. No, he didn't.

"Humh?" Kasper said.

"You a mess."

"Shid—you keep lookin'. I'm tryna grant you access. I can unzip or I can unfasten."

Lacey said, "I'll tell you what—pull it out so I can see it." Kasper wasted no time. "I'm still young but it's fat ain't it?"

"You is a silly ass boy," Lacey said.

Kasper sagged down in his seat. "Suck it fa me."

"So, you can tell how many people?"

"You worried 'bout who I'ma tell? I on't think nobody would care." Holding his manhood Kasper said, "Fascinate me."

"You crazy." Lacey smiled and took hold of Kasper. "Mmhhh." She let her mouth slide down Kasper shaft.

He looked down at Lacey's work, her head bobbing up and down with inspired ecstasy. She would snake her neck making the boy feel great. Then squeeze her jaws around that penis, so concentrated that Kasper very slowly tried to ease away putting his hand on Lacey's back. She kept him grounded and even went throat deep.

"Uh-huh!" was the sound that escaped Kasper's lips.

That sound was the model of a person taking a stomach blow. Lacey came off Kasper. While stroking his saliva- soaked shaft, she said, "This is what you wanted so don't run." Kasper chuckled. "Damn, I wonder how you gon' act when I let choo up in the pussy?"

"Let's find out," Kasper dared.

Kasper moved between Lacey's legs as she was laying in her bed. He guided himself in and began to stroke. Passion sparked fire in Lacey magnifying instant feelings for the young boy. She had her hands on his ass cheeks while working her lips.

This was to Lacey more than lustfulness. "Ahh!" Lacey let out a hot cry, her body was alert to an orgasm.

Her toes curled as her estrogen gravitated in degrees. This rendezvous would force Lacey into a wall of regret. There midsection clashes with sexual punches as Kasper stroked her. Lacey got on top when she and her partner rolled over. Those long breasts were the shape of two slopes. Lacey took Kasper's two braids into her hands as if they were reins and rode him. This reprehensible sex would be coverted.

"Ooh!" Lacey whined. She couldn't help giving herself to Kasper. "I'm about—ahhh!" She wrapped those braids around her

hand. "I'm gonna cum." Kasper eye balled Lacey's breasts. "Baby," she cried.

"Hunh?"

"It feels good?"

Kasper grunted before he said, "Yeah—yeah!"

"Ooh!" Lacey sucked in air with a hiss. "Squeeze my titties." He did just that as Lacey began to bounce up and down. "Shhhhit!" Lacey then went down and gave Kasper a sloppy kiss. He couldn't handle Lacey on the first night. The sex lasted forty-five minutes before he came inside her. "Kasper?" Lacey spoke softly after lying beside her love for several minutes.

"Yeah?"

"Oh, I thought you were asleep."

"Nah, I ain't."

"Mm." Lacey smiled and snuggled up against Kasper.

Twiddling a braid with one hand Kasper hugged the other arm around his bitch. "What's sup?"

Lacey said innocently, "Nothin."

Then Kasper's pager went off in his pants, so he got up to look at it. It was his sister Stacey. "Where yo cordless phone?"

"On my dresser." Lacey pointed.

Kasper picked it up to dial. "Hello?" Stacey said.

"Yeah, you paged." That was a statement, not a question.

"Lil' nigga where you et?"

"My chick spot," Kasper said.

Stacey began speaking to someone in the background. Right then Kasper knew she was making a sale. Then— "Hello, hello?"

"I'm here"

"Get your ass over here," Stacey ordered.

"Why, what's wrong?"

"Phat-Man bring yo ass. Dess all you need to do."

"Man," Kasper huffed "What time iz it?"

Stacey said, "Da perfect time, get here boy." She hung up.

Kasper sighed and looked down he was tired, worn out and wanted to get some sleep.

"What's wrong, baby?" Lacey sat up and asked.

"Lemme use yo' cah or you can drop me off," Kasper said.

Lacey sucked her teeth. "You gotta go?" Kasper disregarded the question and began putting on his clothes. "Huh?" Lacey prodded for her answer.

Plainly Kasper said, "Yeah."

Lacey sucked her teeth again and laid down with a huff. After getting his clothes Kasper went over to kiss Lacey's lips though they did not respond.

"You mad?" He asked. Lacey only replied with a huff. "Are you?" Kasper asked again. With an elbow, Lacey only gave Kasper a light push. "I'm all yours tomorrow," Kasper promised. "Tomorrow night man, I'ma cut my pager off and eh' thang." Lacey only shifted. "Don't be mad." He kissed her nonresponsive lips again. "I can't get no kiss?"

"Mmm," Lacey moaned.

Kasper said, "Tomorrow night, Lacey. Now kiss me."

"No Kasper."

Kasper kissed Lacey again, then he got up saying, "You gon drop me off?"

"Gone!" Lacey snapped. "Take the car, I have to be at work by eight in the morning so please be here before then." Kasper went into his pocket and gave Lacey two grand.

Chapter 6

Stacey was out on her platform and had just tossed a blunt clip away. One of her legs was crossed over her lap. A couch pillow sat on her lap concealing the Glock 9mm hidden under it, which she held just in case. Down by her feet rested a pocketbook that she had her weed in for selling purposes only. Two, brick columns sat on either side of the platform, she had to herself because not only did she have the three-bedroom apartment, she also stayed on the end.

"Fuck dis' lil' nigga at?" she asked then flipped her wrist to see the time. A car came around the bend, but it kept going. "He gon make me fuck him up."

"Stacey sale me a dime." Stacey leaned forward, looked around the column to the left and saw that it was Sheena.

She stayed one door down standing on the edge of the platform visible for Stacey to see. She motioned for her and reached down into her pocketbook. "Sup?" Sheena asked holding out the money in exchange for Stacey's product. "Takin' shit easy man you know?" Stacey said and came up with the weed. "Here, you go."

"Thank you, Stacey"

"You know you good." Stacey put her hand on her pistol again. This was only at night when she was cautioned like this. Another car turned the bend cutting the darkness with its headlights. "Dis betta be him."

The car pulled into a parking space on Stacey's side of the parking lot. Her hand constructed around her gun and her index finger communicated with the trigger. Everyone knew Stacey was cool, and as far as weed went, she was the one that had it and was making money. For folks that would scrape up change to get a bag of weed, Stacey sold two-dollar bags well worth the money. She took it all pennies, nickels, food stamps, Stacey was about money period. Her index shied away from the trigger when a familiar body got out of a Lexus.

"Bout time yo' ass popped up."

Kasper walked down the walkway leading up to Stacey's platform. "Sup, big susta?" He stopped in front of her.

"Who cah you got?"

"My chick."

Stacey said, "Who da hell let choo trick dem?"

"What choo call me over here for? I was in bed."

"Kuhmere." Stacey laid the gun on the chair when she got up, covered it up with the pillow and took up the pocketbook to move into the apartment and out the back door to the stoop. "Around one thurty dis nigga named, Kush gon' pull up ova dere." Stacey pointed up past the bridge that went on the creek at a parking lot contributing to the outreach center up the hill. "Park and go to the chick spot det stay dere." Stacey turned Kasper around showing him the apartment that was in the next row beside Stacey.

She put her arm around his shoulders and with that hand pointed. "I believe he messin' wit det girl and stashin' shit dere. He moves like he on the low. Da chick like me to herself and don't fuck wit' nobody. But da nigga got it."

"How you know?"

"Come on, bra, I hustle. Stacey gon' know what's goin' on 'round here and who doin' what. He not fucking around down here, he jus' fuck that chick and stash shit up in there."

"You know him?"

"Not like that. His name ring bells issa lil' early." Stacey turned over her wrist. "Almost twelve-thirty. We got some time before he pulls up over there. I just wanted you to be prepared," Stacey said.

She closed down shop for the night and sat on the back stoop with her brother. They spoke for a while then Stacey got Kasper ready.

Kush parked his black Chevy Impala, got out with a purple Crown Royal drawstring bag, took the bridge over the brooke that led to the back of Piedmont Courts. After he got to the clearing that led to the steps over the hill, a voice came behind him.

"You know what time it is!"

Kush spun around abruptly. Some young boy held a gun, wearing a dark-colored hoodie and a bandana around his face.

'What the fuck!' Kush thought. *'Where this mothafucka come from?'* He walked across the bridge that was only two arm lengths apart.

There was absolutely no way that the boy could have come from nowhere, or did he? Kush would have seen the boy when he got on the bridge and off. He also would have heard him coming up behind him because the bridge had a little gravel on it. Kush looked the way of the bridge with his hands up.

He said, "The hell you come from man?" He looked back at Kasper.

"Nigga, you just get me to tha money or that's yo' ass."

"Take this," Kush said offering him the Crown Royal bag. "It's money in it, you can have it."

"Nah, you hold on to that and take me where you goin' cuz I know there's mo' money."

"Take you to my spot?"

"Dog I'm not gon' talk no mo. You not get movin' I'ma crack fire."

"You got it." Kush turned around and began to walk. He had a pistol in his back pocket, but it was in no use against this shit.

"Keep yo eyes straight ahead," Kasper said "Look back and we a done deal. I part wit' the cash and yo' life. Don't look back, just walk."

Kush walked on. They got over the steps and Kush tried brushing his chin with his right shoulder so that he could steal a look behind him. Out the corner of his eye, he did it with the other shoulder. When he saw it was clear he looked back, *nothing*. He turned around, looking for the boy, searching the area in jerks.

"You looked back!"

"Aaargh!" Kush spun around moving backward with his hands out as if a dog was about to attack.

"You looked back," The boy said again.

"What the fuck is you?"

Kasper had the gun down by his leg. "I told you not to look back."

"I'll get you to the spot man!"

Kasper had gotten Kush into the apartment and robbed him for money. There was a shoebox full of money and some drugs in the small refrigerator in Kush's girl's room. He shot Kush and took it all.

"This Heroin?" Stacey was holding the product wrapped in wax paper. She stuck her nose to it and smelled it again. "Yeah, this a brick a dog food."

"Why was it in a fridge?"

"Got to keep it cool. Oh, nigga did you shoot them?" Stacey asked. Kasper only looked at his sister. "Answer me you lil' mothafucka."

Kasper shrugged a shoulder.

"I shoulda known. Man, you done made my damn money hot. You had a damn bandana on, Phat Man?"

"She wasn't there if it makes you feel any better."

"Now she gon' discover his body. I gotta hustle an apartment row down, and here you is 'bout to make tha hood hot. That's my fault though, I shoulda said somethin'."

"Aye, you can have that cold stuff."

Stacey said, "Oh I was."

A smile formed on Kasper's face. "Don't say it like that"

"Well, I was gon keep it anyway, mothafucka. Did I say it betta? More politely?"

"A'ight."

"A'ight what? Want me to call, Kandy?"

"You always threaten me wit' her."

"Cuz you know she pop yo' ass lil' nigga," Stacey said, and Kasper just smiled. "Yeah, that's what I thought." Stacey smelled the package again. "I hate choo shot him, but fuck it it's life.

It had been two weeks since Kasper hit Kush, Piedmont Courts were hot. Detectives had been asking questions, but no one had any answers to give. Kasper now had five money signs the size of dimes tattooed on his face like teardrops. Blood drops were tatted coming

40

out the corners of the mouth and an upside down ankh was tatted between his eyes.

The ankh symbolized the millions of years to come. The loop was the perfect symbol of what has neither beginning or end and stands for the soul which is eternal because it has sprung from the spiritual essence of the Gods. The cross represented the state of trance in which the neophyte struggles of more precise stages of death. The crucifixion was the chosen victim and in some temples, the priests used to lay the neophyte on a bed shaped like the cross.

The possessor is the geometric key that resembles when turned upside down to the hidden mister of which the symbol was. This very looped cross was able to open the gates of the kingdom of the dead and penetrate the hidden meaning of eternal life. The symbol was sometimes held upside down by the hook especially in funeral rites when it suggested the shape of a key. In reality, was the key that opened the tomb into the fields of Lord Enki the realm of the dead.

Kasper sat on the trunk of the Lexus Lacey had given him. She had gotten herself a Lexus truck. Her parents were real estate agents and she was their only child. The boy was in Stacey's parking lot and she was at the gym. He was dressed in a white Coogi shirt, white and red Dennis Rodman's 8's, white and red Nike shorts and a red bandana.

Then Lacey pulled up alongside him. "Hey, baby."

Kasper jumped down and moved over to the windows. "Sup?" He kissed her. "You get my clothes?"

"I got em."

"How much you spend?" Kasper swatted a bloodthirsty mosquito.

The sky was the perfect untroubled blue of a television screen making its impression at the dead-end of a movie tape. Kids were chasing away tubby pigeons that would burst up into the air astonished.

"That don't matter sweetie, I spent *my* money."

"A'ight."

Lacey put the truck in park and said, "What choo out here doin'?"

"Chilling." Kasper turned his head away. "I know I promised to put some rims on your Chevy. I ain't forgot about choo."

He looked back to Lacey, "A'ight."

"Why did you do that to your face? It was beautiful. Now you look evil."

"So what?" Kasper grew mad, squinting like a sailor peering through a high wind. He did not want anyone criticizing him about his face and what he did to it, it was his face.

"Okay." Lacey put her truck in drive. "I see an attitude coming. I'ma go on and go to the house. Do you want me to cook?"

"Nah, put a pizza in the oven."

"Be careful," Lacey said.

"I got choo."

"Bye." Lacey waved.

Just as soon as Lacey pulled off. Stacey pulled into the parking space.

She got out with her gym bag saying, "You missed Big susta, baby?"

"Hell, you ain't been gone long enough," Kasper teased.

"So, I miss you when you leave me fo' even a minute."

"Well, I'ma 'bout to walk to da store. Let choo miss me a la bit." Stacey smiled as she pushed her brother's head playfully.

Because Stacey stayed all the way in the back of Piedmont Courts at the bottom it took every bit of fifteen minutes for Kasper to walk to the store and it was only across the street from the projects. He bought grapefruit juice and a pack of Starburst. He gave the change to another young boy that came in with his little sister. Kasper got back down to Stacey's apartment and saw another one of his sisters sitting on the platform with Stacey. They did not speak to one another because they did not see eye to eye. Anition was her name, she was 5'5, with caramel skin, thick and plump, with gray eyes, fat cheeks, neck length hair and a gap between her teeth. Anition was twenty-seven years old and worked as a deputy at the

Mecklenburg County jail. She was the second born of Victoria's eight children.

"Phat Man, you want some a dis?" Stacey asked. She was stirring duck sauce into her fried rice Anition had brought for her.

"I'm cool."

"You positive?"

"Man, I'm 'bout to eat deez Starburst. I don't want cho Chinese food."

"Bet," Stacey said. Then some guy breezed up toward the platform. "Sup, Tay?"

"Sup, Stacey? Sale me a quart." Stacey had left her pocketbook in her apartment so she set her food down on the chair and said, "Hold up." Then she stepped inside.

Tay said to Anition, "Hey, what's up?" He had embedded her in one of his fantasies she had no idea of. "Nothin' what's goin' on?"

"Shit." Tay's gaze sloped toward Kasper. "Aye what da fuck you get those tattoos on yo' face for boy?"

Stacey went into her room to grab her pocketbook and more weed for supply. "I need to hit the shower," she told herself. *Fop! Fop!* Two gunshots echoed outside in the front. "What da hell!" *Fop!* Then another, she ran out of the room, took the steps down two at a time and grabbed her gun from off the couch, then leaped out onto the platform. "What's goin' on?" She could smell the gun power Stacey also saw Tay limping off holding his leg.

"This crazy ass nigga just shot det boy!" Anition waved a hand towards Kasper.

"For what?"

"Shit if I know! He only asked him why he had dem tattoos on his face!"

Stacey looked down at Kasper who was seated on the ledge opening a pack of Starburst with a 9mm Glock resting beside him like an infant child. She said, "And you just gon' sit 'round like it's okay?"

"Idiz okay," Kasper replied. "He gotta worry 'bout me, bitchass."

Stacey looked up to see Tay disappear around a row of apartments. "Done ran my money off."

Anition scolded as she looked down at Kasper who was getting rid of the lemon-flavored Starburst and said, "Shit ain't make no damn sense!"

"Fuh real Phat-Man, give me my money. Twenty-five dollas."

"He ain't ask him nuttin' wrong! You done did det to yo' face!"

Kasper didn't give a fuck, for the last time—it was his face! Not even his mother questioned him about it. She only frowned at him. The following day Kasper entered midtown corner store across from Piedmont Court which people referred to as the top store. That was because it sat at the top of the hill and another corner store sat. at the bottom that people call the bottom store.

"Lemme holla at cha when you come back out la' cuz," Trump had requested of Kasper when he passed the boy coming out.

Kasper only threw his head up and kept moving he grabbed his usual grapefruit juice and three packs of Starburst. Trump blew the horn when he saw the boy leaving the store.

He slid into the passenger seat. "Yeah, what's up?"

"Heard you bussed on det nigga, Tay? He's a real bitch ass nigga, soft! Det nigga walkin' round on crutches lookin' silly!" Trump was disgusted with Tay. "Folks laughing at det soft ass nigga! Dey lookin' at det nigga in shame. You got deez niggas shook down here lil' cuz, dey scared." Trump was thirty-four-years old brown-skinned, had a short haircut with a part in the middle and one gold tooth.

"But dig dis out—dis nigga name Petro I need you to squeeze on I'm fo' me. I'ma pay you some bread."

"How much?" Kasper wanted to know what the money was looking like. He didn't know Trump that well, only that he was one of Stacey's clients. Kasper was using his teeth to open up a Starburst. "You gon' get seven grand and I'ma give you a pound of weed upfront."

Check dis out." Trump went under the seat and came up within a 9mm Beretta "You can use dis." He presented the chromed weapon the object of Petro's fate. "Cause I know you gon' do it—" Trump's next move was pulling out a knot of cash and counting out the amount said.

"I'ma pay ya now."

"A'ight, where da nigga be et?"

"He cut hair in a barbershop." Trump pointed to the barbershop that was connected to the top store. "Light skin puss ass nigga, bald head, wit' glasses. He leaves out da back round nine-thuddy."

"Kill him?"

"He's a snitch lil' nigga, yeah. To do you a favor, I can scoop you up on the getaway."

"Nah, I got it."

It was 9:23 PM Kasper was still waiting behind the barbershop. He thought he was standing where no one could see him. Firearm anticipated Kasper was ready to remove Petro from life and amputate the supply of air he was breathing. "—she thinks she is—" Petro was saying while coming out the back of the barbershop with a fellow barber in tow. "Bitch know she can't pay det—" Kasper appeared and fired off four shots.

Petro tried with a hand to block the bullets that burst through his right side. The other barber had renounced and ducked back inside, but the outburst of gunshots was loud. Kasper had run up on Petro trying to reach for the gun holstered on his waist. Six more shots had stolen his breath away. Then Kasper vanished getting away.

Stilloan Robinson

Chapter 7

"Real nigga," Trump said to Kasper as the two of them sat inside of Trump's 92 Monte Carlo in Stacey's parking lot. This was the following day. "You need some 'em you holla et me."

Kasper thought about that for a second and said, "Yeah, I need somebody to rob."

"Oh, yeah!" Trump's body slanted towards the window. He was taken aback by Kasper's petition. "You rob?"

"Yeah," Kasper said bluntly.

"Okay." Trump bobbed as he took in the young gangster. "Yeah, I know somebody, my baby mama's brotha. Fuck det police ass nigga. He da feds straight up la homie, his name, Chris." When Trump told Kasper everything he needed to know, he dapped the young boy and watched him get out as he left.

"Aye what's up la cuz?" a person who Kasper knew to be Jeremy spoke as he pulled into a parking space in a 98 Mercedes C-350.

This was one of Stacey's clients and had been since high school. "Sup?" Kasper gave Jeremy dap.

Stacey came up to serve the five ounces her client came to get. She got the money saying, "Tell yo susta I said hey, Jeremy."

"A'ight now." He backed out to leave and Stacey curved her arm around her baby brother. "My sugar pie, you good hon'?" They both started for the platform.

"Yeah, I see you made some money today."

"Nigga dess eh-day." Getting to the platform Stacey sat on her chair and Kasper sat in his usual spot. "Phat-Man, I want cho' ass to be careful about what choo do."

"I will."

"You're big susta's baby but choo get outline you know who I'ma call."

Kasper looked back at Stacey and smiled saying, "Man Kandy ain't gon' do nuttin'."

"Okay, boy if you say so. But don't tell ha cuz she will whoop yo la ass. You know it."

"I ain't scared of, Kandy."

It was the next night when Kasper had followed the directions to Chris' home. He went around the nice house to the back. Two dogs in a kennel began barking immediately. Kasper stopped in an abrupt pause and rendered his ability to vanish becoming unseen. He discovered this intelligence when he was five years old.

He had been spending the weekend with his aunt Yazette and it was around three something in the morning when he entered the kitchen for something to drink. Attempting to put the pitcher of kool-aid back into the refrigerator footsteps came sweeping up the hall and it brought Kasper to a freeze. He flinched, Yazette stopped at the threshold of her kitchen.

"Why's the refrigerator open?" It was the only administer of light the kitchen owned at the moment.

She surveyed this scene because it was strange. The refrigerator door opened. Not only that Yazette knew something or someone was present. Gradually Yazette advanced, her slow gait was graceful like that of a woodland beast; each careful step testing the ground. Something was just too inept, looking and trying to decode this Yazette brows crinkled. A presence could be felt. Kasper was standing there looking directly at her standing as if assigned.

'*Why my aunt can't see me?*' he thought.

"Ciphadeen?" Yazette stopped and called while looking about. For some good reason, she knew he was there. "Are you 'dere?" she asked. Yazette started moving again very slowly moving her hands as if washing the hood of a car. "Ciphadeen? You dere?"

"Why can't she see me?"

"Ciphadeen?" Now Yazette's voice came in telepathically. "Ciphadeen?"

The boy responded back in his mind saying, "Ma'am?"

"Whe you boy?" Kasper was surprised by this communication that he did not answer back. "I say whe yoo?"

"Right here."

Looking in a certain spot Yazette said "Whe?"

"Here Auntie."

Yazette looked by the refrigerator and saw some kind of energy a form of vapor that made up Kasper's body.

"Deeh yoo?" she asked waving a hand towards that energy. Yazette subtracted from the energy because it shocked her a little. Touching it was the equivalent to touching a nine- volt battery to the tongue.

"Ciphadeen? Deh yoo dere boy."

Kasper's simple reply was, "Yes." Yazette studied the energy "Sho yo' sef."

"I'm tryin'." Kasper was trying to reappear, but nothing happened.

"I seh sho ya sef." Yazette was tempted to touch the vapor with both hands. She was trying to figure out a way to help her nephew.

"Why can't choo see me?"

Yazette was frustrated. "I seh yoo no dere. Only see ya energy." She touched it and drew back. "Try again, Ciphadeen."

Kasper tried but nothing was accomplished. "Did I?"

Yazette sucked her teeth and called her mother who showed up with Aunt Jean.

"Ciphadeen?" Aunt Jean's voice became telepathic.

"Ma'am?"

"What yoo do boy?"

Kasper became afraid. "Why y'all can't see me?"

Aunt Jean walked around the vapor of energy, trying to figure out what the solution was rather the problem. She stopped. "Bwoy suck di air in."

Kasper sucked in air as hard as he could and was normal holding that pitcher of Kool-Aid. Yazette nicknamed him Kasper a.k.a The Ghost.

Magically waving a hand the dogs scoured into their houses. Kasper reappeared and snipped the alarm located in the telephone box. He traveled up the patio steps and peered into the curtainless French doors. Force was put into the blow he threw with the butt of his gun, shattering the window. The more force, less noise.

Kasper extended his hand through the broken glass and unlock the door gaining unlawful entry. He moved through the kitchen and

slowed when he heard television voices punctuated by bursts of laughter. Someone was in the living room under the cover sleep. It was a seven-year-old girl. She was awake and taken with a note left behind.

At 6:30 AM Chris was in Atlanta, Georgia at his side chick's house when his phone rung startled him out of his sleep. "Yeah?"

It was his wife in tears. She was telling him about the ransom note left by some unknown perpetrator.

"The fuck you mean?" Chris barked, sitting on the edge of the bed. Rage began to surge through him unhindered.

When he registered that his girl was sleep, he turned to see if he had awakened her. She was looking up at him appalled.

"They got her," the wife was saying. "I got up—to wake her for school and she was gone, Chris—gone!"

Chris stepped out into the hallway. "Who took her?"

"Somebody, I don't know, Chris!"

"Shhhit!" Chris shook his head. "Read the got damn note!"

"They—" She sniffled. "They said please don't call the police, that would be a mistake. That will not cost you a penny—" The wife stopped reading as she cried more.

Chris snarled, "Read it!"

"—but it will cost your daughter her life. I only—I only want the money. I know you got it—so cough it up and call the number."

"Fuck man!"

"What we gon' do, Chris?"

"Give me that number."

"Is there a lot of parks in um—Haiti?" The little girl asked.

Her name was Alexis, she sat up against the wall in what was supposed to be the living room of a vacant house in one of Kasper's aunt's neighborhood beside Kasper eating a big bag of M&Ms. Kasper was eating a big bag of Starburst the lemon flavored ones were thrown out on the floor.

"Some," was the boy's reply.

"So, you talk French and Spanish?"

"It's not talk French and Spanish. It's speak French and Spanish."

"You speak French and Spanish?"

"Yeah." Kasper chewed his Starburst candy. "But I promise you gon' go home."

"Why do my daddy owe you?"

Kasper explored his thoughts for a feasible answer. None was available so he said, "He jus' do. We're gon' get some ice cream when I take you back."

Alexis became excited. Her smile was exuberant. "Oohhh, I like strawberry ice cream!"

"Dess what we gon' get den."

"Why you don't like da yellow kinda Starburst?"

"Lemon, I don't like lemons. Dey tastes nasty. You do good in school?"

"Yeah, I always do my homework," Alexis said.

Kasper's phone rung, he sat his candy down and answered it. "Yeah?"

The voice on the other line growled. "Da fuck is dis?"

"You don't ask doze type of questions."

The voice on Kasper's end said, "Lil' nigga you sound like you can be my son. Who you workin' fo'?" Kasper fired a firecracker and Alexis shrilled. He didn't want to fire off a live gun around an innocent child. Anything could have happened.

"Dere you go askin' questions."

"Da fuck you want?" The voice in Kasper's ear asked.

Kasper said, "Det wuzza good question. I heard you was da man. I need det bread, one million."

"A million? La cuz—I ain't got det fo' ya." Another firecracker popped off and Alexis shrilled again.

It was all planned, Kasper had told the girl to scream whenever he popped off firecrackers. "Lil' cuz' listen—I can give you—"

"Det million." Kasper urged.

"Work wit' me la buddy. I can't give you what I don't have."

"No exceptions, dog."

"Lil' cuz?"

Another firecracker detonated and Alexis played her part. Kasper grew mad. "Next bullet won't be in the air! It's gon' take it away." This was another one of Kasper's bluffs.

Alexis was a child he would not harm in any way. She reminded him of his deceased cousin, Blusha. Blusha was the same age as Kasper or would have been the same age had she still been alive. She had gotten shot in the mouth during a home invasion. Some people had run up in Kasper's mother's house to rob the place right after his father had gotten killed and Blusha was the example of what was to become of everybody in the home had Victoria not come up off the money. Kasper was not there that night. Only his mother, his younger sister Yaziki, other sister Zya and Blusha.

"Listen, la cuz please!" The voice pleaded.

"Speak!"

"I got a quarter million for ya and ten birds."

"Fifteen."

The party on the other end huffed. "A'ight you got it."

"Cawl back when you have my shit."

"Can I hear my daughter's voice?"

"You heard her scream?"

"Yeah, I heard her."

Kasper said, "Then, you heard a voice." He hung up.

Chris got on the highway later to get the ransoms for his daughter heading back to Charlotte. He was on the phone with one of his boys.

"What choo mean kidnapped?"

"They or somebody got up in my house and got Alexis, dog. Some ransom shit. Sound like some la young ass peewee ass nigga. I'ma get dis mothafucka. Find out who it is and it's game ova fo' that ass."

"You say a peewee?"

"Yeah, dog, I believe he works fo' somebody. He knew what he was doin'."

"Sho nuff?"

"Yeah, but let me get dis shit. I'ma get witcha."

"Okay, Big C, get at me."

"You know."

Chapter 8

Kasper called Chris and gave him very brief instructions that included if he had anyone follow him it would be a tragedy. Alexis was in a stolen car with her strawberry ice cream at a shopping plaza.

"You bet not try shit!" Kasper reminded Chris. "Get in a car wit' my shit and drive to where det piece of paper say. When you get 'dere leave my shit and take off on foot. You look back you gon' see bullets comin'."

Later that day Stacey stopped by the old folk's home where she'd resigned before moving out. The two sisters were out at the grocery store.

She went down the steps into Kasper's room. "Phat Man?"

"Sup, Big susta?" He was in the mirror putting two fresh braids into his hair.

"You baby, what's up?" Stacey held her baby brother to her breasts in a one-arm hug.

He pointed. "Check det on my bed."

Stacy directed her attention that way. "Da bag?"

"Yeah," Kasper said.

Stacey went over, pulled it to her and unzipped it. The many kilos in abundance enthralled her. "What da fuck?" She extracted one. "Where da hell you get dis shit from?" The boy recanted the story back to Stacey as he went and lied down.

"So, you pulled off a ransom?"

"If that's what it is."

Stacey looked serious when she said, "You ain't hurt det la girl did you?"

"No!"

"So, what choo gon' do wit' dis?"

Kasper shrugged up one shoulder saying, "You said if I eva run cross some throw it to you. So, dere you go."

"Aww." Stacey collapsed on her brother. "Baby, I love you."

She stroked his sister's hair and said, "You my, baby."

Stacey kissed the boy's lips and got up to check out her product. "How many iz it?"

"Fifteen."

Kasper called Trump when Stacey left to offer him some money.

"Oh nah," he said. "Det lick fo' you. Boy, I see you official. You a real ass lil' nigga, homie, cold. Stay real!"

"No doubt." When they hung up Lacey called. "Sup girl?"

"You comin' over, baby?"

"I'm et home chillin'."

"Can you please come over? Please," Lacey begged.

Kasper sighed and said, "I'm tired, Lacey."

"Come over here, I'll tie you up." They both laughed.

"You come over here."

"Okay."

"And bring me a chicken salad sandwich from Subway on your way and a big bag of Starburst and hurry yo' ass up."

Lacey said, "I'm comin', baby."

"I'm waitin'."

"I'll be there in a few, bye."

Kasper hung up. "Gotta change my numba," he said to the screen on his cellular, Chris had the number.

<p style="text-align:center">****</p>

In the wee hours three men Nico, Hollywood and Tank Head pulled into the parking lot in the back of Piedmont courts at the out-reach center.

"Tank Head dis' some bullshit dog," Nick claimed. These three men were from a small neighborhood called North Charlotte which was five minutes in walking distance. They were on a mission to-night. "Man listen—" Tank Head said. "I know dis bitch got some money up in her shit. All she do is sit on the porch and push weed."

"All day," Hollywood chimed in.

"She don't eva run out cuz she keeps reefah. Stacey sittin' on bread, my nigga."

"She good people man, she looks out for da struggle. We'd be dead wrong to hit dis bitch."

"Dead wrong! Nigga anybody can get robbed. Ain't choo shootin' bad, right now?"

"Yeah, but got damn—"

"A'ight den. Man, Hollywood you ready?"

"I don't know what he talkin' 'bout." Hollywood chambered a round. "I'm ready to get dis' bitch bread."

"Come on."

Nico sucked his teeth and got out. He admired Stacey, but these were his homeboys and he had to come through for them. After crossing over the creek, the three men took the steps over a small hill.

Lookin' at his pager Tank Head said, "It's fo' eighteen in the morning. Dis hoe should be sleep. We gon' kick in the door and run up in there." They had stopped yards from Stacey back stoop. "Yaw ready?"

Nico said, "Dis shit crazy."

Nico said, "Yeah, we ready."

"Les' do dis." Tank advanced Stacey stoop.

Their negative energy triggered the tumise balls on either side is Stacey's stoop. Two Thrase Jaxelz popped up. They were 6'7, their bodies were covered in a black mesh robe that had hoods covering their faces. The hands on the Thrase Jaxelz were massive in size. Three times the size of the men. In the inward struggle against empty self-inflation, the Thrase Jaxelz was invited to a banquet by Annunaki Gods. Marduk, Ishkur and Nergal. The Thrase Jaxelz whose real name was Indankuz had been an under God to Dr. Faustus who has soon betrayed his soul to the Prince of Darkness. Once that happened Indankuz turned to enlil who was the illegal heir of Anu the supreme Annunaki Gods for support. At the banquet of his own and when he served up his own wife. Indankuz was ill reputed by Lord Enki. He was cast down into the Poviks where he would serve as security for the Kovijcii Goddess and was cloned for that cause and were called Thrase Jaxelz. Indankuz himself was

placed in the Pocomi temple where he watched over the Pocomi dwellers.

Hollywood and Tank Head had been seized as they yelled out their horrors. The Thrase Jaxelz vanished with Tank instantly. Nico tried running and the Thrase Jaxelz that took hold of Hollywood teleported in a quick flash, then appeared in front of Nico clutching him by his neck and vanishing, leaving a swirl of black clouds before they too evaporated. Total oblivion would befall each man and their souls would become Helots in Ikedele.

Stacey's eyes opened in a sharp snap. She hadn't been sleeping only resting her eyes. Stacey had a sleeping disorder called insomnia where she could get little to almost no sleep at all. She snatched the covers off her body as she got up in a hurry. Her Glock 9mm found itself gripped in her hand. Barefoot Stacey stormed the steps, twisted the lock on the back door and jerked it open.

When she stepped outside on the stoop, she immediately spotted three pistols on the ground and turned her attention on both sides of her stoop. The Tumisc balls were gone.

"Yeah, somebody was gon' try me," she said to herself and went for the guns that would go to Kasper.

Then Stacey went into her apartment and got two more Tumisc balls that were black, shiny and the size of pool balls to place back there. When grounded these balls hovered a quarter-inch above ground and couldn't be moved by anything man-made. Only Stacey could move them.

Over the next few days, Chris had been asking around about anybody young who's name rung bells. Nobody had any information. He went to the barbershop just to kick it with one of his boys who was sitting in the barber chair waitin' for any customers.

"Toney, what's good, bro?"

"Ah man, Chris I ain't been up to shit, my boy. Only out here workin'. Know what I'm sayin'?"

"Yeah, homeboy."

"What choo got goin' on partner you still down in Atlanta fuckin' wit' det la strippa chick?"

Chris chuckled. "Boy, you crazy. Nah I just left from down that way."

"Oh, word up?"

"Yeah."

Then Chris thought about askin' Toney about any young boys, he knows his homeboy wasn't out there. He also knew it wouldn't hurt either. "Yo' Tone—you know any pee-wees out here makin' any noise?" Looking through the contacts in his phone, Toney slowly shook his head. Chris said, "I thought choo wouldn't."

When the question finally enrolled Toney laid his phone in his lap sayin', "Oh, yeah! Lil' young ass nigga, Kasper."

"Kasper?" Chris repeated the name tasting it on his tongue.

Pointing in no general direction while snapping Toney said, "Yeah, he be in uh—uh—" He closed his eyes to remember because of the collision of temporary amnesia. Toney brought them back open. "Piedmont Courts."

"You know him?"

"Nah, I don't know him. I seen him and heard niggas speak of him. You know my aunt stay down there so I be over there to fuck wit' ha."

"How he look?" Chris asked.

"Lil' nigga brown-skinned." He waved his hand in front of his face. "Got tattoos and shit all on his face." Now he began combing back his hair. "Long ass hair and gold teeth. Mothafucka ain't but 'bout twelve or thirteen."

Chris looked down trying to draw a little picture of the description. '*Yeah, I gotta see him,*' he thought to himself.

"Why wassup?" Toney's question effaced Chris envisage of the young boy.

He looked up at Toney. "I think he had some'em to do wit' me gettin' robbed," Chris lied. He couldn't tell how this Kasper had gotten off on him on a ransom. "Where 'bout in Piedmont Courts he be dog?"

"If I'm not mistaken in the back." Toney gestured like he was shootin' a basketball when he said, "Wayyy in the back."

"I'm 'bout to go check him out." Chris dapped Toney.

"A'ight."

When Chris walked out some guy getting a haircut two chairs down said, "Toney, you know det nigga?"

"Who, Chris? Yeah."

"Man, that mothafucka dem people! He got my homeboy Junior from Cummings Ave fucked up on a Fed case. He a bitch—certified!"

As he turned into Piedmont Courts Chris ran into Trump coming out and blew his horn. "Sup Chris?"

"Shid lookin' fo' dis pee-wee that done robbed me."

"Oh, word up?" Trump played the surprised specimen.

"Think it wuz, Kasper, I heard about. I know it wuzza young nigga. You know him?"

"Yeah." Trump looked back down toward the bottom of the projects and pointed. "He back dere in the back. You'll see him."

"Aye I 'preciate det."

"Okay." Trump pulled off.

Chris made his way down and around the back where he could only make a right. "Okay, that's him." Chris pulled up to Kasper. "Holla et me la cuz."

Kasper asked for a minute by holding up an index finger while holding the phone to his ear. The other hand was behind his back holding a pocket revolver. After a couple of seconds, he hung up and said, "Da hell you want?"

"Oh, nah la man, I ain't like det. I heard about cha, so I had a lick set up fo' us. Trump told me to get at cha."

Chris was fishing to see if Kasper would jump on the proposition to confirm his suspension.

"Okay, so what about it?"

"Can I scoop you up about nine?"

"A'ight."

"Be right here."

"I will," Kasper replied. "Make sho' you come back."

"You know it." Chris pulled off saying to himself "Yeah, that was definitely him. I'ma torture that ass until he come up off my shit then it's lights out.

Chris came back as promised. He had his boys waiting in an abandoned building for when he showed up with Kasper. Kasper wasn't at the expected location when Chris pulled up.

"Baby girl, you know who Kasper is?" he asked some female standing by a Cadillac Deville.

"He up in the front. Tole me to tell you to come up det way."

"Okay." Chris pulled off in his car, his eyes were glued to his side-view mirror. "That's a lil' sexy ass bitch, boy." He found the boy and let him in. "You ready lil' cuz?"

"Yeah, it's action."

"Sho' is." Chris smiled with a blissful gleam and left the neighborhood.

Kasper pulled up a .40 Caliber out of his hoodie. "Nigga, I know who you is." He cocked it back and Chris flinched. "Yeah, I got cho' shit but it ain't nothin' you gon' do 'bout it. Put both yo' hands on the steerin' wheel don't even move 'em flick da turn signals and you bet not get pulled for it."

Chris' whole body chilled. It was like something gripped his spine, handicapping his ability. "How you find out who I was?"

"Det was Trump I was on the phone wit' when you pulled up earlier. He told me he was sending you around to me. And you played yourself when you said he told ya to get et me. I was gon' blow yo' head off but I wanted to see how you played it. You ain't know fo' sho' who I was but choo wanted to try me. Det pretty chick det told you where I was—dess my Big Susta. I showed ha where you stayed after yo' punk-ass left." Chris sucked his teeth. "So, you try something eh body in that house gon' get it." Kasper lied about that, it was just a tactic.

"Come on la—"

"Shut da fuck up and get me to da money. So, you was da lick, huh—again?"

"I got—"

"I said get me to it!" Kasper demanded.

Chris took Kasper where his mother stayed. One hundred grand was in her storage house. A single shot to the head ended one person's life. Kasper walked away with his.

"Wha yoo gunn do wit' house tew ya self?" Victoria asked her son. Kasper had gone with her to the grocery store the next day.

"Jus' to have it, ma."

As she read the ingredients on the back of a Zatarain's rice box Victoria said, "I dunno, hoony. Cuz if ya get house tew ya self and people see no udda body but shoo, dey watch yoo. Yoo know wha I say iz t'doo."

"No, iss not true. So, you sayin' you, can't do it?" Kasper asked while moving the shopping cart back and forth. Victoria did not reply. She was more into reading the ingredients rather than worrying about a house her son wasn't even old enough to have.

"Momma?" Kasper said and a smile lengthened across Victoria's pretty, plump, dark-skinned face. "Ma, I know you hear me." He got another mute response. "Ma!" Kasper yelled. Shocked by the outburst, Victoria sort of loped back, looking at her son for a second before she lunged forward and swatted Kasper over the head. He nursed the soft pain with a hand saying, "I'm talkin' to you an' you ignorin' me."

Victoria spoke seriously saying, "Ya dun't yell!"

Kasper grinned. "A'ight dog."

Taking a step closer to him, finger-pointing, Victoria said, "No, I no dog! I no get house! Ya wunn house you ask ya grand-nanny, see is she do it, but I no get house!" She shook her head quickly. Then put the rice box back. "Ask ya Bi Susta. Ya know she do anyting fah yoo."

"I asked you, not her."

"Well, I seh no!" Victoria shot a look to her son that said she was more than serious.

"Don't worry 'bout it."

Victoria picked up another rice box and said, "Oh, I no wuddy. When ya get bi' boy, yoo khan get house." She gave Kasper a silly closed-mouth grin.

Kah-Kah and Tron we're sitting on the back patio in West Charlotte Westchester apartments where they sold crack cocaine. Five yards away was a red, seven-foot brick wall then some woods followed. A two-story apartment building could be seen through the trees. A six by four wooden plank separated each patio. Kah-Kah was approximately 6'6, with plaited hair, a thick build, gold teeth, and brown-skin. He was thirty-three years old and Sheba's husband Victoria's eldest child. Tron was twenty-eight, dark-skinned, 5'11, with dreadlocks and slim built. This was Anition's baby father and the reason why the two siblings did not get along.

"Stacey, blessin' on the work," Kah-Kah said.

"Guess so."

"I fuck wit' Stacey. She gets det money boy."

Plainly Tron said, "She do a'ight."

Kah-Kah looked at Tron for a few seconds, then said, "Nigga you a hater!"

"Man, I ain't hatin' on ha. I ain't thinkin' 'bout det mufucka."

"You only feel det way cause she don't fuck wit' choo or Kasper either."

"Fuck bof dem!"

"You need to keep yo' hand off dey susta."

"They'll be a'ight."

"You my boy but I bet one a dem gon' pop you before it's all ova wit."

"You right, Dere go Lance."

"Sup yawl?" Lance walked up. His expression made him look as if he had just been surprised.

"Shit," Tron said looking up at his friend who had once been a respected hustler.

Kah-Kah said, "Gettin' money."

"Girl actin' all crazy and shit man," Lance said.

"Hell yeah."

"Damn," Tron said lamely.

"Bitch, be trippin'. Kah-Kah, I seen yo' new lac homeboy. She looks sweet too cuz you stay in some 'em nice."

Softly replying Kah-Kah said, "A'ight."

"'Bout da nicest ones I done seen," Lance said.

Tron snickered. "Den, I see you wit' the J's on—"

"Nigga, what da fuck you want?"

"Bra I know I owe you, let cha boy get a la gram, so I can flip some—"

"Nah, get da fuck on!"

"Come on, homeboy"

"Bye."

"Kah-Kah—" Lance tried reasoning like a desperate Jew.

Kah-Kah pulled out a Glock 9mm that was resting on his lap under his shirt and said, "If you don't roll up out my face—"

"A'ight den." Lance walked off

"Got til' tomorrow to have my shit."

Three days later Kasper was over at his mother's house. She and Anition were at the kitchen table talking when he walked in to get something out of the refrigerator. A scratch on Anition's eye jumped out to him.

He shook his head, sucked his teeth and said, "You stupid."

Anition snapped like a violated mouse trap. "Nigga fuck you!"

"I should kill yo' punk ass baby daddy."

"Oh, now you a gangster?"

"Been one a dem," Kasper said. "Let det nigga hit choo."

"Don't worry 'bout me! Betta worry 'bout det nigga you shot!"

Kasper said, "He look ova his shoulda fo me! I look ova my shoulder to make sho eh-body followin' my lead!"

Anition sucked her teeth. "Punk—ass—lil' nigga."

Kasper stormed out of the kitchen and came back waving his 9mm Baretta. He cocked it. "Get cho dumb ass out, my momma house."

Putting up a hand trying to halt action Victoria said, "Kasper don't do dis! You put that gun away."

"She betta get da fuck out!"

"What I say—" Victoria's words were caught in her throat when five gunshots rang out.

Anition held her hands up, with her face turned screaming and attempting to block shots from coming. Kasper left quickly.

Stilloan Robinson

Chapter 9

Stacey was coming out of her apartment as Kasper was stepping onto the platform. "Nigga why the hell you shoot at Ann?" She sat down with her gun and pillow. "I took the shells out da case wit' some pliers." Looking up at Kasper who was still standing Stacey said, "You made some blanks?"

"Yeah."

She looked out into the parking lot shaking her head. Kasper was a handful. "Phat Man you don't do shit like det boy! Yo' ass—is—in—trouble. Yo' grammy jus called looking for you. Told me da tell you when I saw you to come home." Stacey threw up the peace sign.

"Man."

Stacey looked at Kasper. "You shoulda did det. Gon' see what Aunt Jean wants."

Aunt Jean fussed Kasper out about what he had done and smacked him with a hard clap. It was his mother that phoned her up. Mother Eba wanted no parts of it. She was in her room with the door closed. Aunt Jean was more like Kasper's second grandmother rather than a great aunt. That's why he called her Grammy and referred to Mother Eba as granny.

The smack hurt Aunt Jean more than it did Kasper. She had gone into her room and weeped because of the position Kasper forced her in. She nor Mother Eba love hitting their children but Kasper could get way out of the hand at times. During some of his tantrums when he was a younger boy Kasper would sometimes climb on top of the roof of the house and pout threatening to jump. Then the family would spend countless hours convincing him to come down. He would also dress up as a demon and go around the neighborhood vanishing and disappearing before neighbor's eyes. He had caused five heart attack deaths.

Kasper ate the snack and moved on. He went to Trump's Crack spot on the Northside in the McArthur's Park Community.

"You my lil' nigga," Trump said while sitting at the table chopping up a half kilogram of Crack cocaine. "I fuck wit choo harder

than I fuck wit' mosta theez niggaz. You a real nigga. Stay real, homie. Only da real survive, and you surviving off that sayin' alone."

"My gotdamned susta be lettin' her baby daddy put his hands on her."

"Who, Stacey?"

"Nah, my other susta."

"Well—crazy as it sounds you got some chicks that love to put up wit' shit like that." Kasper sighed.

"It's da truth, she stupid man," Trump said.

"You gotta let her worry 'bout that. Dey still togetha?"

"Yeah."

Trump said, "Well if she ain't left yet that's her stupidity. Who da nigga is?"

"His bitch ass name, Tron."

"Tron," Trump whispered to himself. He was trying to see if he recognized the name. He said it again, it did not click. "How old is he?"

"Him and my susta da same age, she's twenty-seven."

"Oh, nah I wouldn't know him. What he do?"

"Sell crack," Kasper said.

Trump said Tron's name once more to see if it sounded familiar. It didn't. "Fuck det, nigga," he said. "What school you goin' to, la homie?"

"Management school."

"Well, at least you still in school, nigga like me," Trump's words were interrupted by a loud *Bang*! The front door had been kicked in by the Feds.

"Found a .357, some pot and four grand on the kid," one of the agents said to a fellow colleague. "Let's get him down to headquarters to see what he knows."

"I don't know shit!" Kasper lashed. He was being interrogated by Us Marshalls.

Agent Muller said, "You're thirteen—how'd you get those?" Circling his face with a pointer. "Tattoos?" Kasper only grilled him.

"Rolex watch, you one of Trump's runners?"

"I don't run, I walk cracka!"

"So, you rather go to juvy?"

Agent Volinski said, "That's where you wanna go kid?"

"Get me dere."

"What's your name?" The staff asked while sitting in the office doing Kasper's intake. He had state charges consisting of possession of marijuana and possession of a firearm.

"Kasper," the boy said.

"I didn't ask you for a nickname," the black staff member said as his forehead beaded with sweat.

Kasper said, "Well, you got one."

"You wanna give me a hard time, son?"

Kasper's brows furrowed he did not like being called *son*. "I ain't cho gotdamned son, mothafucka!"

"You watch your mouth!"

Kasper snapped, "You heard me!"

"Son! You heard—" The staff member's words were clipped off when Kasper lunged and connected with a straight blow to his mouth. He was stunned, the boy hit hard.

Gaining apprehension Kasper was body-slammed on his thigh letting out an, "Urrgghhh!"

<p style="text-align:center">****</p>

"There go my, homegirl" Stacey said excitedly. Her first cousin, Cantrell had just gotten out of the car after pulling up.

"Suuuppp?" When she got to the platform she stopped to kiss Stacey's cheek.

"Les' go inside hon," Stacey said and grabbed up everything.

The two cousins sat in the living room watching *7th Heaven* on the TV. Cantrell said, "So, what's been diggin' cuz?" She was twenty-four-years old, slim, standing 5'6. Cantrell looked just like

a light-skinned Angelina Jolie. Her hair was one long braided ponytail. She worked a job as a bank teller at the Nations Bank in downtown Charlotte.

"Da usual, sellin' my weed and shit," Stacey said.

"Where yo' son?"

"Det lil' nigga in juvy."

The news came as a surprise to Cantrell. She looked at Stacey appalled. "The hell he in juvy for?

"Got caught wit' some weed and a gun."

"So, what the hell is this I hear about him shootin' blanks at Anition?"

Stacey may have had something stuck in her teeth because she sucked them and said, "You already know they don't see eye to eye."

"Yeah," Cantrell said.

"Dey got into it, Cantrell. Something about, Tron," Stacey finished. Cantrell looked away shaking her head. Stacey said, "Phat Man just crazy."

Looking back at Stacey, Cantrell said, "She can't leave him alone, huh?" Stacey waved off the topic. Then Cantrell asked, "You been gettin' any sleep?" Stacey only shook her head slowly. "Damn, Stacey."

"I'm good."

"I wanna get DMX's new CD, man."

"Flesh of My Flesh?"

"Yeah, I might go get it when I leave here."

"He comin' to da summa jam comin' up. You wanna make plans to go, cuz?"

Cantrell said, "Yeah, lest do that."

"Me, you, Justice and whoeva else wanna go. I wanna see Mystical."

"He gon' be there?"

"Yeah, he is." Stacey's phone rang on the couch beside her. She answered the phone, "Hello? Yea, you pulling up? Okay, I gotcha." When she got off the phone, she stood up sayin', "Cantrell what choo 'bout to do?"

"Nothin' why?"

"I'ma go make dis sale then we gonna get somethin' to eat," Stacey said. "On me." She went to bag up some weed and went outside as one of her clients pulled up in a grey Lincoln Town Car with gold Vogues. "Hey, Treon."

"Sup, girl?" Treon flashed a white gold smile.

"Here you go." Stacey had the product in exchange for its worth in cash.

Treon said, "So, what choo been up to?"

Shielding her eyes from the blazing sun Stacey said, "Hustlin'. You?"

"Same shit. Look—what's up?"

"Wit' what?"

"I can slide back through later on?"

Stacey inclined her head. "And do wha?"

"Smoke and see what's up."

"Nah, Treon." Stacey, it seemed, was waving a hand good-bye. "I ain't like det."

"Check me out right—" Treon reached into his pocket for his money. "I got det bread."

"Are you serious?"

"Listen, Stacey—"

"No, come on, Treon. I thought we was people?" Stacey lowered her voice. She couldn't believe Treon was coming at her like that. "Don't do me like dis," Stacey pleaded. This was for the benefit of the doubt. Stacey was feeling violated and wanted Treon to stop making sexual passes at her.

"I got it," Treon pressed. He looked at his money and flashed one thousand dollars. "You wanna grand?"

"Les' stop, Treon please," said a desperate Stacey. She didn't want Treon to end his life because that was the way it was going. "I've known you since high school, you can't come off on me like det. We do business, nothing more nothing less, Treon," Stacey said. "I'm askin' you to stop disrespectin' me."

"What choo want fifteen hunnid?" Treon asked.

Stacey stared a hole through Treon. She weighed her options. Treon was being foul. "I said no, Treon. I don't rock like det mixing business with pleasure."

"Damn, I'm payin' you a chunk."

"Come here." Stacey reached into the window to touch Treon on the forehead. "Leave da neighborhood when you get to da first red light—kill yo' self somehow." She removed her hand, tossed the money she had gotten for her product in the window on Treon's lap and walked off.

Chapter 10

In Gatlin's Detention Center, Kasper had been placed on what was called 'the cross' handcuffed and shackled to his steel bunk and four points wearing only a pair of boxers. He was thinking about a lot. Kasper felt like he hated Anition. If it had not been for his niece, he would have killed Tron and gave no thought or care in the world about how Anition felt about it.

Tron was a stone-cold coward. Then it was that smack Aunt Jean gave Kasper that left a lingering burn on the side of his face. 'It's Anition's fault!' he thought.

Lacey became associated with the boy's thoughts. He liked Lacey a lot. She was his bitch, but yet she was real aggravating always wanting him to be up under her. She was not trying to let him grow up and that he knew. Despite all that, she had good sex. The way she moaned and cried would arouse him even more. Kasper's thoughts were intruded by the sound of keys jingling and someone descending the hallway.

"Damn." Kasper had a hard-on and the staff was coming to check on him. Peering into the four by six-inch window the staff chuckled. Kasper raised up his head. "Faggot ass nigga!"

"Shut up lil' pussy! You hard, huh?"

"You lookin' at my dick?"

"I'ma go home and fuck some pussy while you in here thinking 'bout it," the staff said.

"You up here lookin' at my hard dick thinkin' bout cho' momma did det!"

The staff snickered. "Lil' bitch boy." He went back up the hall whistlin'.

"I'ma try da knock his bitch ass out when I catch him!" Kasper promised. "Gay ass!"

Treon had been given a demand by the Kovijicii Queen and had to follow the order all the way through. Treon knew he had to do what was commanded. When he came to the entrance of Piedmont Court, Treon went under his seat for his .45 Colt and held it. He

turned right into Siegal Avenue and pulled up to the light. Treon stuck the barrel of the gun into his mouth—
Poow! He slumped into the steering wheel.

"Stacey, you okay babes?" Cantrell asked standing by the bathroom door. When Stacey came back into her apartment she started crying and stormed up the steps into the bathroom slamming the door behind her.

Cantrell could hear her sniffling but Stacey didn't answer. "Baby, Stacey, you, cool hon?"

Stacey sniffled and said, "Yeah." Then unlocked the door.

Cantrell went in and found Stacey sitting on the edge of the tub. "What's wrong?"

Stacey told Cantrell about the incident with Treon. It hurt her so much to have done Treon the way she did. *But he did it to himself,* she reminded herself.

<p style="text-align:center">****</p>

After four hours on '*the cross*' Kasper was let off and moved to room one, there – unlike many other cells- was a stationary toilette and sink. He was placed on status three *out of cell restriction* and labeled a threat. A T-shirt, socks, khaki pants with no pockets, a bedroll and a mat had been issued to him, not to mention a pair of shower shoes that had to stay outside of the door.

"Aye room one!" Someone yelled. Kasper was making his bunk. "My nigga wit da long hair?"

Kasper paused and turned his head toward the door bellowing, "What!"

"Come to the door."

"Man—" Kasper went to look out the window. "Yeah, dog?" he said while poking around.

A dark-skinned, juvenile with a small afro, waved from the window diagonally across from him. "Ova here."

"Sup?"

"What dey put choo on a cross fo'?"

"Da cross? Man, I don't know what choo talkin' 'bout!"

"When you was shackled to the bed."

"Oh," Kasper said. "Because dey thought I was da Lord and Savior."

The other boy laughed. "Nah what choo do, though?"

In a flat tone, Kasper said, "Cuz I stole on a staff."

"So, what choo locked up fo?"

Kasper said, "I do not feel like talkin'." Then moved away from the door.

"What? Fuck you den, lame ass nigga."

Kasper ignored the comment and went back to making up his bunk. When he finished, he went to look out of his back window. Wasn't much to see but the parking lot and some trees. Dinner had come and the *gay* staff was serving the plates of food held on top of a large round tray. He opened the door to give Kasper his rations. All that could be heard next was the tray falling, crashing the few plates of food to the ground with wet *thunks!*

Next, there was scuffling against the door, someone being knocked up against the wall and shoes scratching, then loud thumps and grunts.

"Girl's side! Girl's side!" The staff needed some help subduing the out of control juvenile. "Girl's side!"

There had been females housed here in Gatlin but was removed in 96. Kasper had been restrained and admitted to '*the cross*' again. Court was the following day, yet, Kasper was detained. Raged pervaded his emotions like an AID's takeover. He started something with one of the staff when he got back to the detention center. That staff suffered a broken nose and Kasper was back on '*the cross*'.

"Every time," Kasper said while being shackled. "It's gon' happen every time." The next week at court Kasper was detained once more.

"Have a seat, young fella." One of the supervising staff had taken Kasper into the office to have a one on one chat.

"What choo want?" Kasper exclaimed as he sat down.

"I just want to talk. Now listen, you don't know why they keep kicking you back, right?"

"They ain't say."

"What did you do to the judge. When you youngstas leave for court, notice the sheriff that transports you guys has envelopes." The supervisor emphasized by making a figure with both thumbs and index fingers. "In these envelopes are reports on each of you." He pointed a finger around the room. "On how you all acted, you got—" He softly jabbed Kasper in his chest with a knuckle. "Assaults—assaults—assaults." He held his hands out shaking his head. "And they're all on the staff. Before long they give up on you and send you off."

The supervisor lowered his voice. "Cause these crackas gonna say you're a threat to society. You already have a gun beef and you're only thirteen. You need to chill, my man, and be cool so you can get out." He dropped his voice again. "I know you be getting pussy. You are no slouch from what I see, with your face tatted up, gold in your mouth and long hair. Get out of this place man and quit being so aggressive. You're a real hostile cat. But I'm willing to write you a good report providing that you behave. I'll even let you read it. Deal?" He stuck his hand out.

It didn't take long for Kasper to agree and shake his hand. "Deal." The following week Kasper went to court and was released with a one-year probation.

"Glad you out, Phat Man," Stacey said with an arm around her little brother. She kissed his cheek and said, "I missed you."

They were leaving the courthouse along with their mother, grandmother, Aunt Jean and Aunt Yazette.

"Missed you, too."

"Trump wrote choo a letter."

Smiling, Kasper said, "Oh, yeah?" He had mutual respect for Trump. Trump was solid, down to earth, he kept it real and in him, Kasper found an uncle.

"Yep," Stacey said.

Kasper kissed the rest of his people and went with Stacey.

"I rented another apartment," Stacey said from the driver's seat of her 95 Mustang GT. "Got two of my young boys sellin' out of it for me."

"Where et?"

"The one yo' ass went up in that night."

When Stacey and Kasper got back to the apartment, she gave Kasper Trump's letter from out of her drawer.

"How you doin' wit' that dope shit?" he asked.

"Doin' good. Com' here, baby." Stacey led the way to Kasper's room and went into his closet. She took down a shoebox off the shelf and gave it to him. "I put twenty grand up for ya."

Kasper shook his head. "You don't owe me."

"No, I'm giving it to you. Big susta want choo to have it."

"A'ighd. Thank ya, then."

"Go ahead on getcha self together." Stacey left out the room and Kasper sat on his bed and opened the letter Trump wrote.

Cold K

Sup, real nigga?

Them big boys got me, cuz. I'm fucked up bad—real bad. I appreciate you not telling those crackas shit 'bout me. They got me lookin' at some time, gangsta. I had my girl run by yo' susta's spot to drop this letter off to you. Need some favors from you. I feel you're the only one I can trust. A jigsaw wouldn't dare trust these sucka ass clowns out here. These niggas is snakes.

Check this out it's this nigga named, Cola that be in Savannah Woods in the Southside. He owes me five grand, snatch that up for me la cuz. Also, another nigga named, Mika that be in JY Williams on the Westwood owes me twenty-five hundred. Touch that for me, too. Give it all to my woman, Valencia. Her number is 529-0495 call her, she knows what's up. That Fleetwood in my driveway yours, you can have it.

It ain't nothing I can do with it, except sell it, but I'd rather give it to you. My lady will give you the title. It's a pump at the house, an AK-47, two twin Glock 40s and my other .357. So, don't worry about the one you lost. And forgive me for gettin' you hemmed up.

"I ain't worried about that," Kasper said to the letter, then continued reading.

One more favor: that nigga Peanut in PC, drop the top on that nigga. He an informant on my case. I appreciate you again. Aye,

those niggas in Piedmont Courts can't fuck wit choo. Cold K, you a real official nigga. Be easy homeboy and stay in touch wit' my girl but burn this letter. Peace,
 Trump

Chapter 11

Remembering all the information Kasper took a lighter, burned the letter and flushed the ashes down the toilet. His Erickson mobile phone rung.

"Hello?"

"Hey, baby." It was Lacey.

"What's up?" He sat down on his bed and twiddle with a braid.

"I missed you," Lacey claimed. "I'm glad you're out. Why you ain't write me back?"

"You ain't write me."

"I wrote you every week you were in there, Sweetie."

Kasper said, "I ain't get no letters." Kasper had been a problem and that resulted to his mail getting misplaced. "I was in there actin' up."

"I know, I tried to come see you and bring you money, but they said you couldn't have either."

"Yeah, fuck it."

"Did you miss me?" Lacey wanted to know. Kasper told her about the erection he had while on 'The Cross' and they both laughed. "I couldn't come to court this time, baby. I had to work," Lacey said. "I saw your sister, Kacey and she told me you'd gotten out. I got somethin' to tell you."

"Tell me."

"Nooo," Lacey whined. "I wanna tell you later."

"A'ight."

"Well, let me get back to work."

Kasper said, "Pick me up et my susta Stacey's spot in PC."

"Okay, when I get off, I'm straight over there."

"See ya."

"I love you," Lacey said innocently

The boy smiled. "I know."

"I love you too is what you should say."

Over a chuckle, Kasper said, "Come on, man."

"Okay, baby!" Lacey said. "Don't worry about it. You don't have to say it. I'll be over there to pick you up when I get off."

"I'll be waiting."

"Bye."

Kasper hung up and went downstairs and out the door to the platform.

"You pregnant?" Kasper repeated. He was lying naked in the bed with Lacey. She'd just told him she was pregnant.

"Yes," she confirmed. "With your child."

"So, what choo gon' do?"

"I wanna have it, Kasper, what you mean?"

After a sigh, Kasper said, "I was just' askin'."

"But choo know we gonna have to keep it quiet."

"Okay, but my kid gon' call me Daddy."

"If anybody finds out I can go to jail. Ain't nothing wrong with it calling you by your name."

The boy protested, "Yeah, right! You better come up wit' a betta solution."

Lacey sucked her teeth. An abortion was out of the question most definitely. She was having this boy's baby. Lacey turned over, she'd never loved anybody the way she loved Kasper. *However, did this come to happen?*

After about five minutes of silence, she said, "As long as it knows who its father is—"

"You shoulda thought about that, Lacey," Kasper said causing a grimace on Lacey's face. "We gon' think of something."

"Goodnight."

The next morning Lacey got up to shower, then let Kasper drop her off at work so he could keep the truck. Kasper went home, took a shower and chilled until 12:30 pm. Kasper went out to look for this Cola dude on the Southside. When he pulled into the neighborhood there was a handful of guys standing out in the parking lot, so he pulled up to them.

A knock came from the front door as Stacey was coming down the stairs. "Justice!" She sang once she saw who it was through the screen. "Come in, babes," she said, embracing her best friend since childhood. "I missed you friend."

"I missed you too, baby, Stacey."

"You been gone a minute." Stacey went and sat down as Justice sat beside her.

"It was only 'bout two months."

"Two months too long. How was Cali?"

"Stacey, I really enjoyed it. I did not know my family was that big." Justice was thick, with a honey-colored skin complexion, cornrowed hair and was twenty-four-years old.

"Glad my girl's back." Stacey smiled. Justice was the only friend Stacey ever had.

"You is?"

Stacey said, "Yeahhh, I really missed you, my buddy. Where's Asia?"

"She et my mom's house," Justice said. "Yo' brotha get out?"

"Yeah."

"My lil' Indian boy."

Stacey threw her head back and said, "Oh, Lawd." Justice laughed. "Girl wait till you see this nigga's face and what he did to it."

"You was telling me about his tattoos."

"That boy crazy, J."

"That's yo' son." They both laughed. "I ain't lyin'."

"He shot that boy on the porch fo' nothin. Then sat his ass down and started eating Starburst like it was nothin'." They both laughed again. Then Stacey said, "C'mon, I gotta go down here and check on my spot. I got another apartment. Two of my boys sellin' out of it for me."

The two friends found their way to Stacey's spot and went inside.

"Sup, Stacey?" Tonio spoke. He had a big head with cornrows.

"Y'all good?" Stacey said to Tonio and Santario as they played the video game.

Santario said, "Yeah, we good." He had a low cut with a head full of waves.

Santario was seventeen-years-old and Tonio was sixteen.

Tonio said, "Stacey, you wanna play?"

"Shut up," she teased. "I do not play video games." Tonio chuckled. "Can one a y'all go to the store for me?" Stacey asked. "Please, I need a Mountain Dew."

Tonio decided to take the walk to the store and as he was coming out, he ran into Santario's girlfriend, Kita. They started talking then she asked, "You gon' let me suck yo dick?" The words escaped Kita's lips like a jailed inmate.

Tonio was surprised. "You serious?"

"Yeah!"

A smile formed on Tonio's face. It was now a matter of sexual satisfaction not a matter if Santario was Tonio's boy.

"Where we gon' go?"

"Come on." Kita started walking. "My momma and susta's gone."

Tonio followed Kita back to where she stayed. Inside the apartment was a trifling mess. There were dishes in the sink, stacked and crawling with bugs. Grease clunks were splotched on the stove and the floor was dingy and sticky from spilled tea. Tonio and Kita went into the living room, where a TV set on a steamer trunk, a wire hanger was used as an antenna. The material over the cushions was ripped away on the couch.

Kita instructed Tonio to sit down, then she sat beside him, unfastened his pants and pulled out his manhood. "Don't slip up and tell nobody," Kita demanded.

"I ain't."

"Mmmm." Kita went down and Tonio sucked in a quick breath of air. "Ooh!" He flinched when his boy's girlfriend pulled on his dick head as if she was trying to pull it off.

She popped it out, spat on it and went back down.

"Uuhh!" Tonio's eyes became bloodshot red. Tonio relished this moment of sexual glory, it took him all of five minutes to come. Kita went into the kitchen to spit it out into the sink.

"Y'all know who, Cola, is?" Kasper asked the men.

They all looked around at each other, one guy moved over to where someone was sitting halfway inside of a Buick Roadmaster.

"Yo', CoCo some lil' young ass PeeWee want choo."

Kasper softly tskd, "This man had no clue."

CoCo got out of the Buick and approached the truck. "Sup, lil' cuz who you?"

"Cold K," Kasper told him. "Trump got locked up and sent me to get five grand that somebody named Cola owed."

CoCo's eyebrows furrowed. "Trump?"

"Yeah, you Cola?"

"I am but my question is—" he thought. "—why would he send you?"

"That shouldn't be yo' concern dog. Trump got his own reasons," Kasper said, as Cola stared at him. "Iz it gon' be a problem?"

Cola said, "Look here man—you roll up here like—"

"Fuck all that, I'm only doin' what Trump asked. It ain't my money but gotdamn—respect tha fact he sent me da get it. If you owe him evidently, he did some truism. You gon' payback what choo owe. But if you can't pay and I holla et Trump. He gon' send me da get it anotha way." Kasper raised his eyebrows. "And I'm comin'."

"Lil' cuz I don't know who you comin' et like that, but I don't play 'bout no threats."

"Bra just pay da bread. The man locked up and gon' need his money. If it was you somebody owed you'd want cho bread. Let the man get his money."

"You got that lil' cuz, I see you official, too. Come holla et me tomorrow 'bout one. I'll be here wit' the money. That straight?"

"Nah man, I'ma be in school tomorrow et that time. I get out et three-thirty—try four."

"That'll work."

"A'ight."

"You tell Trump he snatched up a real ass lil' nigga."

Only throwing his head up as a response Kasper pulled off.

"Damn, Stacey, how tha years came and went," Justice said.

She and Stacey were on the platform of the drug spot. Stacey had been waiting for Tonio to come back from the store.

Justice said, "Seems like it was just yesterday when we started high school."

"Time's flyin' friend. You know what's funny, J?"

"What's that?"

"When we were younger, we wished we could be grown. So, we could really do what we wanted to do, but now that we're grown—"

"—We wanna be kids again." Justice took the words right out Stacey's mouth and they both laughed.

Stacey said, "It's a crazy thang."

"Ain't it?"

"Mmmhhh-huh." Stacey looked to the right and saw Tonio coming. She snapped, "Where my damn soda? Yo ass been gone almost an hour! I ain't sending yo' ass to tha store no damn mo' dog, for real! You take to mothafuckin' long!"

"My fault." Tonio gave Stacey her soda and she snatched it.

"This shit hot! What the fuck wuz you doin'?" She was scowlin' at him.

"Talkin' to somebody," he replied.

"Next time you bring yo' ass. That shit and yo' conversation down this way!" Stacey got up and said to Justice, "J, you want somethin' outta here?"

"Nah, I'm good."

"A'ight." Stacey went inside and Tonio tried to go in behind her. She threw a blocking elbow saying, "What tha hell you want?"

84

Tonio chuckled. "I'm tryna get in?"

"Fa wha? You need to get cho head knocked. Tonio I can look at choo and tell you been doin' somethin' you ain't have no business doin'."

"I ain't been doin' nuttin'."

Stacey walked on inside saying, "Beat cho ass." She wanted to get a cup of ice, when she came back out, she saw Kasper. "There go, my baby." Justice looked and saw a smile across her face. Waving a hand like a person stranded out to sea Stacey said, "Ova here!" Kasper came over. "Hey, baby."

"Hey, Big Susta." Then Kasper said to Justice. "Sup, J?"

"How you doin'?" Justice was checking out Kasper's tattooed face.

He said, "You been gone a minute ain't choo?"

"Yep."

"I got cho welcome back gift."

Justice sucked her teeth. "Where?"

"Unzip me an get it out." Kasper smiled and Stacey hunched over laughing as she held both her cup of ice and soda.

"Wow," Justice said.

"Want me to show you tha tip of it?"

Tears came to Stacey's eyes as she laughed. Justice looked down at Kasper, for a glimpse, then looked back up to him and said, "You know you need to stop."

"I just saw you go down there. You was lookin' for it, wasn't ya, huh?"

Justice said to Stacey who couldn't stop laughing. "You hear yo' brotha? Ya son." Stacey gestured as if she did not want anything to do with it.

Justice then said, "Yo' lil' badass."

"You gon' invited me over to yo' spot tonight?"

"Fa what?"

"Cause I wanna see yo eyes lookin' up et me while you—"

Smiling, Justice cut Kasper off, "Shut cho dam mouth."

"Well—can I smell it?"

"What?"

Stacey's laughter grew louder.

"You heard me, let a real nigga smell somethin'. I wanna smell it from the back."

Justice shared in Stacey's laughter. "Aye, you know how to spit slop and do all that nasty shit?"

"You a nasty lil' nigga."

"Yeah, let's get that nasty."

"Oh, my God."

Kasper waved Justice off. "You bullshittin', I gotta phone call to make."

Chapter 12

Trump's girl, Valencia, picked Kasper up from Piedmont Courts, so he could get the car and guns. He gave her seven thousand five hundred dollars. The money Cola owed, Kasper would pocket that. The money Mula owed Kasper was going to pay out of his own pocket and not worry about Mula. Kasper did not have time for the conflict that would come with that. He parked the Cadillac at his aunt, Zhale's home in Huntersville on the outskirts of Charlotte. She had the big farm that contributed to the two-family owned restaurants called, *The Fancy Napkin* which sold island foods.

The car was put up under one of the sheds. Kasper stayed a while before getting a ride back to PC. He got in the truck around 6:45 to pick Lacey up from work and let her drive. As she was taking him home she started talking shit because he wouldn't come to her place and he wouldn't tell her he loved her.

"Don't try and come back to my place," she said when he was getting out.

"I hope you wasn't worried," he fired back before shutting the door.

"You know what—" Kasper heard Lacey say in a muffled tone. He was walking around the car headed towards the house. "—you got a slick ass mouth!" Kasper shrugged. "Stupid ass nigga!"

He shrugged again, this was how he got Lacey. She wanted an argument. Lacey snatched the truck in park and got out.

"Give me my key—now!"

Kasper turned on his heels. "Lacey gone now."

"I want my key!" She held her hand out like a corner beggar.

"Fuck you! You ain't gettin' shit!"

When Lacey got closer, she tried to slap Kasper, but he jumped back.

"A'ight now."

"What?" She walked up on Kasper as he was moving backward. Lacey jolted forward and grabbed the boy's shirt.

"Stop dog." He smiled

"I want my key!"

"Cuz I ain't gon' argue witcha?"

"Just give me my key."

Kasper said, "Please believe me when I say you ain't gotta worry 'bout me comin' back to yo' place."

"I hate choo!" Lacey slung Kasper to the ground and fell on top of him.

"Glad you ain't say you loved me," Kasper said.

"Nigga fuck you!" Lacey was tussling with Kasper.

"How you look out here fighting with a thirteen-year-old?"

Lacey got up saying, "Yo' ass make me sick!" She had tears in her eyes. When she got back into her truck, she screeched out of the neighborhood crying. *How could the boy I would give anything to hurt me so badly?* Lacey thought he was the sweetest thing. "Damn Kasper!"

"Why what happened?" Stacey asked from the top of the stairs with her hands on her hips looking down at Kasper who stood at the bottom of the steps.

"Somebody wants me da murk em. Sayin' he an informant."

"And you jus' gon' go up there shootin'?"

Kasper stood there looking at his sister. It gave her the indication that he would do just that.

"No man," Stacey said. "You know somebody gon' tell on you. No!"

"Well—he gotta go. The person that told me to do it said so."

"Have they paid you to do it?"

"Yep."

"I don't know what to tell you then, Phat Man. But choo ain't 'bout to go up there and jus' pop him in front of everybody."

"I know what to do then," Kasper said.

A short while later, Kasper left out of Stacey's back door dressed in an Atlanta Falcons pullover and his hair was tucked

away. He had a .357 Magnum, shorty was ready as he vanished into the night.

Peanut was standing in front of a platform talking to some females along with a few homeboys about the hood and what the word was on anything.

"We gotta keep it real," one of the females was saying. "How many times y'all think LuLu hit that shit? They say Maurice wasn't fuckin' her."

"Girl, Maurice, was fuckin' everybody."

"Even you, Monique?" Peanut asked

"Hell, no! What tha fuck?"

"Well, a'ight then."

Monique said, "Shut tha fuck up mothafucka! Yo' lame-ass fuckin' ole dirty butt ass, Kim."

"You won't tell her that."

"You, act—" Monique stood to her feet. "—like she gon' do somethin'. Nigga that bitch ain't gon' do shit! I bet choo that!"

One of the other girls said, "Y'all don't start that."

"Nah, Shanice this nigga gon' make it seem like—"

At that moment everyone but Peanut saw a figure appear behind Peanut holding a pistol with both hands. *Boom!* A loud explosion blew Peanut's head in half and the figure vanished. This happened within a split second.

"*Oh—what the fuck! What the fuck!*" One of the guys yelled out while cowering behind one of the females.

It felt like everyone was trying to out yell one another. Not only because Peanut had gotten shot but also because of the way it happened and how they saw it. This could not register. How could they explain this to detectives when they came around asking questions?

Kasper ignored the phone call from Lacey the next morning.

Eight months later, in the year of 1999 Lacey gave birth to a baby girl. Kasper was there but could not sign the birth certificate. It was Stacey that named her niece, Kanazi Anjari Pecoise.

"You a grandma now," her cousin Cantrell teased.

Lacey came clean to her parents about Kasper. They respected her honesty but didn't agree with her choices. She was their only child so they went with it and was surprised that the boy could hold a conversation on a college level.

Stacey had sold out of crack cocaine but she still had Tonio and Santario around selling weed. Kasper got Stacey to get him in a three-bedroom house with two full bathrooms, and a two-car garage. The house was two-story, and in Stacey's name. Stacey had a condo on the Southside but still had her two apartments in Piedmont Courts.

The Texaco gas station in Eastway and Shamrock was a hangout spot for small-time hustlers and gang members. Kasper pulled up in his Cadillac, some dude wearing a blue dickie outfit and a blue bandana spotted Kasper wearing his black Bulls jersey, Girbaud jeans, and a red bandana.

"Sup, lil nigga, choo blood?"

Opening the cooler Kasper said, "Ain't no gotdamn blood!" He took out a grapefruit juice. "I don't gang bang. If anything I bang gangs."

"Fuck that 'pose to mean fool?"

Turning to walk away Kasper said, "Fuck you think, nigga?"

The guy sucked both lips, cocked his hand back, leaned forward and smacked Kasper so hard that he reeled back, and the drink flew out of his hand, as he crashed into the cooler. The dude ran up on Kasper and rammed his head into that cooler, snatching off the red bandana in the process. Kasper's right hand reached quickly grabbing the Glock 9 on his waist, as he slipped it out like an outlaw in a Jon Wayne movie. He banged out four shots in rapid secession until the gun jammed then Kasper ran off.

Chapter 13

The police had been by Kasper's mother's house because of the surveillance footage catching his tag number, but he wasn't there. Officers told her that he needed to turn himself in as soon as possible. The next day, Kasper turned himself in and later in court the Judge ruled his actions self-defense but unfortunately because the camera showed Kasper in possession of a firearm, he'd violated his probation and was sentenced to serve ten months in the boys reformatory school that most called a training school named Swannanoa.

He was transported by the sheriff. The only thing on his mind was his baby girl. Kasper had heard that Trump took a plea deal and received fifteen years in prison for gun and drug possession. His relationship with Lacey was shaky. The sheriff had made it to the mountains of Swannanoa North Carolina. When they got to the compound campus, security let them through the gates. The boy was scanning his temporary home away from home as he released a heavy sigh.

To the left they passed a second building, to the right was a street that snaked left right before climbing a hill past the chapel getting to the cottages Frye and Gilliard. Just right after that was the cafeteria, and across the street from it was the gym then came a street and another cottage suite. The sheriff took a right past a large basketball court, to the right of that was Sloop Cottage. The sheriff made a quick left pulling up in front of Greenwood cottage the main cottage and processing. All of this was kept inside of a twenty-five-foot fence shaped like a lowercase f. Kasper was still handcuffed and shackled down, as he was let out by the sheriff. He was escorted to the double set of doors that stood as a small vestibule.

After the sheriff rang the doorbell, a tall, white, muscular guy who looked like he was in his mid-forties came to unlock the interior set of double doors. Locking them back he unlocked the exterior set of double doors to let the sheriff and the juvenile in. The staff repeated the same unlocking and locking ritual once more in a practiced fashion to get back inside. Now they were in a lobby that was cold. It sounded like an exhaust fan was on. To the left of the large

lobby, a day room could be seen through tempered glass. Juveniles gave the new arrival cold hard stares.

Kasper sighed inward, knowing it would only be a matter of time before he would have to prove himself. Juveniles here on the A-wing were either on DI: *Detention Isolation* or doing their fifteen days of A.T.W: *Assigned To Wing*. Straight ahead slightly to the left was the B wing. The juveniles were doing a three-month A.T.W program called IDP: *In Door Prison*, for numerous infractions. They too had the same welcoming stares for Kasper. Beside B wing was the supervisor's office. To Kasper's right was the C wing. Juveniles were doing their thirty days orientation before going to the yard for programming.

Their looks were somewhat different as if Kasper could be familiar. A small sofa sat up against the wall in front of the C wing where Kasper was told to have a seat. The sheriff stepped inside the supervisor's office, where he signed over custody. After about ten minutes the sheriff and the staff returned. It was time for the shackles to come off.

Standing, watching with one hand on his waist and the other holding a cup of steaming coffee the staff said, "I'm Mr. Sharpe. The supervisor here in Greenwood. You know you're going to have to cut your hair don't ya?"

Kasper's knees were on the sofa as they were trying to get the leg irons off because the sheriff was having a hard time with the key.

Kasper looked over his shoulder with a scowl. He snapped his head forward and said, "I ain't cuttin' a gotdamn thang!"

As he smacked on a piece of gum, Mr. Sharpe studied Kasper for a moment, then said, "Have a smart mouth, huh?"

"You heard me." Kasper darted his eyes from Mr. Sharpe and turned toward the window looking into the C wing. One of the juveniles was up close saying something Kasper couldn't make out. "What!" He frowned. The boy was not in the mood for anything.

"You're not going to last long here," Mr. Sharpe stated.

"Alright," the sheriff said. "Turn around so I can get—" he let his voice trail off as Kasper turned around. The sheriff said, "—I know you're ready to get out of these."

"Well, unless you have religious reasons, you're going to cut that hair!" Mr. Sharpe stated again.

Kasper was looking down at what the sheriff was doing.

"That's all I need to know."

The waist chains were brought to a release. "Wish you the best of luck," the sheriff said.

Kasper looked at him. "You should wish these mothafuckas tha best of luck."

The sheriff chuckled and was let out. Mr. Sharpe came back to give his own brief orientation. He pointed to C wing and said, "Let's move it, you'll be over here."

Kasper's nose flared. He wanted to say what was on his mind but instead let it go. The now juvenile inmate was directed to a rubber sofa that sat beside a staff's desk. Each wing had staff stationed at a desk.

Mr. Sharpe said, "You let me know if this kid gives you any problems, McCoy. I'll put him on DI."

"Do tha clock stop tickin' while on it?" Kasper asked.

"Yeah, you're not going to last, I'm willing to bet." Mr. Sharpe walked off mumbling.

Only one phone call was permitted but since McCoy liked Kasper, he was granted two. Kasper called his mother first, and then he talked to Kandy.

"You bet not let them boys' chump you around," Kandi said. "You ain't no punk so you betta put blood on the flo' and make it pop without warning lil' nigga. If you got so much as a scratch when we visit, word up cuz that's yo' ass no bullshit. I love you and I'ma write choo and send you pictures every week like you did when I was in training school."

"Okay, I love you too!"

"Peace nigga."

After the phone call, Kasper got to take a shower. He was given a pair of socks, T-shirts, shower shoes and some USA sweatpants

to put on. His street clothes went into a mesh bag that would be stored away until his release. The rest of the clothes would be issued out by the program director. Kasper was free for day room activities. Lockdown was at 10:00 pm. He looked up at the clock on the wall it was 8:19 pm. Then he sat on one of the rubber cushions and watched TV. The making of *TLC's* hit single *Scrubs* video was on MTV.

"I was askin' what part of the city you from?"

Kasper looked up at a tall, lanky juvenile who then sat down beside him. "Part of tha city I'm from?"

"Yeah, I could tell by the sheriff that you from Charlotte."

Kasper looked back at the TV and said, "Shamrock."

"Tha Eastside? I'm from the Westside, Beauties Foes."

"A'ight."

"What choo locked up fo'?"

"Got caught wit' a pistol," Kasper half lied.

"You goin' to Sloop."

Looking back to the juvenile Kasper said, "Sloop?"

"Serious offender cottage. It goes down ova there. You got diamonds in yo' mouth?"

"Yeah." Kasper's eyes found the TV again.

"How much you pay fo' 'em?"

"Dog—" Kasper looked back at his interrogator. "—you come ova here and start askin' me questions and shit. I don't even know you or yo' name! Then I ain't gon' mentioned how you tried to put fear in me by telling me it go down in Sloop." Kasper pointed a finger into his chest, sayin', "I'ma problem! If it go down in Sloop, then whateva cottage they put me in go be Sloop!"

"Bra, I ain't mean it like that. I was jus' puttin' you on point."

"No, put cho' self on point! Put y'all on point cuz I can go off now."

"We both from the same city, calm down. My name's, D-Lo."

"I'm Kasper." He raised his eyebrows. "Or Cold K."

Chapter 14

Ten-o-clock lockdown came. Kasper was sitting on his bunk thinking. The cell was 7 x 14 with a large sink that sat by the door. The bed ran quadrilateral on the back wall with an 80-inch square window. A toilet sat parallel behind a small wall. Sometimes millipedes would sneak their way in through small cracks in the wall at the bottom.

"—part of tha city that nigga from?" Kasper all of a sudden heard a voice.

"Oh uhh—Shamrock," that was D-Lo.

"Call, him to tha door."

"Kasper?"

Kasper got up slowly and shuffled toward the door. "Yeah.

"Sup, bra?"

"Who you?"

"Dre, you from the Eastside?"

"Shamrock."

"I'm from Windsong Trails, tha southside."

"A'ight."

"How long you got?"

"Ten months."

Dre said, "Dog, they gon' make you cut cho' hair?"

Kasper snapped. "They ain't gon make me cut shit, nigga, bet that!" He didn't play about his hair.

It was only one time in the boy's life where he'd had to cut his hair off. He was eight and in his Aunt Chattajmas neighborhood. Two older women were on the porch talking, one sat on the steps and the other stood. They saw the child, smiled then spoke. Kasper was on his bike looking to get a thrill.

"Hellow," he said in French.

"What he say?" The woman standing asked.

"I don't know."

Kasper got off his bike. "Y'all wanna see magic?" he said in French.

"Baby what are you sayin'?" That's was the one sitting on the step.

Kasper repeated his question again and this time pulled out a lighter.

"Lord, la boy," said the women standing. "What choo doin' wit' a lighter?"

"I'm 'bout to show y'all some magic."

"We do not know what choo sayin'." the lady sitting down said. This was her house.

Kasper flicked the lighter to the flame. "You see it?"

"What in tha world is this child sayin'?" The women sitting asked.

"What is he doin'?"

Kasper put his mouth over the flame and came off it still holding down the gauge. He showed the lighter as if he couldn't say nothing because he had his mouth close. Then he put his mouth back in the flame pocket as if spitting on it and replaced the flame and showed it.

"Wha that—" The sitting woman asked. "—a trick lighter?"

Kasper smiled. "You think so, don't you?" He flicked the lighter again and the flame raged. Kasper took his index and thumb, picked the flame up and showed it to the women.

"Ooh!" The standing woman shouted as she ran up the steps frightened. "Tha Hell," the woman said.

"Child you gotta gone from here."

"Lord have mercy!"

"Gone child and take that devil mess on."

In English Kasper said, "Well, tha devil just showed you his fire." And left.

The fire magic was illicit and prohibited because the time and place were very inappropriate. One of the Amudakis sent down a black dove to mother Eba bearing a message that the boy had to clip his hair. He was also made to wrap it in a kerchief. When a month passed his hair was restored to its full length.

A husky voice spoke saying, "Man y'all niggas take y'all asses to sleep! Ain't nobody tryna hear y'all talk! It's bedtime!"

"Who is that?" Kasper asked Dre.

"Nigga—" feet came rushing to the door. "—I'm Abe!"

"Fuck you, mothafucka! You ain't tha staff!" Kasper spat.

"Tell you what—I can see what choo hands like tomorrow when Baily come!"

"Yeah, you gon' see 'em comin' straight to yo' face! Man, I ain't 'bout to talk to you about it."

Dre pleaded with Kasper as Abe kept talking saying, "Chill Kasper."

"Knock his lil' ass out, beat those tattoos off yo' face!"

"Fuck that, nigga," Kasper said to Dre.

One voice chimed in saying, "He don't know you do he, Abe?"

"Oh, Ima show him!"

Dre said, "Jus holla et ya tomorrow."

"Yeah, I'm 'bout to lay down anyway," D-Lo said. "Been up all day."

"Y'all gon' let that bitch ass nigga turn y'all from the door?"

"They gon' run yo' ass to tha hospital!" Abe said and somebody laughed and clapped at the same time. "Punk ass lil' nigga."

"Get et us," Dre said.

"Scary ass niggas!" Kasper moved away from the door.

Abe kept going. "Whoop that nigga ass tomorrow. He think I'm playin'!"

The next morning staff showed up and brought the breakfast trays. Two personal bowls of fruit loops, a sausage patty, eggs, and biscuits was served. D-Lo had given Kasper a pair of state-issued black converse sneakers.

"You can use these to scrap in."

Kasper said nothing.

"Abe talkin' to Bailey now."

When Mr. Bailey went to Kasper's room he said, "Y'all fight and let it go. You get whooped don't snitch."

"Shut tha fuck up, go tell him that!" Kasper snarled.

"I wanna see how you come outta this one." Mr. Bailey smiled.

"Tha same way I'm goin in." Kasper said with arrogance.

Stilloan Robinson

Chapter 15

Abe was standing by the back wall in the shower area when Kasper walked in. He was a lot taller than Kasper, maybe about 5'10, and weighed about 171 pounds, was about seventeen years old and black as tar. Kasper was little, much shorter and weighed much less than Abe, but he knew he had one advantage and that was speed. Because Abe had size over Kasper, he thought he had the win. Kasper assessed his opponent. The boy knew the chemistry of fighting, staying calm was one of them. Staying calm could help you see the fight instead of just being in it.

"I'ma beat cho ass," he said to Abe.

Abe sized up the match, he wanted Kasper on the ground so he could lumber him thereafter. Kasper knew this, so Abe came rushing in, with one hand reaching out to grab Kasper and the other cocked back to drive blows to the boy when he got him onto the ground.

Kasper used Abe's momentum against him. Abe was reaching with his left hand, Kasper sidestepped to that side, pulled Abe's arm onward and down, then chopped him right in the solar plexus and let go. Abe crashed to his knees gasping and fell forward. He flopped around like a fish out of the pond, then tried to get up. Kasper kneed his opponent in the face breaking his nose.

"Man—o—okay—" Abe could hardly speak because of his throat. He was sprawled on the floor, ready to give up on the fight. Kasper stomped the back of Abe's head. "Please!" Abe cried out. "You got it you got it!"

Kasper took his victory to the day room. He pointed to Dre and said, "You a bitch!" To D-Lo, he said, "You a bitch, too! You want cho shoes back come take 'em back!" D-Lo didn't.

Everybody at Swannanoa knew about the fight between Kasper and Abe. Respect was won for one and lost for the other. After doing the thirty-day orientation Kasper was moved to C wing in Sloop. When he came through the door, escorted by staff carrying his bin, everyone stared. Some juveniles thought he looked crazy and would stay away from him.

"He's all yours," a female staff was told.

She was sitting at the desk eating a bag of Doritos. Kasper saw that this cottage looked different from Greenwood. The wings were shaped with rubber cushions in four long rows in the center of the day room facing the TV. A table for four sat to the side for tabletop games. An activity room was also available. In each corner of the wing was a small hall, with four rooms on each one and the rooms were a double bunch. Each of these halls was labeled as units, numbered one through four with one double bunk on each hall.

The staff grabbed a blue magic marker and said, "What's your name?" And went to the whiteboard.

"Cipherdeen Pecoise"

"Ooh!" She jerked her neck back. "Spell it." When Kasper was spelling it, she was writing it. "So, it's pronounced "Peh Swah?"

"Yea."

Capping the marker, the female staff said, "Come on." She took Kasper down to his room. "This is unit one. You can call me, Duryea or Miss Duryea, don't matter." Duryea had copper skin, brown eyes, brown hair, and round hips. To, Kasper, she looked about thirty-four years old. She stopped at room five, then turned to him. "This is your room. And look at you. You just thugged out ain't you?" Duryea smiled down at Kasper.

"Money," was the boy's only reply.

"They ain't make you cut your hair?"

"Hell no! My Aunt put togetha some bullshit documents sayin' it was against the Vodou religion."

"Are you goin' to be good?" Duryea asked

"If I can."

"Let me know if you need something." Duryea went back up the hall.

Kasper checked out his room, it was smaller than the one in Greenwood, it had no toilet, but it did have a metal stationary shelf and desk. He sat his bin down on his bunk and took out his hygiene, mail and pictures.

Kasper was allowed to have packages mailed in. He also had his shoes. Two pairs thanks to D-Lo, two pairs of grey sweatpants,

seven white t-shirts, four Dickie khaki pants, a brown coat, along with winter skull caps and gloves. He also had two teal shirts and two turquoise shirts that would be alternated each school day and two white, golf shirts for Sunday chapel. These would never be needed.

"You Kasper?"

Kasper turned, a light-skinned juvenile stood in Kasper's threshold. He was skinny, with sandy brown hair and a spray of freckles on his face.

"Yeah," Kasper said looking the other juvenile up and down. "Why?"

"I'm just askin', I'm from the city, too." The juvenile advanced into Kasper's room and made a W with his hands. "Tha Westside, Clanton Park. My name's, PJ."

"A'ight." Kasper went to fill up his shelf. "Lot a niggas from the city in here?"

"You made seven."

"Sup, my nigga?" Another juvenile entered Kasper's room.

"Who you?"

PJ said, "That's Jimmy, he from Southside homes."

Kasper said, "I'ma holla et everybody in this wing from the city."

Kasper took his home fronts into the bathroom. He wanted everyone on one accord and moving as one unit. Unity equaled power and control. Everyone, PJ, Jimmy, Ray-Ray Walter Murdock, and Toney was down. Other home fronts would too agree to these terms. Kasper didn't want to deal with anybody, but he had to make the best of his situation.

He went up to holla at Duryea who was talking to another juvenile. "Let me holla at her, right quick, dog."

Chapter 16

Stacey and Justice had begun trudging to the store. "What choo goin' down South Carolina for?" Justice asked.

Piedmont Courts was fully awake, kids were getting off school buses, as adults went to check their mailboxes for anything promising. Car systems thumped and blotches of clouds hovered in the sky like small UFOS.

"I'ma take some herbs to some folks," Stacey said as they crossed the parking lot.

"What time?"

Stacey flipped over her wrist to see the face of her watch. "Like seven o'clock we pulling out."

Getting up on the sidewalk the two friends went between a row of apartments. "Who they say it wuz that kilt they self, up here?"

Stacey said, "Treon." She waved his name away.

"That's crazy."

They came up between another row of apartments before crossing over another parking lot. "Yep," Stacey said. "Nigga tried to pay me to fuck."

Justice frowned. "How much?"

"His last offer was fifteen hunnid," Stacey said while they crossed over that parking lot and came up between some more apartments.

"Fifteen hunnid?" Justice was bewildered.

"Yes."

"Damn! Wish he woulda came et me wit' that."

Stacey glanced at her. "Justice—" Stacey began as they took that sidewalk to the right. "A real woman values her self-worth." Stacey pointed a finger to her chest. "I could never be bought, my womanhood is priceless."

"Stacey, you got some weed?" Sabrina one of the locals asked. She was sitting on her platform, holding a jar of ice water. From somewhere in the apartment, *Lauryn Hill* was singing her single *X-Factor*.

"Nah—" stopping Stacey remembered the smoke sack she had in her shorts. "Here."

"What choo want fo' this?" Moving on, Stacey dismissed the weed with the wave of her hand. "Thank you, Stacey."

"Okay, anyway Justice, neva let a man think he can buy you, homegirl. That's why I despise pimps and women that let themselves get pimped. How could you allow another human being to own you? You, sell yo' body to keep clothes on another man's back!" Stacey scoffed.

She and Justice took the steps to the left so they could cross yet another parking lot. A woman Stacey knew as Jelissa was up on her platform arguing with her baby father. Something about some shoes he was supposed to give her the money to get. It was already plated indelibly into Stacey's subconscious to get the shoes herself.

Justice said, "So, how you feel about stripping or strippers, period?"

Making a puzzled face while slightly shrugging shoulders Stacey said, "I would say it's an art, an advantage women have to make money. I don't wanna take my shit off though. I ain't got nothin' against strippers."

The two friends got to the entrance and made a right on a sidewalk. To the right down a small hill was a row of apartments facing them.

"Hey, Witchy," Stacey spoke to one of her friends.

Witchy was sitting on her platform picking at her nails, one leg bouncing. She'd gotten turned out on crack a year ago. Witchy lips that were there to curse, kiss, smoke or complain were white and chapped. "Hey, Stacey, you 'bout to go to tha sto'?"

"Yes." Stacey stopped.

"Can you get me a packa cigarettes?"

"I gotcha, babe."

The store was straight ahead across the street on the corner.

"Was he talkin' 'bout money?" Kasper sat down.

"Nah, he was talkin' 'bout his neighborhood"

"Well, how could you understand him?" Kasper said cutting Duryea off, causing her to laugh. "Yeah, laugh et him."

"You silly."

"What's up, wit' cha? You doin a'ight?"

"Yep, what choo locked up fo, man?"

Kasper explained the whole story. "I can wear what tha fuck I wanna wear."

"What choo 'bout fourteen—fifteen?"

"Fourteen."

"And yo' momma ain't have nothin' to say about you doin' that to yo' face?" Duryea asked with a frown.

"She only gave me an exaggerated frown."

"Where you from?" She looked and saw that juvenile staring.

"Charlotte, but check this out: I'm tryna take some of this money off my face and put it in yo' hand."

Duryea gave a high pitched laugh that got attention.

"How you gon' act?" Kasper said. "I only want my phone and some weed."

"Look et cha. You watch too much TV. How much you got?"

"How much I gotta have?"

"I know you ain't got what I need on you?"

"Nah, tha bread only one call away."

"Well, you call yo' bread and tell it Duryea need five hunnid. You got that?"

"In bread."

"Okay." Duryea chuckled. Then she flicked a hand down as if bouncing a ball saying, "Gotta keep it on the low."

Kasper rose to his feet. "My people comin' this weekend. I'ma get choo my susta numba, but let me make that call."

"Okay."

"Tell ya boy he can come back and whisper sweet nothings in yo' ear," Kasper said. "I'm gone."

"You gon' split on me, huh?"

"Holla et me."

"Well, tell lil crazy to come on back ova here so I can listen to some more of his lies. I need tha entertainment."

"A'ight."

"Oh, and he say, he into Vodou."

Those words got Kasper's attention. "Oh, yeah?"

"Mm-hmm, he ain wrapped to tight though. Sometimes I don't pay him no mind. He just likes to talk."

"Okay, I'ma holla et cha."

Chapter 17

Kasper waited until the juvenile that Duryea had said was into Vodou finally went to his room, then Kasper made his way down there shortly after. His name was Darious from Greenville, North Carolina. Darious was sitting on his bed about to open up a Vibe magazine when Kasper knocked and walked in.

"Yo' dog what's sup wit cha?" Kasper asked.

"Nuttin' what?" Darious asked. He was about 5'7 and sixteen-years-old.

Kasper said, "A home front of mine told me you into that Vodou shit," he lied.

"Yeah, I do Vodou. Why?"

"You *do* Vodou?"

Darious said "Yeah. Why what's up?"

"How do you *do* Vodou?"

"Man," Darious said. "Why?"

Kasper shrugged one shoulder. "I jus' wanna know."

"Roots, put roots on people."

"Oh, that's it?"

"Bra, I don't wanna talk about doin' Vodou and roots."

"Okay, well listen—stop sayin' you *do* Vodou because it's clearly evident you don't know nothin' 'bout Vodou."

"Nigga, how you gon tell me? You *do* Vodou?"

Kasper looked at Darious for a few seconds, then pointed to himself. "Yeah, I practice Vodou."

Darious sucked his teeth and said, "You don't even know what Vodou is. You *practice* Vodou."

"Aye, yo' listen dog." Kasper took a step closer. "You really need to stop sayin' you—" He couldn't find the right word so he said, "That shit is nothin' to play wit'." He looked serious when he said, "It can get choo kilt."

"Whateva man I do Vodou. Ain't nobody gon' tell me shit."

Kasper put up his hands in a surrendering way as he backed up slowly and said, "A'ight." Then he pointed to himself again. "I *do* Vodou," he said.

"You don't do no Vodou." Darious waved Kasper off.

Kasper stopped and stared at Darious. Then he looked and saw a sharpened pencil on Darious' desk. He grabbed it and stabbed himself in the palm hard enough to bleed. Kasper turned toward the door looking over his shoulder he said, "Vodou." Then smacked the wall with the bloody palm and walked out of the room.

Darious put the magazine down saying after Kasper, "Bra you got blood on my wall?" Then he got a roll of tissue off one of his shelves, rolled some off and wiped up the blood saying, "Ole bitch ass nigga."

That night Stacey and Justice were coming back from Charleston, South Carolina and decided to pull over behind an elementary school to rest and smoke.

"Geechi, down there in Charleston ain't it, Jay?"

"As hell," Justice said looking around. "Ole South Carolina."

Stacey lit a blunt that was already rolled. As smoke rolled from her mouth, she said, "That's a racist ass state, homegirl. Where part of tha Civil War took place. These crackas was fightin' to keep us in slavery." Stacey puffed on the blunt again then she passed it to Justice.

"I can't ever get past why they don't really like our ass." She took the blunt from Stacey.

"Crackas want America fo' they self. Like they bought this shit."

Justice snickered. "Jay you been my homie girl for a hot minute now."

"Since elementary school."

"That long? I wanna show you somethin'."

"What is it?"

Stacey held her hand out as if accepting somethin' and said, "Ripe," in Krepesk, which meant appear. A golf ball size stone appeared in her palm, it was purple and glowing.

Justice moved slightly away. "What tha hell!" Then she said, "What's that?"

"Cleprque grain," Stacey gave another demand. "Meküt ēm Jorko." *Come to me, Jorko.* Just then a six-foot-nine Povik Valkein appeared in front of her, the brown face was made like a hockey mask, its eyes were round like Cotton balls and glowed this same purple Stacey held. Its hands were that of brass, head writhing of snakes and wings of gold. The Povik Valkein was the great-grand-son of the Cthonian Monster Medusa.

The blunt flew out of Justice's hand when she jumped up yelling and almost backflipped off the picnic table.

"Vēlsë Jorko."

The Povik Valkejn disappeared. Stacey closed her hand around the Cleprque grain and said, "Awē." Then it left also.

"What the fuck was that?!" Justice asked standing back behind the picnic table. Stacey looked that way and chuckled.

"Stacey for real! What was that?"

"A Povik Valkejn"

"A *Povik* what?"

"Valkejn Valkejn." Stacey related and got the blunt.

"Tha hell it, come from?"

"Come sit down," Stacey said. "It came from the Poviks."

"Jason, he lyin!" The female cried out in distress. She held her shirt up to her nose that was bleeding, while in a truck sitting between her now ex-boyfriend and his homeboy that was driving.

"Love, shut tha fuck up!" Jason bellowed.

"Zino," she pleaded. "Please tell tha troof!"

"You did."

Jason scowled out of the window. "It's a'ight."

"But it ain't true!" Love said and caught a paining elbow.

"Yo' ass gon' get lost tonight."

"What's tha Poviks?" Justice asked Stacey after she had told her where the Povik Valkejn came from.

"It's an island on Empyrean. A dark island that analyzes hell from the ethical and psychological angle. It's also an island stuck in darkness, cold and haunted with demons and monsters. Jorko was the great-grandson of Medusa Queen of Gorgons. His mother is Satari granddaughter of Zeus. She had been raped by Medusa grandson and left the baby in the temple of Athens the Greek Goddess because Satari thought that Athens would take care of the child being as though Athens attribute consisted of serpents and Jorko had a head full of them.

But what Satari did not know was Athens was Jealous of Medusa because of her half serpent body, she knew the baby was of Medusa's descent. She damned Jorko and threw him into the ocean in hopes that he would drown. One of the Amudakis Yemoja Goddess of Seawaters and Maternity saved Jorko and took him in. He served and protected the Poviks. My emergency security."

"What is Empyrean?"

"Empyrean is a place that the souls of black people go when we die. But y'all only go to either Ikedele or Vashir also know as the Red Horizon."

"You said *y'all* like you don't go."

"I'll go to the Poviks. Don't ask why I'll explain that some other time. But I will let choo see Empyrean."

"When?"

"Tomorrow."

"Ain't nothin' gon' happen to me is it?"

"You'll be okay."

"Okay."

Then Stacey said, "I love you, homie."

"Well, I love you too"

They saw a black truck pull around the back. Stacey reached for her pistol. "Who this?"

"I don't know." Justice was curious as well. People were seen getting out and some chick was yelling and crying while being pulled out the truck.

"Tha hell goin' on?" Stacey began moving.

"No Jason!" Love kicked and screamed. Jason threw her to the ground. "You know what it is bitch!" Jason pulled out a .44 Magnum.

Zino stood as an onlooker. This could have been him.

"Zino please tell tha troof!!!"

He only stood silently.

Jason pointed that big gun at Love with both hands. "Well—it *was* love."

Two shots cracked and Jason almost fell onto Love but she managed to roll out the way. Zino didn't try to see where the source of gunfire came from. He knew it didn't come from Jason's gun so he ducked and tried to flee.

"Nah," said the gunman taking four quick steps to gain purchase and five shots found its intended mark, Zino was gunned down.

"What's yo' name?" Stacey asked from the rearview mirror as headlights passing by flashed across her face.

"Love." Love was a thick chick with dark skin and was twenty-seven-years old.

"You want me to take you to tha hospital? It sounds like yo' nose broke."

"I'm straight."

Stacey sighed. "Where you from?"

"Concord."

"You right outside of Charlotte."

Justice said, "What tha hell happened?"

"My ex's homeboy tried to pay me to fuck him. He got mad when I turned him down. Then went and told my ex that I came off on him."

Stacey glanced at Justice. "See what I was telling you, Jay?"

"Yeah."

"Fuckin' coward. So, why you ain't say nuttin' to yo' ex, Love?"

"I ain't wanna fuck up they friendship."

"Fuck that! He wasn't no damn friend! So, where you stay?"

"I was stayin' wit' him and his sister."

Stacey sighed again and took a moment to think. She then said, "I'ma take you to my place. You can stay as long as you need."

Chapter 18

Darious was half asleep when he heard a loud *Boom!* It was like someone had kicked his door open. He jolted gun up on his elbows, then swung out of bed and trudged over to peer out the window. It was unusually dark in the hallway on his unit. He couldn't even see, it was like someone had blacked out his window.

Behind him, his chair slid across the floor and crashed up against the wall.

"Arrghhh!" He spun around and was slammed back against the door. That's when he noticed he was still laying on his back in the bed. This was his out of body experience. The door behind him boomed again, Darious felt the bang. "Arrgghhh!" He ran over to his physical body and began shaking it and yelling, "Get up! Get up!" Darious tried to wake himself out of what he thought was a nightmare. "Wake up!"

Something swept down from the ceiling and landed on top of Darious's physical body. Darious flailed back, thumping up against the desk, yelling. The thing that landed on the physical body resembled a Banshee or some type of witch but far more scary. It was straddling Darious's physical body maybe so he couldn't wake up. Darius cried as he ran to the door and tried banging on it, but nobody would hear.

"Come open the door! Open the door!" He tried cutting the lights on, nothing happened. Darius kept flicking the light switch yelling and looking back at whatever this was. The door boomed twice more and Darious fell toward the chair that had slammed against the wall.

Kasper was laying on his bunk, eyes closed and fingers up to his temples, concentrating. He was controlling everything that was happening with Darious. What he was doing was calling Nefele N' doki. It was Red Level Sorcery used in his *old folks* Vodou line. He had studied their program, but this was a level of sorcery he was not

authorized to do. But under the circumstances, it was okay as long as he did not kill Darious. He could but he wouldn't.

The Banshee moved off Darious's physical body and swept toward the out of body.

"Leave me alone! Leave me alone!" Darious held up a protective hand. The Banshee cocked its head to the side as it hovered over Darious.

It spoke in a Darth Vador like voice, "Do you do Vodou?"

"No, I don't do Vodou! No, I don't do Vodou! No!"

The Banshee held out a hand that was all bones and long. It suddenly closed it into a fist and the chair flew into the wall behind it before it crashed to the floor and skidded across.

"I don't do Vodou!"

"Hush," the Banshee whispered and suddenly Darious rushed up from his sleep, toward the door, yelling. Keys jingling as a staff came running. He opened it and Darious rushed out.

Kasper didn't get up to go to breakfast the next morning. He was too tired, that Red Level Sorcery had taken a lot of his energy. He needed to eat but he just didn't have the energy to get up. Before school, he forced himself to get up, went into the bathroom, drank a lot of water and washed his face. Then the wing was ready to walk to the school building in two lines with the staff bringing up the rear. At lunchtime, he wolfed down his meal.

By the time school was out at a three-o' clock Kasper had the names of his home fronts and cottages they were in.

Duryea was there to walk her wing back.

"You learn something?" She asked Kasper who was walking in the back with her.

"Same shit tha fifth grade taught me."

Duryea laughed. "I talked to yo' susta. She seems pretty cool. By tha way she was talkin', I can tell y'all close."

"Yeah, people tease us saying we mother and son."

"Oh, it's like that?"

"Pretty much."

"What's wrong with you? You look tired."

"I am."

Everyone got back to the cottage and had to lockdown until it was time to walk to chow. Kasper couldn't wait. Duryea came around sliding mail under doors. Kasper got cards and money from his old folks, and mother, a letter and pictures from Kandy. He opened the letter.

The Ghost,
Sup, young cousin? Hope you are maintaining your aura. Me and all tha girls were just talkin' about you the other day. We miss whipping up on yo' lil' ass boy. Just don't let no one else do it, or we gonna refreshin' your memory. You know who your Devination is. Eleggua the solitary warrior. You gotta be that cuz real, my nigga! You know my punches hurt, you felt enough of em. Dog you know I don't play.
You locked up so you better believe your card is gonna get pulled if it ain't got pulled already. So, I want you to be on your shit. You know how to fight. As much as we all used to just hop on your ass nigga, you know how to handle yours. This weekend we up there. So, you bet not have no bruises. Just want you to be tough, nigga. It's thug life dog. I love you!
P.S sent you some pictures to reminisce with.
~Kandy~

Kasper smiled, it was always Kandy that wanted him to be tough. He looked at the pictures. One was a picture taken in 1989. Kandy had her arm around four-year-old Kasper who had his hair back in a ponytail, drinking a Pepsi in the living room at home. Kandy's face was pinched up in a sneer. She was eleven. Another picture was Kandy's sister Sotra and her mother Lusha in 1992 at Kandy's Middle School graduation. The other pictures were of other female members. Kasper knew how his second cousins were. It was mainly them being a little too rough.

"You, betta be tough," Kandy would say.

Other people told Kandy she was being more of a bully. He recalled one incident when he was seven. Kasper was down in his

room watching *'The Money Pit'* starring *Tom Hanks*, laying in his bed chilling. *Footsteps came down the stairs and the doorknob twisted, then there was banging on the door.*

"*Open the door punk!*" *It was Kandy.*

Kasper sucked his teeth and said, "*Man, she always messin' wit' me.*"

"*Open up tha door!*" *Kandy banged.* "*I know you in there!*"

"*What choo want, Kandy? Leave me alone, man!*"

"*If you don't open up tha door I'ma pick it!*" *Kandy threatened while twisting the knob.*

Kasper sucked his teeth again, got up and went over to the door. "*Why you always gotta mess wit' people!*"

"*Cause you a punk!*" *Kandy gave the door a bang.* "*Open the door!*"

"*No, you play too much, Kandy!*"

Trying the knob with hard twists, she said, "*You gon' make it worse!*"

"*I don't care, go away!*" *Kasper said.* "*Always messin' wit' me!*"

"*You know why!*"

"*I ain't no punk either!*"

Twisting the knob still, Kandy said, "*Well open the door then!*"

"*I said no!*"

"*I'm tellin' you, Kasper—*"

"*Go home.*" *Kasper went and laid back down.*

"*When I catch choo I'ma knock yo' lil ass out!*"

"*Shut up, Kandy!*" *Kasper yelled from the bed.* "*That's why you stupid!*"

Twisting the doorknob Kandy said, "*You won't open the door!*"

"*You just want me to, well, I ain't!*"

"*That's cause you a punk!*" *Kandy banged.*

Kasper ignored her and she left him alone until she could get a hold of him.

Duryea came around to open doors so everyone could prepare for chow. But first, everyone had to sit in the dayroom so two

appointed juveniles could pass out laundry. PJ would get Kasper's, he went to talk to Duryea.

"My lil' entertainment went up to Greenwood."

"Oh yeah?" Kasper seemed surprised.

"Bugged out late last night."

"Damn look here—" Kasper gave Duryea two hundred dollars he had gotten.

Usually, it would be recorded and every Monday the behavior specialist would come around to whoever had money and they could request up to seven dollars for the week to go to the vending machines with quarters to buy two snacks and a soda.

"You keep that, I may need you fo' somethin' else."

"Now how you gon' charge tha phone?"

"You charge it when you here and I'll get extra batteries comin'."

"If you get caught wit' all that shit—"

"They can't give me no mo 'time, fuck it."

Chapter 19

Tonio was upstairs putting his clothes on, he had just finished having sex with Kita. "I wanna get choo pregnant."

"Hell no, Tonio!" Kita said putting her legs through her pants. "Nigga, I can't have yo' baby, I'm only fifteen! My momma would kill me!"

"You fuckin' me behind Santario back."

Kita snapped, "Look who's talkin—tha fuck!"

"You bullshittin', you know you wanna be my girl."

"No, I do not! I fuck you when I get mad at Santario."

"So, you use me?"

"No."

"Well, what choo call it?"

"What choo wanna call it."

Stacey and Justice were sitting on the back stoop enjoying the uptown view.

"So, when you gon take me to see this place?"

"You ready?" Stacey stood.

"Yeah." Justice stood.

They went up to Stacey's room, she went into her closet and pulled out an oak, framed full-length mirror that was engraved with the symbol of the Sovakites. This symbol is called the Beswaze ce Taukuse. The Sovakites were also Demi Gods and symbolized unknown spiritual powers. Those energies contained with the Amudakis which would neither be calculated or spoken of and which is dangerous to unleash in the fashion of Sorcery. The Beswaze ce Taukuse was given to the Sovakites by the Amudakis as devin Mediums.

"What choo 'bout to do with that mirror?"

Stacey sat it up against the wall. "The portal."

"The who?"

Stacey had her hands out. "Ripe."

"Nah ahn!" Justice recoiled. "Don't call that thang." Stacey laughed. "I'm serious."

"Jorko? Nah, I ain't callin' him. Look don't say nuttin' to nobody."

"You ain't goin'?"

"No, you'll be okay."

"I don't wanna go to that dark place by myself."

"You definitely ain't goin' to the Poviks. You goin to the civilized part. A region, not no island. You wanna get back say *epitise*."

"What that mean?"

"Just say it, Jay." Stacey put the Cleprque grain against the mirror.

"Okay," Justice said looking at the Mirror. She took a deep breath, it felt like her heart was going to skitter off.

"Go, Jay"

"Okay, epitise?"

"Yes."

"Okay." Justice reached out to touch the mirror. She drew her hand back with a laugh when it sunk through.

"Jay, if you goin' go."

"Okay, okay." Justice took another deep breath and went through the mirror. Within seconds she was gone—no longer on earth.

"Bra what choo gon' do when you get back out!" PJ asked Kasper while sitting in the boy's bunk, with his headphones halfway on his head, flipping through a *Source* Magazine.

"Get back to gettin' money dog," Kasper said.

He stood and gazed out of his screened window that looked out past the campus beyond the fence where cars were going up and down Old Highway 70.

PJ said, "You still ain't tell me what choo do."

Kasper looked back at PJ then back out of the window saying, "You'll see, I'ma put choo up on some bread when we get out."

"I get out a month before you do."

"We gon' get out of here and do it."

"A'ight." PJ smiled thinking of the future.

A few more of Kasper's home fronts came in. He looked and saw that it was Ray-Ray and Walter, then turned back to life outside his window.

"What y'all up to?" Ray-Ray asked.

PJ said, "Shid—chillin'."

"Check this out y'all," Kasper said as his eyes diverted to two squirrels fighting. It was funny how even the smallest creatures had their quarrels. "I gotta visit tomorrow and I'ma get some weed," he lied to cover Duryea. "We gon' smoke but it ain't nobody business. It's only fo' the home fronts in here." Kasper looked at them.

"Ray-Ray said, "Ain't gotta worry 'bout me sayin' shit."

"Me either," PJ agreed.

"I gotcha," Walter replied.

"A'ight then." He looked back out of the window. Another thought occurred to him, he looked to the home fronts again. "How they do room changes?"

While messing with Kasper pictures, Walter said, "Duryea or any other staff can do it anytime."

Kasper looked back out of the window. "Make this unit all Charlotte. That way nobody won't be in our business. They can't come on this unit unless invited."

Stilloan Robinson

Chapter 20

"Nigga, you can't beat me," Santario told Tonio after finishing a game of Madden 99.

"That's cuz you cheat!"

"How I cheat?" Santario smiled. "Huh?"

"Every time I throw a pass and catch it you pause tha game to fuck me up.

"Man stop crying." Santario picked up the butt of a cigarette out of the ashtray and lit it.

"Nigga, fuck you, is there some mo' cigarettes left."

"No, you see I have to put the shit out."

"You smoked 'em all up!"

"Only some 'em."

At that moment, Stacey walked in. "My thugs."

"Sup, Stacey?" Tonio said. "You came to give us some money?"

"Shut the fuck up," she teased passing through the living room heading for the kitchen. "I jus' gave y'all money. What the hell y'all do wit' it?" Then she saw how messed up the kitchen was. "Oh, hell no!" Stacey made an about-face.

"What?" Santario said.

"Let me hit that cig," Tonio said with no regard to what Stacey was inquiring about.

Aiming a thumb over her shoulder Stacey said, "If y'all don't get the hell in there and clean that kitchen—"

"What's wrong wit' it?" Santario got up.

Tonio was holding up his finger for the cigarette but Santario ignored them.

"It's fuckin' nasty! Nah y'all ain't 'bout to do this." Stacey stormed over toward the TV and unplugged it and the PlayStation. "Hell no!" Then she pointed toward the kitchen. "Clean up y'all fuckin' messes! Take that trash out, sweep and mop. Come on now! Y'all old enough to know betta! Stacey ain't gon' have it! Don't plug shit back up till that kitchen's spick! Don't make no damn

sense! Y'all clean this apartment or get out!" Stacey left out pissed off.

Justice stood looking around the room she was in. It looked just like Stacey's room but everything was inverted. "Stacey," she called out with her eyes plucked toward the window and she went to investigate. What she saw were high rise, four wind project buildings made of white concrete with tinted windows. "Damn," Justice said softly.

Then she noticed how red the afternoon was. She turned to go out of the room and down the steps but there was none. This was a one-level apartment. Justice stepped out in the foyer and looked around before she let the door close. After going up the hallway, she came to a small lobby of elevators that directed down and up. Down was the way to go. Getting on the elevator, she came to an abrupt pause. This was because it was her first encounter with the realm's entity. There stood two black dudes. One of them looked around nineteen-years-old, he was skinny with a dreaded Mohawk. The other guy was around thirty, with black skin and built thick with a fade. Both of their eyes were very dilated.

Justice moved on for the first floor but the floor icons were in shapes that she couldn't understand. She looked back to try and ask for help but remembered Stacey telling her not to say anything to anyone. Justice touched what she thought would take her to the first floor. Those two guys got off on another floor, the last stop down, the door pinged open and Justice got off. She went outside through a set of automatic doors and a foul stench smacked her in the face.

"Ohh!" Justice stopped and covered her nose with her shirt and closed her eyes because they burned. "The fuck!" Then she had to open her eyes back up to look down at her feet, it felt like they were no longer there but they were. "Shit!" Justice noticed she was as high as she'd ever been. It took her a minute to get herself together.

Justice moved along, with her nose still covered by her shirt. Three females were there sitting on a bench in a court area to the right, smoking. The color of the smoke was a bluish purple.

'*What the hell is that?*' Justice thought. These female's eyes were dilated as they grilled Justice.

The next day was Saturday, Kasper got his visit. Kandy didn't have to jump down his throat about nothing. When he got back to Sloop he had to wait to be stripped searched by a male officer that was taking each juvenile into the laundry room to search them.

"Under yo' mat," Duryea mouthed.

When Kasper finally got to his stuff there were two ounces of weed, a cell phone, and three batteries.

"Damn, man," he said to himself. "Forgot to get lighters."

"Aye bra" PJ knocked and came in.

Kasper dropped the mat after taking the weed. He wouldn't tell nobody about the phone. "Sup?"

PJ's eyes moved downward to Kasper's hand. "I see you got the weed."

Kasper looked at the weed. "Forgot to get my people to bring a lighter."

"I can pop that socket."

"Bra you still gon' make that move happen?" Jimmy had found his way to Kasper's room.

"Oh, yeah." Kasper had forgot. "Get Walter and Ray-Ray."

"Walter and Ray-Ray playin' spades."

"Well get Murdock and Toney, then get those two niggas that sleep in that double room shit."

Jimmy left to go up to the day room to get Fly Boy and Slim.

"What's up?" Fly Boy said, his heart pounded as his suspicion flared anew. They were being confronted by Kasper and he had his home fronts with him.

Kasper said, "Y'all step in y'all room."

Everyone followed his order and went there, which was the room next to Kasper's.

"Yeah?" Fly Boy said once they were in their room. He made sure he was by the bunk in case he had to get under there if things got ugly.

"Dog check this out man," Kasper began. "Y'all gotta move out the room."

"What?" That was Slim, he pointed a finger with his thumbs up.

PJ said, "Bra you want me da smack him?"

Kasper frowned sourly and put a hand up to PJ. That move was not necessary at the moment. He said to both boys, "My home fronts want the room."

Fly Boy sucked his teeth. "That's fucked up."

"I know, tell Duryea y'all switched rooms. One of y'all take Jimmy's room the other take PJ's."

The switch was made and two more had to happen. Gregory, a nobody Indian switched with Murdock. A big, white, country boy named Joey bucked on switching rooms. "Guy—I'm not moving anywhere!" he proclaimed.

"A'ight," Kasper told him. "You ain't got to, don't worry 'bout it."

Kasper got with two juveniles named Adrian and DeeDee who claimed to be Crips. He paid them both a gram of weed.

"Get that white boy Joey up outta here in blood."

The Sally Port slider doors opened in Pod 5500 in the Mecklenburg County Jail and Lieutenant Pecoise-Moody walked over the podium.

"Hey, Susta," she spoke to Anition as the sound of dominos was slapping the table, as well as men carrying on in their own conversations.

"What's goin' on?"

"Chie—" Sheba rested both elbows on top of the podium. She was Victoria's eldest child, she was twenty-eight, with smooth

dark-skin, light, grey eyes, had long hair pulled into a ponytail and stood 6'3. "An inmate down in medical just knocked out Corporal Spencer."

"Whaattt!"

"Laid her ass out, she deserved it."

"Is she okay?"

"She'll be straight."

"They went to see yo' lil' brother today, huh?"

"Don't act like he ain't cho brother too."

"He said when he was shootin' at me, he kilt me, so I'm dead to him."

She looked over to the inside basketball court where some inmate was playing while others were huddled in a corner freestyling.

Sheba said, "Y'all need to stop."

"I ain't messing with yo' brother. He be in my dam business to fuckin' much."

Sheba looked back at Anition. "He's just protective over us."

"And maybe he a lil *overprotective*."

"Y'all squash this shit and you need to write him."

The advice made Anition snap, "I ain't writing him!"

"He cares about yo' well-being. Kasper the only man in the family. So, you know he feels like he got a position to play. Gotta expect that from him."

"Well, I'm still not writin' him. He shot et me!"

"Wit' some blanks!"

"So, he owes me an apology, then we can go from there."

Joey was in the day room talking to a few of his buddies about how the blacks had approached him about his room.

"He and some other *coloreds* trying to run shit."

His line of family were Klansmen. Joey also kept his eyes on Kasper who was in the activity room. *That nigger is a problem*, he thought.

The impact of a blow to the left ear caused Joey to jump up out of the rubber cushion. Dazed, he ran in to the wall trying to move away. Before he could assemble himself, DeeDee rushed up to him. Fists were coming like mother birds trying to protect their nests.

Miss Duryea was on the radio calling campus security for assistance. The two juveniles had Joey on all fours beating him savagely and bloody. Now Joey's room could be filled. Kasper would later be questioned about whether he had his hand in the fight.

As she moved down the sidewalk, Justice felt she was smoothing along like a ghost with her nose still covered. She was looking up at the project buildings. Just like New York, there were so many of them and they looked luxurious. The air smelled of salt and palm trees. Children past by her not playing or laughing out loud. People out in a field where playing with Spears, trying to throw them long distances like it was a game, and observers manifested themselves like it was a tournament.

Justice stood on a curb looking around, clouds of that bluish-purple smoke rose into the air as people spoke. Her eyes came to the left there was a parking lot. A familiar face was sitting on the hood of a car that had no wheels. It was hovering off the ground somehow. It looked like a futuristic hoppy. The guy was sitting with one knee up. The other leg was swinging, his arms resting on his knee and he had a long knife in his hand. His hair was twisted in knots. He wore a lair of Suede boots, black pants with green stitching and a black vest on top of a green shirt.

Regardless of the dude's eyes, Justice knew him. She let go of her shirt covering her nose and eased over. "Ricky?"

Chapter 21

Lacey came to see Kasper that Sunday and brought Kanazi and some lighters. The visit didn't last long at all. She asked Kasper if he was moving in with her when he got out.

Lacey got in her feeling when he said, "Hell no, Lacey. I got my own spot, my susta still paying on for me." Kasper knew living with Lacey would be a disaster.

"Please, do not say it like that," she said. "You know what—" Lacey gathered her child. "I'm gonna let choo go because I see that we about to fall all the way out!"

"Well gone, Lacey! Yo' aggravatin' ass!"

"Nigga, fuck you!" she said loud enough to be heard. At this point, she didn't care.

Back at the cottage, Kasper passed the lighters off to Jimmy before being stripped searched, then everyone went to Kasper's room to smoke a few roll-ups before he went out to talk to Duryea.

"You look mad. What's wrong?" she asked. Kasper told her about Lacey. "It be like that sometimes," Duryea added.

Folding his arms across his chest, Kasper said, "You got kids?"

"None."

"Where you from—here?"

"No, I'm from Memphis Tennessee. Been here with my mama for a year. She been out here for three."

"And you like it out here?"

Duryea frowned. "Ain't staying forever, it gets too cold in the winter. I might go back to Memphis, I don't know."

"Well, don't let these mountains get in ya way."

The guy moved up to her, he spoke in a language that Justice could not understand. No one would have reacted to her had she spoken. She was a failure to speak, she didn't belong. She was out of territory. Who she thought was Ricky held his weapon speaking

hastily. Who she was and where she came from was what he wanted to know.

"I don't know what choo sayin'," Justice said.

The guy did some type of a whistle that was quick. It was like everyone looked and started moving in. Justice had to get out of there.

"Epitise!" She found herself back in Stacey's room.

The mirror was there, and she went over to touch it. When her hand entered she was automatically put back into it. But something had followed her back.

Stacey was out on her platform feeding her bird Tashki strawberries. A squad car rode by slowly. The officer looked down at his computer, then checked the surroundings.

"He lookin' fo' chuck," Stacey said to herself. "Chuck done robbed the gotdamn sto'."

The police pushed on, then the screen door burst open and Stacey looked in time enough to see it was Justice. Before she threw her hand in front of her bird's face as its wings came up and its mouth open.

"It tiro ōn Tashki!" Stacey spoke in the Krepesk language that only the bird understood. It slowly lowered its wings as it watched Justice. "Ti elon, Justice." Stacey had to reassure Tashki that it was okay and it was only Justice.

"Girl, you, betta watch how you comin' up outta there! She was 'bout to tear yo ass up with that acid, thinkin' you was a threat!"

"My bad."

"I missed you, go get a chair and tell me all about it."

Justice went and got a chair, came back out and said, "Why is it dark?"

"Girl, it's Sunday night." When Stacey said this Justice's soul had been a night creature frozen in her headlights.

"You bullshittin'."

"Nope. Sit down."

While positioning the chair to sit down, Justice said, "I only been gone 'bout fifteen or twenty minutes."

"Homegirl—you was light years away."

"That's crazy." Then Justice told Stacey everything.

"I told you not to say nothin' to anybody."

"It looked just like him, Stacey."

"Ricky Truesdale, that got kilt robbin' the sto' on Beattis Ford?"

"Yeah, man."

"It coulda been," Stacey said. Tashki was finished, Stacey kissed her bird and lifted it into the air, so it could take flight. It flew upwards and they watched as the bird vanished into the sky.

Justice said, "What language was he speaking?"

"Krepesk, he wouldn't have remembered you, anyway. Nobody's memory of their past life exists. I don't know why so I don't ask."

"So, I won't remember nobody or my spirit won't come back?"

"Nope, but your loved ones will remember you. Astenan Greshu."

"Huh?"

"That's where you was, Astenan Greshu, the name of the projects. Depending on the season you can see clovers floating in the air all day and night!"

"So, you been out there?"

"Yeah."

"Do they grill you and do you have to be quiet?" They both laughed. Stacey said, "Jay, you silly, but no they can see us as being a person that belongs."

"Why so?"

"I'll tell you that story soon, Jay, but not right now. Did you see the beach?"

Justice crinkled her brows. "The beach?"

"Yeah. Stacey directed a finger back over her head and said, "It's behind the complexes."

"That's why I smelled salt?"

"That's a tropical region, called Panasonic."

"What's a region?"

"How we got states they got regions. It's on the North Coast."

"That stuff they was smokin'?"

"Looked like dro' wit' a lot of crystals in it, huh? You high to ain't cho?"

"As hell."

They both laughed.

"You tried it?"

"Nah. Did you have a good time?"

"Hell of an experience."

"Please don't tell nobody else."

"They would think I was crazy."

Stacey reached and hugged an arm around Justice. "Glad to have a homegirl like you."

"Glad to be yo' homegirl," Justice said as she hugged one of her arms around Stacey.

Stacey said, "You wanna go see Martin Lawrence's new Life movie?"

"Let's go."

During school the next day, Kasper was in the gym talking to a few of his home fronts, J-Penny, Bee-Bop, Showtime, Marco and a Juvenile from Winston Salem named, Reggie. Showtime owed Reggie a dollar out of his seven-pack money and wasn't trying to pay it back.

"The man gave you his cheese, Showtime, and you ain't gon' pay him?" Kasper said.

"Hell nah, this Charlotte fuck that shit!"

"What that got to do wit' it?"

"I ain't payin' him shit! He wanna do some 'em we can do it," Showtime was speaking.

Kasper shook his head. "It ain't but a dolla," he said.

"I don't give a fuck!" Showtime bellowed

"Hold on! Who the fuck, you talkin' too?"

"Nah, I'm just sayin'—"

Kasper said to Bee-Bop, "You got a dolla?"

"Yeah," Bee-Bop replied.

"Give it to that nigga and I'll give you two back dog."

"A'ight."

"I'm 'bout to go ball." Kasper went over to pick his team.

Later in math class, Kasper handed Marco, who was sitting in the desk in front of him, a note. He opened it and read it. Then he turned his head to the side and nodded.

After the staff unlocked the doors in Suite Cottage B wing so that the juveniles could prepare for chow, Marco, Bee-Bop and another one of their home fronts named, Corey had gotten together.

They found Showtime and moved on him fast.

"Why y'all jumping me!" He yelled while being pummeled. They were beating him up under the small table. "What I do? What y'all jumping me fo!" Then he yelled for the staff to call campus security which he was already doing anyway.

Kasper heard the call go to campus security over Duryea's radio. That was what he wanted to hear. He got up and motioned with his head for PJ to follow him to his room.

"They did it?" PJ asked.

"Yep." Kasper went into his weed so they could smoke a roll-up.

"I can't stand petty ass niggas," Kasper said. "The nigga felt like he had a gang of niggas that was gon' ride wit' him. So, he got petty ova a dolla. All he owed the man was a dolla. I could see if it was a hunnid dollas. Then he got loud wit' me. Nigga I'll beat choo ass." PJ laughed. Kasper said, "I owe Bee-Bopp two dollaz. Anyway, aye you wanna fuck, Duryea?"

"How bra?"

"I got that, I'ma get choo the pussy. You want it?"

"Shid." PJ smiled at the thought.

Kasper waved off the idea. "Fuck it, man." Then he rolled up a blunt.

"Man, she ain't gon'—how you know?" PJ let his voice trail off.

Kasper smiled, then said, "Listen dog—don't worry 'bout all that. You gon' fuck her or you straight?"

"Yeah." PJ was cheesing. "Okay!"

"Bra." Kasper shared the roll up. "Don't tell nobody, I'm serious."

"I gotcha."

Chapter 22

"Say what?" Duryea was taken aback by Kasper's request.

He said, "You know shit wit' me is real. If I'm vouchin' fo' a nigga then he official. I don't vouch fo' lame-ass niggas. Two grand says my nigga can stay back from school? He gon' play sick tonight. You come in early so the mornin' staff can leave early, then let my dog get right. He ain't gon' say shit and that's on me."

Duryea was looking at Kasper pondering. "Three grand?" she finally said.

"I'ma get my susta to meet halfway."

Later, as he walked back from school Kasper said to Duryea, "How it go?"

She sucked her teeth and said, "Your boy was scared."

Kasper hung his head in disappointment. He'd put up a lot of money for his boy's pleasure and he was scared of pussy.

Duryea laughed, then said, "You not gettin' yo' money back so you might as well man up, and act right."

"Where that Love chick et?" Stacey's twin sister Kacey asked.

The two sisters looked very much alike it was only the glasses Kacey wore that allowed people to tell them apart. They were born five minutes apart and Stacey stood an inch and a half taller than Kacey. Kacey kept her hair cut in a light buzz style and she was in the military. She was tough as nails and as hard as stone. Stacey always wondered where her sister had gotten such will.

Kacey was a S.E.A.L who was on active leave for an incident involving one of her fellow S.E.A.L. As a S.E.A.L. woman, Kacey got scrutinized often by other men on her team. One of those men she'd got into an argument with and he pointed his finger in her face calling her soft.

"Do it again," Kacey said and the man pointed in her face again.

Kacey quickly pulled the man toward her, then she came around with a right hook to his kidney, sending the man pissing to hell. When he gripped down to one knee, she moved in behind him and pulled his own knife from his waist, putting it to his throat.

"If you disrespect me again, it'll be a twenty-one gun ceremony for you."

So here she was on leave until further notice. It had been nine months. Now her job was working at the county jail. Kacey was holding the punching bag for Stacey at the gym. when Stacey said, "She work et, Walmart."

"Oh, et work?"

Stacey gave the bag a four-piece combination and said, "Yeah." She hit the bag again.

"Okay, you gon get back in the ring—go pro?"

"Nah," Stacey said as she bounced from foot to foot. "I love boxin' but I'm straight, I grew out of it." She hit the bag with a three-piece. "Your round," she said.

They switched places, Kacey took a deep breath and started jabbing at the bag.

"Kandy has a nice fight game, too. And she hits hard," Stacey said.

"Yeah, but Kandy has real bad sportsmanship. She don't like taking a loss."

"Who does?"

"She isn't built for the ring and she be in the streets too much."

"Amber is, too, but she still go to that jujitsu class with Barsuesha and Sotra."

"Kandy know we come to the gym to work out. If she wanted to come she woulda."

"I let Justice cross over," Stacey said.

Kacey paused. "No, you didn't?"

"I did."

"Stacey, you know you cursed her."

"Cursed her?"

"Yes, you can't let non-blood cross over. You ain't read the book? Ask Zya, she knows the whole book from both ends. You

sent that girl to land of the dead. Why would you do that?" Kacey was on the verge of crying. "Now the Amudakis might penalize you."

Zya was at home studying with her legs curled up on the couch. She had honey-colored skin, long hair that she always wore draped over a shoulder, grey eyes, high cheekbones and was about 5'5. Zya was an A honor roll student that attended Providence High School, she was only sixteen and yet, very well-mannered.

The door chimed to someone's entrance and the alarm started beeping away like a bomb count down. Stacey went over to the key-pad and entered its code.

"Hey, lil' susta," Stacey said heading her way. "You studying?"

Zya showed the cover of her book. "Science."

Stacey bent down to kiss Zya's cheeks and turned hers for one. "Momma et work?" She sat down beside Zya.

"No, she et the restaurant."

"I wanna ask you somethin'."

"Uh-huh?"

"If we let somebody cross over, that ain't family—"

"It's a curse," Zya said cutting her instantly.

"You sure?"

Zya closed her book using a finger to hold its place. "That's what the book says."

"Can you show it to me? I wanna see it."

Zya got up, taking her science book with her to her room where she laid it down. Zya went to her drawer and got a purple velvet bag that was rolled up like an Oxford Encyclopedia that was solid white and had a large 14kt gold symbol of the Beswaze ce Taukuse on the front cover. She was looking for the page while heading back downstairs.

"Right there." She pointed to a paragraph and gave it to Stacey as she sat don't.

Stacey started reading. "And for Empyrean is a place that only the Sovakites are fingered access to cross into and are awarded immediate respect of the clash names. Cursed be upon mankind that shall dare cross over for death will follow you back and be with you until you are claimed." Stacey slowly closed the book. She was crushed like a mashed ant caught under a foot. She looked at Zya. "Is there a way to lift the curse?"

"Not even," Zya replied. "What happened?"

Stacey looked Zya in the eyes for a moment, then told her what it was. Zya looked down at the book in thought, then lifted her gaze back up to Stacey.

"Ain't nothing anybody can do. It is what it is, I'll be surprised if the Amudakis don't come at choo with a penalty. But the curse will still stay."

Anger raged within Stacey choking her in convulsing agony. She told Justice nothing would happen to her. Her careless actions would now cost Justice her life. She would meet her demise due to Stacey's lack of knowledge.

Zya spoke saying, "The book of Dookari was not given to us to hold onto only. We're Sovakites, we have to read, understand and respect it."

Stacey doubled over and sobbed. As quick as she made another friend in Love, she'd lost one in Justice. Zya moved to console her sister.

The moon reflected the sun that was far off in the Western Hemisphere as it shined delicately in the sky. Stacey was in the conceals of the woods behind her aunt's house about to perform the Arupa. This was a form of necromancy.

She used combulik stones a luminescent precious stone the color of pomegranate that she formed a large circle with.

"I niv-Ed ëtēd," Stacey began chanting calling forth her deity. "I lok nape wy ni teleykami thaf!"

Then in the center of what was called the Zocialgram Stacey sprinkled black Persian powder. Then she took a white handle Athens blade and stabbed it in the center of her palm. The wound was

painless the blade being coated with Komodian oil, the magic oil that relieved pain instantly. Stacey continued chanting as she turned her palm over the Zocialgram. When she felt enough blood was given Stacey took a niquen cloth that would absorb the blood that continued to flow before it stopped the bleeding completely, pretty much telling the wound to stop bleeding.

She would have to wait until afterward to doctor her wound, she had a choice. Bowing her head while on her knees, Stacey said, "Zelp Mek throf!"

"Lift your head to me, my child," a telepathic voice demanded.

She lifted her head to Olokun who wore a black and gold dress, a gold strapless Moretta face mask. Olokun was associated with ocean floors sometimes visualized as a beautiful siren and other times a hermaphrodite. She was not only a Vodou deity but, too, an Amudakis for Empyrean a Goddess.

"Mother Goddess," Stacey' voice quivered, "Please—"

"What have you done my child?" Olokun knew already.

Stacey explained the situation with Justice. Olokun did not respond right way, when she did, she said to Stacey, "One must never let the outside being cross over into the body of Empyrean. Only to see this realm is through the eyes of the departed soul if not a Sovakites. We must not forget what the book of Dookari shows and teaches us. A penalty has been set forth for you but has been revoked by councilors of some of the Amudakis. Your own actions befall someone else child—"

"I beg you, Mother Goddess, to lift the curse."

"Child—nothing can overturn the decision of the curse. The curse stays—"

"So, no sacrifice of any?"

"I'm sorry child but the Dookari has been written so the laws of it cannot be changed for anyone. Not even an Amudakis."

Stacey began to weep, this was terrible. All of it was her fault and it was tearing her up inside to know she would be responsible for her homegirl's death and there was nothin' she could do about it.

Olokun said, "Child as you know you are the Kovijcci, Queen Lord of the Poviks of which you will rule when your time here on earth expires. And I do say Aliyscious," she used Stacey's middle name, "you should have known what the book of Dookari speaks. Bewitching your friends because of your lack of knowledge and wisdom was foolish. Now what I can say is that she will have appropriate living in the Poviks if which we will let her reside to."

Stacey looked up with tear-filled eyes. "You promise?"

"An Amudakis makes no promises. What an Amudakis say is true words from the heart."

"I understand."

"Stay strong and uplifted. When your time comes you will be reunited with your friend, who will then be restored with memory of her last life and most important you will have your throne. But child—you must read that book first and you will be tested."

"Yes, mother Goddess."

"Be sweet child." Olokun vanished.

Kacey was in her bedroom crying. How could Stacey be so careless? Justice was a friend to her as well, even though, Stacey was closer to Justice. Kacey felt awful, she wasn't mad at Stacey, only sorry that she did not read the Book of Dookari.

"Damnit, Stacey!"

Chapter 23

As months progressed J.E.C. had become worse than it was already. It was Kasper that had been calling out of school early and escorted back to Sloop by staff. He was instructed into the activity room where his case manager, a behavior specialist, and administration were seated at the table.

"Sup?" Kasper sat down.

"Mr. Pecoise," the behavior specialist began staring at Kasper. "Your name has come up on numerous occasions."

"So, what?"

"Since you've arrived at this school, there's been vicious beatings, pencil stabbings, and other violent offenses. Many say that you're the man behind it all. It doesn't seem like you're fitting in here at this school. So, we're transferring you to Dillon. There you'll be placed in IDP."

"Man." Kasper rose to his feet. "Y'all can suck my dick! Fuck all you hill crackas!" He spat on everyone, including his case manager. For all he knew, she was in on it too. Then a jackknife appeared.

Campus security had been radioed but they too were held at bay. It took a supervisor that worked well with Kasper to talk him into surrendering. He was sent to Greenwood with all of his belongings. When he came through the doors, Mr. Sharpe was standing right there, dressed in a brown, plaid shirt, tan-colored pants. He had one hand on his hip, the other was holding a cup of steaming coffee and he was smacking gum.

"What I tell ya?" Mr. Sharpe let his words hang in the air for added effect. "Knew you weren't going to make it."

"That's cuz I had this place wrapped around my finga. I snap two fingas yo' ass will get hopped on cracka!"

"Move your ass on to B wing. You're going on IDP status.

"Fuck you, bitch!"

"What happened, bra?" Demond asked Kasper as he stood at his door.

Kasper would remain on lockdown until he got shipped. Demond had been on IDP status for two months for stabbing another juvenile at the chapel. That call had come from Kasper.

"I don't know, dog," Kasper said from his window. "Say my name came up in shit that happened. So, either tha mothafucka it happened to told, or the mothafucka that made it happen told. Somebody told, now I'm goin' to Dillon."

"That's the worst trainin' school."

"Well, they really in trouble now."

"They say Miss Duryea got fired."

Kasper sucked his teeth. "Hell no, she moved back to Memphis."

"How you know?"

"She told me somethin' came up, so she had to go back. Quit listenin' to these niggas, 'Mond," Kasper said.

Commotion up the hallway broke out and Demond looked. The campus security was bringing in PJ.

"There go bra."

Trying to look up the hall Kasper said, "Who?"

"PJ."

"Where's Kasper?" PJ asked in a hyped tone while being put in his room.

"He right here. That's who I'm talkin' too."

"Kasper?"

"Yeah?"

"Goin' to Dillon man! They say I was yo right hand."

"Fuck these crackas!"

"You pulled a knife on everybody?"

Demond started laughing.

Kasper said, "This shit ain't no game."

"Same shit applies."

"All day."

Sadly, Demond said, "I wish I could go wit' y'all."

"Nigga, you gonna be a'ight, you from Charlotte."

Ghost Mob

The next morning Kasper and PJ shipped out. Getting grilled up on entering the wing, "Betta make it pop off without warnin' nigga." Kandy's words boomeranged.

"PJ come in my room when you put cho stuff up."

After setting up his stuff in his room PJ went to Kasper's. "Sup?"

"I don't know how you feel?"

"Bra you seen how those niggas was grilling us?" PJ interrupted Kasper.

"That's what I'm—"

Three juveniles came down the hall and looked in Kasper's room at him and PJ, then headed back up the hall saying something that couldn't be made out.

"They wanna try us," Kasper said. "If you gon' ride wit' me. I'ma go back up to the day room and swing off on who I can. You hit who I miss."

"I'm here cuz, I been ridin' wit' cha. Bet!"

"Let's go."

Kasper and PJ went to the dayroom. Kasper saw those three juveniles sitting at a card table and went straight for them. PJ went for some juveniles sitting on the rubber sofa.

"No!" An older white female staff shouted surprised by the action. She got on her radio and called campus security.

Those three juveniles had Kasper on the table wailing on him, but he was putting up a fight. PJ had fallen between a row of sofas and was getting stomped.

After the fight was broken up all those juveniles were locked in their rooms. Kasper's nose was broken, he had a lump on his forehead and both his eyes had been blacked.

"Whooped they ass, Bo!" one juvenile yelled out of the door.

"Yo—fucked them niggas up!"

Everybody laughed and talked about it for a while. When it got quiet Kasper called PJ to the door.

"Yeah?"

"You straight dog?" Kasper asked while holding a towel to his nose. He had refused medical treatment.

"Hell, yeah! You?"

"If these bitch ass niggas ain't kill us they ain't do shit. Fuck them! When we see the hearin' officer we gon' tell him we was the aggressors so these niggas can come off lockdown."

"A'ight."

Stacey and Kacey were at Sheba's home sitting at the kitchen table eating meat, cheese and crackers, and drinking Bombay Sapphire

"That lil' nigga was in that place actin' up huh?" Sheba asked before shoving a cracker sandwich into her mouth.

"Yep," Stacey said.

"He still got that phone?" Kacey asked while making a sandwich.

"He still got it."

Sheba said, "'Bout time fo' him to come home. We havin' a party fo' him?"

Kacey didn't answer because she knew Stacey would handle that, if so. "I got plans."

"Y'all wanna hit this?" Sheba asked while pouring the liquor.

Kacey put a hand up to indicate that she was cool.

"Yeah," Stacey said.

Sheba gave her the bottle saying, "Knew you wanted some. You a drunk!"

"Shut up," Stacey teased as her phone rang. "Yeah?" It was Kasper. He told her about the current event. "Your nose broke?"

Both Sheba and Kacey's brows went up. "What's goin' on?" They asked in unison.

Stacey put an index finger into the air. "Hold up."

When she ended the call, Sheba said, "What the hell goin' on?"

Stacey repeated Kasper's story, Sheba laughed.

Kacey said, "Wooow!"

"You see," Sheba began. "Our brother is really special, man. Now, why would they do that?"

144

"Damn," Kacey said, shaking her head.

"Y'all leave my baby alone."

"Okay," Sheba said. "We ain't gon' talk 'bout cho' brat."

Kacey said, "And I can't believe he did that to his face."

After doing fifteen days DI, Kasper and PJ came off. The other juveniles had beat their DI due to Kasper and PJ's statements.

"Ready?" Kasper asked while standing in PJ's doorway.

He was tying up his shoes. "Yeah." When he was finished he said, "Let's go."

They went to the dayroom, the juveniles studied these two threats. Anyone who was in reach of these two when they got to swinging was in trouble. Kasper hit one juvenile so hard he knocked out a tooth and cut his hand in the process. The two friends took another L with pride because it was a victory to them. Kasper had a black eye and PJ had a gash in his.

"The fuck is wrong wit' him?" Sheba said when she got the news. "It was funny at first, but this is ridiculous! I'ma call him." When she did Kasper answered his vibrating phone. Stacey had been sending him batteries in care packages.

"Kasper!" Sheba snapped.

"Yeah?"

"The fuck is you doin' man?"

Speaking in a low tone Kasper said, "What choo talkin' 'bout?"

"You know what the hell I'm talkin' 'bout! Why yo' ass actin' stupid? And doin' the shit choo doin? You got somethin' to prove?"

"Yeah, listen—lemme do what I wanna do. You ain't the one locked up."

"You, just crazy!"

"I know—Big bird."

"And I'll kick—"

Kasper hung up saying, "Aw shut the fuck up." He knew Sheba didn't like to be called Big Bird.

When Kandy got the word on Kasper she said, "He doin right, y'all leave him alone. If he feels that's what needs to be done to make a statement, he doin' right. Shid!"

Chapter 24

Fifteen days had gone before the two friends came off lockdown.
"You ready?" Kasper asked PJ.
"Anytime."
When they entered the dayroom, all the juveniles rushed to their feet. One of the bigger boys said, "Why y'all can't be cool?"
Kasper pointed to himself and said, "Cause we like it hot!"
"Y'all trippin', we ain't did shit to y'all."
"That's cause we doin' it to y'all!"
The boy sucked his teeth. "Fuck the dumb shit! Can we be straight?"
"Anyone of y'all try us again we starting all over. We might not swing next time—might start stabbin'! I'm Kasper and this PJ, Charlotte's finest."
Kasper later called Stacey who was crying. Justice had been shot to death by her baby father and he'd gone on the run. Kasper wished Stacey had read the Book of Dookari. He and PJ got adjusted to C.A. Dillon and the other juveniles. This time they didn't have to be from Charlotte to rock with them, as long as they were real.

Santario walked up to where Kita stayed but she wasn't there. He walked through the parking lot and saw her and Tonio getting into the Honda Accord Tonio stole. *Where the hell they goin'?* he wondered.

"Where we 'bout to go?" Kita asked when she got in the car.
"To the mall, I'ma roll this blunt right fast."
"Want me da suck yo' dick while you rollin' it?"
"Come on." Tonio slouched down and peeled the wrapper off an Optimo.

Kita pulled out Tonio's dick and stroked it to get it hard. She was only trying to make sure she had something coming when they went to the mall. As soon as Kita put it in her mouth—

"Oh shit!" Tonio dropped the cigar and pushed Kita off.

"What?" Her eyes went fifty-fifty with Tonio's gaze and then wide when they saw Santario approaching. He had the face of a mad dog from a wild pack.

"Santario, what's up?" Tonio asked as he rolled down the window. "She wanted to go to the sto'."

Santario got up to the window and said, "You ain't gotta drive to the sto' nigga! The sto' right there—I saw—"

"We ain't do—" Tonio's words died in his throat when he saw Santario pull out a .38.

He shot Tonio in the chest six times while Kita screamed. Santario forgot that his gun only allowed six bullets because he went around to the passenger side and tried to shoot her.

Stacey was very upset about everything that had gone down wit' Tonio and Santario. Santario was caught beating up Kita by police who were in the area.

Two Weeks Later

"I'm gone, Kasper," PJ said giving Kasper dap. Today was his release date after doing a year and a half for Common Law robbery.

"Call my susta when you get home, so she can give you that five grand and weed."

Pj smiled. "A'ight."

"We gon' get that bread when I get out, stay tough."

"I am bra."

"Cureton let's go if you wanna go home," the staff said

"A'ight, Kasper."

"Love you, my nigga."

"Love you, too," PJ replied while walking backward. "I'ma—" he let his voice trail off giving Kasper the, 'call you sign' "Soon as I get home."

"Do that, stay outta shit till I get out. We gon get into it all when I do."

"Fasho," PJ said and walked away.

That would be the last time Kasper would ever see PJ.

The money from Kasper had gotten him robbed and killed his second day out. PJ was only seventeen years old. Kasper took the news hard. He'd never wanted friends before, but PJ had grown on him. There were tears to shed for his boy.

A month later, Kasper was released. Stacey threw him a party at their mother's home. He and Anition got into a heated argument and she left. A couple of days after his release, Kasper was enrolled at West Mecklenburg High School. He pulled up in a red Lincoln Navigator at just fifteen-years-old.

As he stood in front of the cafeteria with his backpack on, Kasper was checking out his new school. He was in high school now. Some senior walked by looking Kasper over. Jealous of the young boy's fresh black and red Nike shirt, blue denim Heaven or Hell jeans, black and red #7 Jordan's and on the Cuban link he wore hung a symbol.

This symbol was the Trisada attributed to Marsuk Son of Lord Enki which stood for 'he who watches that the Devon denim god from the belly of the great pyramid' of where Marduk had been buried after the outbreak of the Pyramid Wars after the Deluge. The 'Peace of Earth' arrangements circa of 8650 BCE has left the west while Edin in the hands of the enlilites. That confirmed the decisions of Anu father of Lord Enkinand Enlil but was never acquiesced to by Marduk. He was enraged and took it upon himself to start a war with the gods. Anu was forced to exile his grandson in order to end the war. When Lord Enki refuses to let his own father exile his son Anu sent Enlil to kill him. Marduk was places in the Greek Pyramid.

The five-pointed Blazing star is the symbol for the regenerated individual blazing like light Israel's in the darkness of the profane pyramid. The Crescent Moon being used to suggest death and resurrection.

"The fuck you all in my face fo'?" the senior snapped.

"What?"

"You heard what the fuck I said!"

"What choo think my Nike mean, ho?" Running a hand across the work Kasper said, "Nigga, I'll kill everybody."

Tee was a vicious, stone-cold dyke. She could change her appearance, but not the pretty features. She still had long eyelashes, full lips, thick eyebrows, and a peanut butter complexion. Tee wore shoulder-length hair in double twists and at fifteen she stood 5'9, wearing a white Enyce shirt, Pelle Pelle jeans and some all-white mid-cut Air Force One's.

An altercation looked like it was taking place by the cafeteria. She saw Capone, he was known for being a hater because he had nothing. The other boy with the long hair she didn't know, he was new. Tee was feeling him, he looked like a real nigga. Let Capone try something, and he was gonna get popped. Tee had a car so getting away would be easy. She would worry about the consequences later.

"Man come on, Capone," the senior's homeboy said tapping his shoulder. "Fuck that shit, Nivea waitin'."

"I'll whoop yo' lil' ass, nigga," Capone said and walked off.

Kasper only watched him, not worried at all about the last remark.

"I was 'bout to bust that nigga."

Kasper turned to see a chick, he scowled at her. "Say what?"

"I was gon' fuck around and pop his ass."

"Who you? I don't even know you."

"I'm Tee."

"You was gon bust wit' what?"

Tee hooked her index finger. "My tools, I had my finger on the ready button."

"Why the hell would you shoot fa me fo'?"

"Look like you a real nigga. I can tell you in that thug life shit."

"You gotta pistol on you at school?"

"Shit go wit' my outfits dog."

Kasper snickered. "Let me see."

Tee took Kasper around to the boy's bathroom and pulled her gun out. Kasper reached for it and said, "Let me hold it?"

"I know you ain't gon' beat me fo' my tool?"

"Nah, fa what?"

Tee passed the gun over to Kasper and he looked at it. "Twenty-two?"

"Yeah."

He stuck the gun into his back pocket.

"So, you gon' beat me fo my tool?!"

"I mean—"

Turnin' to walk out, Tee said, "Don't come back to school tomorrow without it cause I'ma make you use it!"

"Hold up, nigga."

Tee about-faced. "What's up?" she exclaimed.

Kasper pulled out a Glock .45 held it out to her and said, "You gotta keep somethin' heavy."

"What?" Tee said her hand slowly moving to it. "What choo—"

"Man, take the gotdamn gun an put it up."

"I can have it?"

"Man—"

"A'ight." A smile took character on Tee's face. "What they call you?"

"Kasper."

Tee gave Kasper dap. "Okay, I ain't neva seen you befo'. You new?"

"Just got outta trainin' school."

"Fa what?" Tee asked and Kasper told her the story. "So, he must a been a Crip or somethin'."

"Hell if I know."

"How old you is?"

"Fifteen."

Nodding her head, Tee said, "We da same age." Then crinkling her brows, she said, "Look on yo schedule and see if you got some

of my classes." They both looked at the schedule and found out they had all the same classes except math.

Chapter 25

During gym class Tee introduced Kasper to two of her homegirls sitting in the bleachers.

"This Tia and Felicia, they're cousins," Tee said. "They fifteen, too."

Felicia showed her palm saying, "Hey." She was 5'4, with blue eyes, was slim with red-bone skin, and brownish, black hair that was naturally curly.

"I like yo' tattoos," Tia spoke next. She was 5'3 ½, with pecan-brown eyes, straight hair, pigeon-toed, and between slim and thick with a fat, round, red face.

"'Preciate it," Kasper said. "How y'all get to school?"

"Drove dog," Tee said.

"What choo drivin'?"

"My Crown Vic."

"Okay."

"You?"

"Drove."

"After school—" Tee was saying, "—I can park my car and we can roll with choo?"

"So, they rode with choo?"

"I told you they my homegirls."

Before going to his spot Kasper stopped by his old folk's home to get his daughter, Kanazi who Lacey would drop off before going to work.

"Hold her for me," he said to Tia. When they got to Kasper's spot on the Northside Tee said, "Who stay here?"

"This my spot. I had my susta payin' on it fo' me while I was in trainin' school." Kasper saw them inside and gave Tee two cigars saying, "I got some weed."

When Tee got the blunts and started rolling, one of them was for Tia and Felicia. Kasper took Tee and his daughter out on the back deck so they could talk.

"So, what's up?"

Burning one end of the blunt Tee said, "Chillin'."

Leaning slightly over the rail with a smile, Kasper said, "Damn it's two thousand."

"Everybody thought it was gon' be the end of the world," Tee said before she took a drag of the blunt.

"In the cottage—" Kasper stood straight and looked to Tee. "It's three wings, A B and C. B wing was empty cause they had shipped the girls out right fo' I came."

"Uh-huh."

"Dog, 'round Christmas time they filled that whole wing wit' gallons of water."

Tee laughed as she passed the blunt and said, "Thought somethin' was gon' happen. Aye, you like that new Sisqo?"

"Thong song?"

"Yeah."

"Hell, yeah! I wanna see that thong, too," Kasper said, and Tee laughed. Then Kasper said, "So, what choo do? Sell dope or somethin'?" Kasper asked and puffed the blunt.

"I run up in mothafuckas spots."

"Kick doors?"

"How eva, lemme in." They both laughed and Kasper passed the blunt back. "You?" Tee asked.

"I put my pistol on niggas. I don't play."

"I run up in houses, I catch the bodies first. Then look fo' tha money and whateva else on my own."

"Vicious ain't cha?"

"Gotta be."

Kasper hurried towards the steps to stop Kanazi because she was trying to go down. Then she started to act up. "Stop!" Kasper said and Kanazi began to cry. He picked her up and said to Tee, "Come out here so she can run around."

"Bra what choo mixed wit'?"

154

"Guinean."

"What is that?" she asked.

"Guinean is a West Africa country."

"Yo' people from Africa?"

As he watched his daughter chase butterflies Kasper said, "Grandma and great aunt, then they went to Haiti. My momma was born there."

"You Haitian too then?"

Kasper shook his head. "My granddaddy was Dominican. He met my grandma while he was ova there doin' work." Then he said, "So, how you and yo girls get tight?" He looked at Tee.

"Me and Tia met first, but we all stay on the same street. They be watchin' out for me while I do shit."

"They straight to fuck wit' on that level?"

"Yeah, if they wasn't I wouldn't be fuckin' wit' em."

"Sup wit choo, Susta? She'd let choo stay out?"

"She don't care. She just don't want me bringin' trouble to the house, that's it."

Kasper folded his arms across his chest and looked to the ground, thinking. He was digging Tee, she was down to earth, and her character reminded him of PJ. Yes, Tee would make a great leader. He looked up to her and said, "Tee I want choo to be my right hand."

"I'ma be both hands."

Kasper dapped Tee and they became best friends.

Two Weeks Later

"Koda, we gon' get that red Navigator ain't we?" Juicey said.

The two friends walked around the school campus during their lunch period. Juicey was fourteen waiting on a birthday to come, stood 5'6 with neck length plaits, and was once chubby which was how she got the nickname.

"Hell, yeah." Koda smiled.

She too was fourteen and waiting on a birthday, 5'6, with her hair in a ponytail. They weren't dykes, they didn't know what they

were because they neither liked boys or girls. They just knew they were *thugged out.*

Koda said, "That navigator fat ain't it?"

"We gon' take the rims off and put them on our Durango."

"Hell yeah."

Then a stench caught Juicey's attention and she put her nose in to the air like a wary dog checking out the new mailman. She said, "You smell that, Koda?"

Then Koda became wary. "Somebody might be behind the gym smokin'."

"Let's go see who."

"Felicia, why you be hot boxin' the blunt?" Tee said. "Please lemme get high wit choo."

Felicia let out a silly chuckle, passed the blunt and said, "My bad."

"I'm tellin' ya."

Putting a hand in the air Felicia said, "Tee you gettin' tall."

"You think so?" Tee said with smoke rolling out of her mouth.

"Shoulda tried out fa basketball. You gon' try out next year?"

"Felicia shut the fuck up," Tee teased. "You know I don't ball."

"Oh, that's y'all smokin'?" Koda asked.

Tee spun around surprised and secreted the blunt behind her back. It was only two other students. Tee sucked her teeth and said, "Oh, yeah."

"Y'all smelt it?" Felicia asked.

Juicey said, "Y'all got some for sale?"

Tee shoved the blunt towards Felicia and said, "I'll give y'all some weed."

"A'ight." Koda cheesed. To Felicia, she said, "You in some of my classes."

"Yeah, yo' name, Koda?"

"Hell yeah. You know Juicey?" Koda threw her head that way.

"Seen her, too."

"Here." Tee gave Juicey a chunk of buds. "Where y'all from?"

"Wonderwood," was what Koda said, "Y'all?"

Felicia was the one to say, "Tuckaceegee, it's two more of us. Y'all wanna meet em?"

"Koda and Juicey?" Kasper asked making sure he had the names right. He and Tia had been in the cafeteria sitting in one of the booths eating lunch.

"Hell yeah," Koda said with a smile as Felicia sat in the booth.

Kasper slid a box of pizza toward them saying, "Y'all good?" It was Dominos.

"We can have some?" Juicey asked.

Smiling, Koda said, "She a greedy person."

"You, can't talk!" Juicey snapped. "You always eatin' somethin'! If you ain't you about to!"

"Juicey, I'll—"

"Aye, y'all gon get some or what?" Kasper interrupted.

"Reach fo' it, greedy." Koda smiled.

"You shut the fuck up! Yo' hand beat mine to a piece!" Juicey slammed.

She wasn't lying because Koda was chuckling as a slice headed for her mouth. Tee, Tia, and Felicia laughed.

Kasper said, "How y'all get to school?"

"We drove our Cadillac Eldorado," Juicey said before biting into her pizza.

"It's y'all shit?"

"Mm-hmm." Juicey nodded.

"A'ight."

Chapter 26

Kasper invited Koda and Juicy back to his spot where everybody sat in the living room of the three-bedroom, two-story home.

"Y'all some kin?" Kasper asked.

Koda said, "No, she my best friend. She stay wit' me at my grandma's house."

"So, what y'all do?"

"Steal cars and sell 'em to tha chop shop."

Juicey came in saying, "Or car jack fools and they rims."

"We ain't know that was yo' red Navigator wit' them rims on it," said Koda

Juicey came back in. "Yeah, we was 'bout to get choo."

"And get y'all whole mouth ripped off." Kasper's words made everyone laugh.

Koda and Juicey had the silliest laughs. Kasper looked at them with crinkled brows. They were peculiar individuals.

"Nah." Koda smiled. "We got 'bout six cars don't we, Juicey?"

"Yep."

Tee said, "What kind?"

Koda's eyes noticed the ceiling as she said, "The Monte Carlo." A pointer had flicked out in her hand. "A Benz." Then her middle finger mocked its neighbor. Koda would count each car with a flick of the finger. "A Cadillac Durango, Cherokee—that's our crime car."

"That's what?" Kasper frowned. "The fuck is a crime car?" Tia's laugh caused everyone else to laugh except Kasper. Smiling he said, "Hell y'all laughing at?"

"Nuttin'." Koda giggled.

"I see y'all two some goof troops. But what's this *crime car?*"

Chuckling Juicey said, "We use the Cherokee to do crimes in."

"Oh, okay." Kasper looked to Tee who was laughing without sound.

"Um." Koda's eyes found the ceiling again. "The Caprice—oh that's it." Then her eyes saw Kasper's.

"All these cars y'alls?" he asked.

Juicey said, "Yep."

"And where y'all keep all these gotdamn cars?"

"Hospital parkin' deck."

Nodding Kasper said, "That's smart. Y'all got pistols?"

"Got twelve pistols," Juicey said.

Koda added, "And we keep 'em all wit' us."

Pointing in that general direction, Tee said, "Out in y'all car now?"

"Yep," Juicey confirmed.

Kasper said, "So, if we go out there, right now, y'all strapped?"

Koda went into her pocket and gave Kasper the keys.

"What the hell!" Kasper said when he opened up the back door.

Tee moved to get a better look. "What?"

Tia and Felicia were peeking in as well.

Kasper said, "These mothafuckas got two pumps, an AR-15, two AK-47s and a MAC 90 on the back seat."

Smiling Koda said, "Look in the front."

When Kasper got there, he said, "Y'all crazy. Two nines, a .357 on the gotdamn flo', a .45 and a .38." He looked back at them and said, "It's only two of y'all—why y'all ridin' 'round like that?"

"In case some niggas wanna try us. We gon give 'em action." Koda's hands were behind her back and then she gave a closed-mouth grin.

"Y'all—" Tapping his temple, Kasper said, "—got mental problems, but I like y'all."

"Hell, yeah," Koda said. "Bra, I like the way you look."

"Oh, yeah?"

"Fasho."

Juicey said, "She acts weird sometimes."

"Juicey, you, act stupid all the time!"

"You, can't beat me!" said Koda.

"I'll lay yo' ass out!" Juicey replied.

Interrupting the moment Kasper gave Koda the keys back and said, "Aye y'all chill wit' that shit!"

"She talks too much," Koda said.

"You talk too much!"

"If I punch you, you gon' cry!"

"Well do it then," Juicey dared.

"Listen man—y'all shut that shit up and go inside. Tee I need to holla at cha." Kasper spoke with authority.

Stacey sat in the middle of her bed in PC, counting money she'd made. Her CD player was playing her favorite R&B album, *Aaliyah's One In a million*. '*Hot Like Fire*' was on repeat as she sung to it softly. She and Love had become close. But Stacey kept her circle of friends very small indeed. She was cool with females in Piedmont Courts there were only a few that she invited into her spot for conversation and high. If anybody needed anything such as food, flour, sugar, or cooking oil, Stacey would give it. She always bought extra groceries to accommodate anyone's needs along with candy for the kids.

It had been her choice to move to PC. She wasn't even on welfare. Stacey just loved the hood. She was a gutter chick that loved to hustle because it was in her blood. Her twin was taking care of her seven-year-old daughter Yoshi to keep her away from the lifestyle she lived.

"Get Yoshi and Asia some clothes," she said. Asia was Justice's daughter.

Seven thousand, six hundred and fifty-five dollars for the month of April was made. It was about to be May. She recorded that in a memo. Lastly, she put a rubberband around five thousand, because that's how much she was putting up. She recorded that as well. The cordless phone rang beside her. It was her weed plug. They talked for a second and hung up.

"Huhhhh boy!" Stacey swung out of bed and went outside. A money green Escalade pulled up and she got in.

"Sup, Prince?"

"You," Prince said.

He was a white guy that acted black, had low cut blonde hair and a mouth full of white gold. Prince pulled out a half-ounce of weed.

"Orange haze." He gave Stacey the bag. "Straight buds."

Stacey smelled the bag. "Mmhhh!"

"Yeah." Prince nodded with a smile.

"Smells sweet."

"My people in Utah growin' it."

"How much choo want fo' this?"

"I charge you five hundred a pound—you, just give me fifty mo'," Prince said. "I just wanted to show you the new product."

"Well, I'm ready anyway, so I'll follow you."

"Can I take you and bring you back?"

Stacey nodded and climbed into his passenger seat.

"How you feel 'bout Koda and Juicey?" Kasper asked Tee as they stood out in the front lawn.

"Shid—" Tee shrugged. "They cool fo' real—a lil' throwed off."

"Yeah, I like em." Kasper turned his head to look at the Cadillac. "Mothafucka ridin' 'round wit' artillery." He looked back at her. "They 'bout that gunplay. I'm 'bout it so I can tell if somebody else wit' it." Kasper looked down and thought about that smile Koda gave him. "That Koda crazy. Juicey is, too."

"Bra you—" Tee laughed, and Kasper looked to her.

"What?"

Tee was finally able to say, "You said that like you was serious. Like you talked to a psychiatrist and found out." They both laughed.

Kasper then said, "Man, I wanna fuck wit' 'em."

"Let's do it."

The TV was off, everyone was seated in the living room Kasper, Koda and Tia sat on one couch, Tee, Juicey and Felicia sat on another.

"Look y'all," Kasper began. "This isn't no meetin' people. It's six of us and numbers won't increase but decrease if they got to." Pointing to himself Kasper said, "I'm the Black Face, I call the shots. Tee—she the Under Bless, so she enforces my calls. Koda and Juicey y'all the chhayoloka Bishops. Tia and Felicia—The Shadow Popes. After tonight we'll all one family. We'll be the Ghost Mob." Kasper laid out his laws. Then he had to take them to meet his old folks to ask for their blessings. Reluctant at first, the two sisters talked about it and gave Kasper the green light.

He had to go to his Aunt Zhales home to get the bare necessities he needed. Tee, Koda, Juicey, Tia, and Felicia had been briefed about the Vodou practice and decided it was faith that they was willing to accept. Kasper swept the garage at his spot thoroughly and waited for it to dry.

"I don't care to see none of y'all," he said. "But we gon have to get naked. Nudity represents rebirth and purification. In my case, I'll have to get naked for the purification of it. Let's go."

When everyone got nude Kasper instructed Tee, Koda, Juicey, Tia, and Felicia to lay juxtaposed, face up with their arms at their side. After he blindfolded them which would keep them from opening their eyes. Kasper lined the garage with candles of red that represented the blood and white spirit. He outlined everyone's body with red pion chalk. If one thing was to go wrong, even if he so much as got tongue-tied while chanting, it was over. Tee, Koda, Juicey, Tia and Felicia's flesh would wither away, and nothing would be left of them but their skeletons.

Kasper slit the palm of his hand as he began chanting. He let the blood run into a gold motif bowl, then wrapped his hand in cloth. He took a Guinea hen from a canvas bag that clucked away until its neck had finally been broken. Kasper split it open and removed its heart offering the body to a statue image Eleggua, his deity, who is the messenger of death and the direct contact to the spiritual world.

He's a trickster who walked the crossroads; his colors are red and black. Kasper bled the heart and covered his body with the blood. What little was left he touched everyone's lips with it before he offered it to Eleggua as well.

Taking the motif bowl, Kasper would kneel at each person, in turn giving them a little of his blood to drink as he used a hand to lift them up than lying them back down softly. By giving them his blood, they would be artificial family and would have limited synthetic abilities of their own. Kasper and his official family on his mother side were Demi Gods, so the HIV Virus or AIDS could not affect their immune system. So, Kasper had no virus in his blood that could affect Tee, Koda, Juicey, Tia or Felicia. But this would not make them immune to viruses that attacked the blood cells.

After he finished, he wrote '713' on each one of their forehead's including himself. Then he went to stand in the center of everyone. Not chanting anymore, Kasper closed his eyes and held his arms straight out in front of him palms down and concentrated. After a few seconds, everyone began to lift out of their outline which was called a cuva. They stopped lifting at twenty inches. Kasper than slowly brought his hands into a fist and squeezed. Paralyzed at this point, Tee, Koda, Juicey, Tia, and Felicia seemed as though their bones throughout their entire body was being crushed.

They were being cleansed of their filthy knowledge the white man had bestowed upon black slaves. That the Lord God was their Heavenly Father and that his son Jesus died for their sins. They would not forget that this is what's believed, this was just to wash it out of them. A part of their rebirth. The pain only lasted ten seconds, then Kasper opened his palms. The pain would be long gone as if there never was. He slowly brought them back down to earth and the ritual was over. Everyone had to take a sweet herbs bath. Tia and Felicia's consisted of perfume Colonial herbs, cinnamon, and Yerba Buena.

Chapter 27

Kasper figured out that Koda and Juicey argued all the time and made frivolous threats towards one another.

"Aye what's really wrong wit' y'all?" he asked.

Everyone was out on the patio hanging out on this beautiful Saturday.

"Nuttin,'" Koda said innocently. Kasper shook his head. Giggling, Koda said, "Whaaattt?"

"And boy y'all silly as a mothafucka."

Tee said, "Juicey who's chop shop y'all was goin' to?"

"Oil Can."

"*Oil Can*? He black as hell wit' a nappy fro?"

Koda divulged laughter so loud she scared off a bird with its volume.

"Yeah," Juicey answered Tee.

Kasper looked at Tee confused by Koda's outburst of laughter, she was still going. He said, "What's so funny, Koda?" She was pointing at Tee as she cackled. "Aye Koda?" Kasper said.

"Huh?" she answered.

"I mean—what choo laugh fo', though?" Koda laughed out again. Kasper waved the question off. "Fuck it."

Tee said to Juicey, "Yeah, I know Oil Can, he stays right beside me."

"That's who we was goin' to. We used to go to this otha man named, Sweet Bread but he's dead," Juicey said.

Koda was still a little tickled about Tee's description of Oil Can. Kasper laughed. "Aye, she gotdam special."

Everyone laughed, Kasper now had someone around to keep him laughing, Koda and Juicey.

When everyone settled, Kasper said, "So, Juicey where yo momma et?"

"She got shot back in ninety-eight."

"Yo pops?" Kasper asked, Juicey only shrugged. "Koda?"

"My momma and my aunt went out somewhere one night and never came back, I was two. My daddy in Georgia on drugs."

"Yo' people never came back?"

"Nope."

"Damn that's fucked up."

Tee said, "My momma got kilt by my daddy back when I was nine. He's in prison."

"You talk to him?"

"My susta says we don't need nobody like that as a father, so no."

"My daddy got shot," Tia said.

"Mmhhh!" That was Kasper.

"And my momma hung herself in prison."

"Why yo' momma go da jail?"

"Back in ninety-five, she shot two men up the street from where we stayed."

"Shit!"

"Yep."

Felicia said, "My dad got beat to death when I was eight. But my momma still alive, you met her."

"Yeah, I still got my momma but my daddy got shot. We all lost a parent or two. I'm sorry about y'all losses. We family now, we all gotta be there fo each other. And as the Black Face—" Kasper put a hand to his heart. "I gotta put y'all before me cuz I'ma have to be accountable fo' y'all if somethin' happens to y'all that I coulda prevented. Come to me or Tee if y'all need somethin', we family."

"You and yo' lil' brother still beefin'?" Tron asked Anition who was folding clothes on the couch.

She waved the question off, she didn't feel like being bothered. Anition was pregnant and moody, and the baby wasn't Tron's.

"Huh?"

"Tron, I don't know!"

"All that attitude—" Tron said.

Anition sucked her teeth. "Please!" she snapped. "I do not fuckin' feel good!"

166

"I was askin' yo' dumbass a question."

"Yeah, I know."

"Don't talk that shit."

"Nigga, you came in here fuckin' wit' me!" Anition looked up at Tron.

"You heard what I said!"

"I'm foldin' clothes, right now." Anition went back to doing that. "I ain't got time fo' yo' bullshit!"

"Ole fat ass hoe."

Anition looked up at Tron again. "You need to grow the fuck up! Childish ass nigga!"

Tron moved up on Anition. "Bitch, you still here!"

"Cause this my shit, and yo' momma the bitch!"

"What!" Tron slapped Anition's face hard.

She had never told anyone when Tron hit her but this time she would tell Kacey.

Sunday afternoon found Kasper, Tee, Koda, and Juicey over at Kah-Kah and Tron's spot. The two homeboys saw the group coming around the back as they sat out there.

"Lil' bra what's sup?" Kah-Kah spoke.

"Ain't too much," Kasper said and looked at Tron who looked away.

Tron didn't like Kasper, but he wouldn't show it, even though, Kasper knew. The feeling was mutual. Then Tron heard a sound, a fast composite rustle of skin and metal. Exactly like the sound of something heavy coming out of the pocket bags. Phenomenally fast, like a magician. First, it wasn't there, then it was—just like that. Tron saw the muzzle of the .38 flash out taking a shot at him.

"Uhh!" The way Tron jumped out of the seat falling to the ground was like he was trying to move over to the next seat. He didn't holler or fall out of the chair because he got hit, but because it surprised him that a gunshot was fired his way. Tron had been shot in his thigh.

Kah Kah jumped up. "Lil Kasper!"

Kasper ignored him and moved over to Tron, standing above him, holding the gun hanging between heaven and earth. Tee reached for her pistol when Kah-Kah jumped up but did not draw. She was going to see how he played this.

Kasper said to Tron, "You love puttin' yo' hands on my susta, huh?" Kasper spoke with a practiced calm like he was reading for a movie role.

Seeing the look in Kasper's eyes, Tron said, "Don't kill me."

"No, Kasper," Kah-Kah pleaded for his homeboy's life.

"Kah-Kah get cho—" a gunshot rang out once more.

Tron rolled over on his stomach, he was shot in the shoulder.

"Turn yo' bitch-ass over," Kasper said as he advanced one big step. Tron grimaced as he turned back over. Kasper said, "This shit been goin' on too long. You got one mo' time—" The boy brought the gun across the air "—that's it." Whap!

Stacey was over at her old folk's home, where her grandmother Eba was doing a Tarot reading for a neighborhood resident. These readings were outlawed to family. When her cell vibrated, she stepped outside to answer. "Yes?"

It was Anition. She told Stacey about what happened to Tron. "So, I'm on my way to the hospital now, Kah-Kah drove him. You need to tell Kasper to sit his ass down somewhere fo' he get hurt."

Stacey crinkled her brows and looked at her phone. She put it back to her ear. "Anition?"

"Yeah?"

"Let me—I'ma hit choo back." Stacey disconnected.

She called Sheba to get Tron's hospital location and room number, she was sure Kah-Kah had called her.

The 713 went to Applebees after they picked up Tia and Felicia. The booth they sat in was filled with pasta of every kind, platters laden with a variety of meats and cheeses and basket of crispy fresh breadsticks, and deserts. They were feasting like the Mafia-

important criminals who had arrived at a position of significance and respect. Silverware clanged as they ate.

Kasper swallowed a little food and said, "I guess we straight on pistols being as though Koda and Juicey strapped and I got my lil arsenal."

"I only have that .22," Tee said.

"We all good," Kasper reiterated

"I thought cho' brotha-in-law was gon' try da do somethin' tha way he jumped up," Tee said.

"Nah."

"Oh, he just be beatin' yo' susta all the time?" Tee asked.

Kasper rotated his wrist with a frown. "A lil' bit."

Koda said, "That was West Chester apartments. That's where we got our Cadillac from." She smiled.

Juicey licked a finger with a smack of her lips and said, "Yep." Kasper dabbed a breadstick in pasta sauce. "Bout two in the mornin'," Juicey said. "Got up in it one minute on that same minute we was gone."

"Oh, y'all ass like that?" Kasper asked with a breadstick in his mouth.

Koda said, "My cousin Ju-Ju taught us how da get them cars." She was twisting spaghetti on her fork.

Kasper asked, "Where he et?"

"He got kilt by one of his homeboys."

Kasper shook his head, his daddy got killed by someone he thought was his homeboy.

"Dude shot him and his baby mama then shot himself." Koda was able to eat that fork full of spaghetti.

"Damn!" Tee shook her head.

Kasper said, "For real?"

"Uh-huh." Koda nodded.

"This shit crazy."

Chapter 28

Carolina Medical Center was the hospital Tron was checked into. Stacey knocked on Tron's room door and stuck her head in, then pulled Anition out.

"Yeah?"

"Come on." Stacey led the way to the stairwell.

"Where we goin'?"

"Stairwell."

"Fa what, Stacey?" Anition sounded tired.

"To talk," Stacey said. Anition followed with a huff. When they got in the stairwell, Stacey turned to Anition. "Listen—all that shit I'm hearing bout Phat Man gon' get hurt. We ain't gon' do that."

"That's what choo brought me out here to say?"

"I mean—" Stacey shrugged. "In case you wanted to do somethin'. Nobody ain't gon' do shit to Phat Man. Specially, yo bitch ass baby daddy and you know it."

"Stacey, I ain't tryna hear that." Anition turned and went for the door.

"Weak ass hoe."

"What?" Anition turned around.

"You a weak ass hoe," Stacey said. "You heard me! You know damn well, I ain't gon' let nobody play Phat Man."

"Yeah, we all know that's yo' spoiled brat!"

"Will lay down for him, but choo ain't gon' threaten him."

"Did you jump down his throat when he shot blanks et me?"

"Blanks is harmless, grow up."

"Thought so, you sided wit' him."

"Right or wrong!" Stacey spoke emphatically.

"You can have your lil' evil ass brother. When you gon' take yo' titty out his mouth?" Anition turned so that she could try again to leave.

Stacey said "I'll be dead wrong to whoop yo ass, right now. Lay you out all ova."

Anition fired back, "Pick on me, huh—you and yo' son?"

"Outta all of us you put up wit' a sorry ass nigga, Ann."

"Why is everybody so worried about Anition?" She pointed to herself, theatrically.

"Maybe cuz you family! You got a fuckin' brotha." Stacey was pointing to the side for emphasis. "That loves you."

Anition's facial expression said that she did not believe Stacey's words. "Kasper don't give a shit about me, Stacey."

"Oh, he shot Tron fa nothin'?" Stacey raised her arms and brought them back down smacking her thighs with them. "Why you wanna nigga like Tron around?" Stacey pointed that way.

"Stacey—"

"Got cho' own like brother fightin' you fo' him. Tron ain't capable of protecting you! He's a coward and you know it. They used to chump Tron in high school. He lucky Phat Man didn't kill him." Stacey left it at that.

That night the 713 was down in Kasper's room that he had at his initial home. Tia and Felicia were laying on the bed, Tee was sitting with Juicey, playing Marvel versus Capcom 2 on the PlayStation 2. Koda was looking at pictures Kasper had. He sat in a swivel chair, swiveling from side to side. Everyone knew about his ability to vanish, he'd taught them a few things.

He said, "We gon' start goin' outta town bringin' pain to them dope boys."

Koda burst into laughter, Juicey had to pause the game so she could get hers.

Kasper huffed. '*What the hell was so funny?*' he thought.

Chuckling, Tia said, "They laugh et everythang."

Kasper said, "Y'all jus' silly all ova, huh?" Everyone else laughed. Kasper said to Koda and Juicey, "What I said was ticklish?" They both laughed out again. Kasper said, "Y'all, we gon' have to start bein' quiet cuz they laugh at everythang we say." Everyone else started laughing, Koda and Juicey's laugh escalated.

I'm glad they around, Kasper said to himself as he swiveled.

School was the next day, the 713 was standing out in front of the 300 building, just waiting on the first-period bell to ring.

When two boys approached Koda, one said, "Y'all said what when you and Jiucey came through the other day?"

"Hol-hol-hol." Kasper held up a waving hand. "Don't approach them like that!"

The other boy bawled, "Nigga, we ain't speakin' to you!"

"You talkin' to them—you talkin' to all us!" Kasper used a head to introduce he and the family.

At that instant Tee reached back and smacked the student. Her hand was in perfect form.

"Ohhh!" some female walking by said when a man's shadow passed nearby and put a hand over her mouth.

The boy grabbed his face, turned his upper body at the throbbing burn. That female moved on but kept looking back.

"Y'all betta get the fuck on!" Tee snapped.

"Gone," Kasper demanded.

Inside their dope spot, Kah-Kah was at the kitchen counter weighing dope. Tron was sitting on a cushioned seat. A bottle of prescription pills sat on the table, as he just sat looking at them, thinking about how he'd gotten shot. Retaliation was far from his mind. It was just that he was so close to death. Kah-Kah looked over his way. Tron was looking pitiful. He shook his head, looked back to the scale to check the weight and broke the silence between he and Tron. "Leave that girl alone, Tron."

Tron broke out of his trance and looked up at Kah-Kah. "What?"

"Kasper came straight over here and shot choo. He ain't say shit, just whipped out and burned you—twice. I keep telling you time and time again—" Kah-Kah looked at Tron. "That lil' nigga ain't gon' put up wit' choo hittin' his susta too much longer, homie. You take him to be a young nigga that wanna be tough." Kah Kah shook his head. "Nah—" he paused. "—boy 'bout that shit. He shot old boy on Stacey's porch and sat there like it was nothin'." Kah-Kah sort of bucked toward Tron. "Merked some nigga in Texaco

and got off. He in trainin' school done swung off on a whole block two times. He done saw a lot in his life. You know who his daddy was and his uncle Juda. The nigga don't like you, Tron. I believe he wants to kill you, next time he will."

"He don't even fuck wit' that girl."

"It don't matta, that's—still—his—susta, homeboy. She's blood, and he can't deny it if he wanted to. What choo want wit' Anition? You treat her like shit, fuck all that." Kah-Kah went back to weighing dope, then said, "Leave that girl alone or quit puttin' yo' hands on her. In the end—she gon be da death of you."

Chapter 29

The whole 713 was in the garage of their spot after school. "I'ma
show y'all somethin'," Kasper said. He took three modeled cars and
sat them down on the floor. Everyone gathered as he squatted. "This
gon' be da day when it's time to go outta town and put this work in.
We gon' use upscale apartments. Tia, you and Felicia gon set these
niggas up. We gon' hit whoeva they might be."

Showing the Dodge Ram car. "Say this is one of our stolen
cars?" He picked up the Lexus model. "This the dope boy or whoeva
car." Then he put that down and picked up a Suburban. "This represents a stolen van. The middle seat gon' be gutted out. So, whoeva
we get they gon' lay on the flo' the best they can, while me and
somebody watch 'em. Koda, you and Juicey, gon' be da ones in the
car.

"Me and Tee gon' be in the truck. Now dig this, Tia, y'all get
these niggas and bring 'em to whateva apartment we use. Me and
Tee—" Kasper positioned the truck the way he wanted. "—gon be
backed in a parkin' space diagonally across the parking lot. Koda
and Juicey gon' be in a parkin' space as well. We gotta make sure
the van is a Checkmate." Kasper had positioned the suburban.

"What's a Checkmate?" Tee asked.

At the same time, Koda and Juicey said, "A van that got sliding
doors on both sides."

"Oh."

Kasper took the Lexus model saying, "We gotta make sure it's
a parkin' space beside the van on the driver's side." Kasper used the
Lexus to show what he was saying, "Pull up in a parkin' space beside the van on the driver's side. Koda you and Juicey gotta be in a
black van, wearing masks, so y'all can jump out when it's time."
Kasper looked up at Koda and Juicey. "Don't play wit' these niggas.
Let 'em know that they need to comply or it's action."

"A'ight." Juicey smiles.

"Juicey you—" Kasper demonstrated his instructions. "—hurry
up and jump out the van wit' choo handgun, open the driver's side
door, wit' cha pistol on 'em. Open it all the way up. The door should

be in front of you. At this same time, Koda you hop out with the choppa and make his ass get out. Kasper squatted back down to the cars. "Tee, you gon' pull up behind the Lexus to block it in." Kasper stood again "And I'ma get out wit' my choppa. If it's one, I'ma make the passenger get out on the driver's side. His ass gon' get in the van, too. Right beside his best man.

"I'ma get in the van to help Koda watch the people. Tia, can you and Felicia drive?" Kasper continued.

"I can but she can't," Tia replied.

"Well, Tia you take the car and follow the van. Tee you bring up the rear."

"What if it's a stick? I can't drive those."

"Y'all get in the truck with Tee."

Tee said, "Where we goin?"

"To an abandoned house we gon have."

"We need code names."

"Okay." Kasper thought for a few seconds. "Juicey, you gon' be Megabyte. Koda, you Sweepstakes. Tee, you're Party Time. Tia, you're Angel Dust and Felicia, you Baby Powder."

"And you Krazy Face." Koda beamed.

Everyone paused for a moment, then laughed.

Anition was lying across her bed brewing over the beef between her and her lil' brother. Everyone had been right, Tron was no good and treated her like shit most of the time. He would borrow money and not pay her back when he had money of his own. He even wrecked her car and refused to help get it fixed. Anition didn't know what she put up with him when she really wanted to be with the nigga she was pregnant by.

Tron hobbled to the room like a man on invisible crutches. "What's wrong wit' choo?" he asked.

Anition raised her head off the pillow, then laid back down. "Tron, I'm sorry but choo gon' have to leave my house."

Tron's neck snapped back. "What?"

176

Anition sucked her teeth. "You heard what I said!"

"Yeah, right."

That made Anition sit up. "Please pack yo' stuff and move out my house! Yes, this is my house, and I'm tellin' you to leave!"

"Man, listen."

"Ain't no *man listen!* Get out or my lil' brother will come get choo out!"

"Fuck you then, fat bitch!" Tron hawked a glob of spit on Anition.

"Oh, hell no!" She got up. "I know you ain't spit on me?"

"I'll shit on yo' ass, too, hoe! Like I been doin'."

Anition said nothing in return, she went under her pillow and got her government-issued 9mm.

Tron said, "You bet not try da burn me."

Coming around the bed in strong stomps Anition heightened her pistol. "A'ight, Tron Warner."

She leveled the gun to Tron's heart and fired a single shot. He stumbled back and his hand went to his chest as he crashed into a wall and slid to the floor, already lifeless. Anition didn't panic. She would claim self-defense, turn it into a domestic violence issue. Being that she was a Sheriff's Deputy, she would stand a good chance of getting off without punishment.

<p style="text-align:center">****</p>

Sitting at the picnic table in the courtyard by the cafeteria, eating pizza and French fries for lunch, were the 713.

"You gotta problem wit' me dog?" A voice came up on the side of Tee.

She looked up and jumped when she saw that it was two boys, plus the one she'd assaulted. Kasper got up and so did Koda, Juicey, Tia, and Felicia.

Kasper stood beside Tee and said, "Nigga, fuck all y'all!"

"What!" One of the other boys jacked up his pants.

Tee said, "Nigga, you heard!"

The first boy said, "Well, let's—"

"Chill, Mario," the boy Tee assaulted said holding his homeboy back. "The principal right there." Everyone looked and saw the principal watching. Mario looked back to Kasper and said, "I got choo, boy."

"You gon' make a nigga kill you." Kasper scowled.

Mario said to Koda and Juicey, "I know where y'all stay." Then turned to leave.

A smile crossed Koda's face as she said, "Yo' house ain't hard to remember either, nigga."

By Thursday night the 713 was on a Greyhound to Houston, Texas. They had what they needed in a large duffel bag wrapped in a sheet. Kasper had $50,000 in cash in a book bag. When they arrived at the Greyhound depot around 12:06 pm, Kasper hailed a taxi van and they took it to a Marriott. He had Koda and Juicey wait outside with the gun bag.

Kasper waited for the right time to approach the desk clerk, who was a white, female who looked to be in her mid-twenties or slightly pushing thirty, with blond hair. She looked like a Playboy bunny reject.

She smiled. "How may I assist you today?"

"I'm tryna get three rooms."

The clerk whose name tag read: *Melissa* cocked her head to the side and said, "Now how old are you?" She waited while drumming her manicured nails on the countertop.

"Not old enough, but I got somethin' fo' ya."

Melissa straightened up and smiled. "What do you have?"

"I'll give you fifteen hundred per room, per night, and I need it till, Sunday."

Melissa thought about the offer. She finally said, "Would you like doubles or singles?"

"Doubles."

"Okay listen—I can't give you the keys right now." Melissa chucked her eyes to the right where her coworker was on the phone. "I go on break at one if you can wait. I'll put the rooms under a fake name and bring the keys outside when I go on break. It won't be

long." Melissa looked at her watch. "About thirty-five more minutes."

"Bet."

Melissa looked over and saw Tee. She was standing a few feet away talking to Tia and Felicia. Melissa said, "Is that girl with you? The tall one?"

Kasper already knew who she was speaking of, he said, "Yeah."

"How old is she? She looks eighteen."

"She's fifteen, too."

"Wow!" A shocked Melissa said.

Smiling Kasper said, "She tall to be her age, ain't she?"

"She is. Does she have any ID at all? I could check her in."

"Nope."

"Well, like I said—I got you on my break."

Stilloan Robinson

Chapter 30

Melissa had gotten her money in exchange for their rooms and included that she knew a guy they could get fake IDs or driver's licenses from. Something would be set up for Sunday before they left town. After getting Tia and Felicia settled in the room, Kasper, Tee, Koda, and Juicy took a taxi to the AutoZone for screwdrivers, then took the taxi to a hospital where Kasper paid the driver and said, "Now get missin'."

They walked to the parking deck for two cars. Koda and Juicey were faster at stealing than they'f said. They pirated a Chevy Silverado and a Dodge minivan. The van went back to the hotel along with the guns until it was needed.

"Let's go," Kasper said as he got into the back seat of the truck with Juicey.

Koda at the wheel said, "Where to?"

"Find us a gotdamn Burger King. I want some Whoppers."

Stacey was out at Target with Zya and Love shopping for appliances.

"They ever catch Justice's baby daddy?" Love asked

"Nah, not yet," Stacey replied while considering an iron. "I'ma catch his ass, though. When I do—" She put the iron in the buggy. "—I'ma smoke his brains."

Love laughed, Zya only looked at Stacey. Her threat was futile. She had been the one that killed Justice, technically. So, trying to take actions into her own hands was definitely in vain.

"He gon' feel the shot fo' he hears the pop," she said and Zya couldn't help but smile.

Love said, "I don't blame you."

"Remind me to send Santario some money, Love. I miss them, man. He ain't even have to do all that. He coulda just beat the damn shit outta Tonio, man."

"Crazy," Love said.

"Now my boy in jail."

"You get him a lawyer?"

"I'ma see how much time they tryna offer him first. Then I'll go from there.

"It's go time this here weekend," Kasper said as he unwrapped the paper from one of the two Whoppers he had, along with a large fry and a Dutch apple pie.

"Hell, yeah," Koda said. She was putting fries between her Whopper.

"Koda?" Kasper said.

"Mm-hmm?"

"Is that all you say is *hell yeah*?"

"Hell, yeah."

Everyone laughed, then Kasper said, "I got my hands full wit' choo and Juicey's ass." He saw a black chick wiping down some tables and called her over.

"What's up?" The girl said.

"You know any strip clubs where the big boys be et?"

"Big boys? You mean like—"

"Ballas," Tee interjected.

"I mean—" She looked down to the side as she shrugged one shoulder, thinking. "You got—" She was still thinking, then she said, "Tip-C, King Angels—" Then she looked up at Kasper. "But if you tryna be wit' all the ballas, then Heads N Tails is where you wanna be."

"Where is that et?"

"Martin Luther King Jr Blvd."

Kasper gave her two hundred dollars saying, "Don't work yo' self too hard. You breakin' a sweat."

After they finished eating, the three comrades rode around to find an abandoned house that would give them a little privacy. It took almost an hour and a half to find one. It was perfect, right on a dead-end street, in a neighborhood with other houses that were run

down. Everyone helped out in remembering where they were. Kasper found a crackhead and paid him to kick in the door and turn the power on. It was time to find the strip club.

Kasper stood outside with Koda waiting on the owner of Heads N Tails to come out. They had caught a stripper going in and asked her to call out the owner.

"Yo' what's up?" He came out with crinkled brows, throwing his head up. He looked more serious than life. He even resembled Bruh Man from the fifth flo'. The big man wore a purple-colored suit and an iced-out chain.

"I'm Krazy Face, dog."

"Okay, so what?"

"Nigga, tryna see what's up wit' da VIP spot in yo' club."

"You gotta be holdin' to reserve that, baby boy, and besides— all my spots accounted fo'."

Disappointed, Kasper looked at Koda for a split second with a huff, then back to the owner. "Look, man—I'll give you more then what anybody else did fo' they spot."

"You look like money, boss," the owner said while checking Kasper out. "But I don't think you holdin' like that. This is Head N Tails."

"I should let choo keep my books since you know how much bread I got."

The owner shifted his weight in a way that looked like he was doing some type of shuffle, as he thought for a moment.

"Tell you what—one of my top dogs gave up ten grand fo' a spot. You do betta, it's yours."

"Twenty," Kasper said. "All hunnids." He went into his pockets to pull his money out.

"Yo' you said your name is what?"

Kasper counted the money and looked up long enough to say, "Krazy Face." He'd finished counting. The owner smirked. "And this my susta, Sweepstakes"

Koda smiled at the owner and said, "Sup?"

"A'ight, I'm Big Bronz."

"No doubt," Kasper replied. He forked over the money. "Whoever yo' *top dogs* is that had tha spot—they can still have it, but I got two college chicks I'm gettin' it fo'. Yo' people can chill wit' them. I'ma be on the flo' wit' my people."

Big Bronze nodded. "Okay, no problem, playa. You want drinks—bottles?"

"I do bad smokin'. You can send 'em up to the VIP."

"I gotcha lil' cuz. What time you plan on showin' up?"

"What time yo' people gon' show up?"

"Eleven."

"Well, expect me 'round ten-thirty."

"Pull 'round back," Big Bronze said while directing a thumb over his shoulder.

"A'ight, I'ma get wit' cha."

"Okay, Killa."

Getting back into the back seat of the truck, Kasper said to Tee, "I need you and Juicey to take the girls and get their hair and nails done. Me and Koda gon' get tha van and get they clothes and jewelry."

"How much—" A woman went into her purse and pulled out some bills. "—do I need?" She showed the money to Mother Eba.

Mother Eba spoke with accented English, "Whateva ya tin kiss wuff."

The woman peeled off three hundred dollars and held it up like it was a novel, saying, "Is three hundred dollars fine?"

Mother Eba's nod was heavy, yet defiant. The woman tried to offer the money, but Mother Eba said, "Ya ahffa shall go to Oshun." She held her arm away, pointing at a statue image of a woman holding a fan in one hand, and clutching her stomach with the other.

She was naked, wearing around her neck three necklaces. Five yellow beads alternated with one red bead in honor of Chango. The other necklace had five yellow alternating with two blue symbolizing maternity. The last being all yellow beads for herself. Pumpkins

were in front of the image that sat on the other altar. Pumpkins were sacred to Oshun. She used them as her bank and that's where the money went. The woman cringed when she put it there. All money offerings had to be used towards bills and any necessities used for worship, not for personal gain.

The woman followed Mother Eba up the stairs to a windowless room that had only a small table, two chairs on each end, and a white candle in the middle. The room gave the woman creeps. Mother Eba closed the door and told the woman to have a seat, then the light went out.

"Ooh!" The woman flinched. It seemed like the room had developed a darkness never seen.

Mother Eba sat across from the woman and reached out both of her hands saying, "Take me hands." The woman took hold of mother Eba's hands after a short struggling locating them. "Don't let go," Mother Eba warned. "No matta wha— don't let go."

"Yes, ma'am."

Silence stilled the room for a few moments, then the woman heard mother Eba inhale through her nose and exhale through her mouth. They were once again with silence. Then a barbeque lighter flicked to life and the woman turned her head to look up and saw Aunt Jean standing there lighting the candle.

She thought, '*What the hell!*' She had seen Aunt Jean downstairs before she and Mother Eba came up polishing some weird looking black African mask. After lighting the candle with the barbecue lighter still aflame, Aunt Jean looked down at the woman and gave just a mock of a spooky ventriloquist dummy blink of her eyelids. When Aunt Jean released the flames' trigger, it was like the room had taken on that darkness once again. It was only an illusion to expel Aunt Jean. The woman wanted to get the hell out of there.

What the fuck have I gotten myself into?' She loosened her grip on Mother Eba's hand contemplating her departure.

Mother Eba tightened her grip so the woman chose wisely. "Oh, spirit of te deces, David Ingram." Mother Eba was conjuring the woman's husband from Empyrean. Once he crossed back over to the earthly realm, his memory of his past life would be restored.

"Kesme into ya," Mother Eba continued. "David Ingram, jur prestas es rekerir." She got silent.

"Hello?" A voice searched.

The woman's eyebrows drew down as she listened intently.

"Don't let go," Mother Eba stated for the last time as she felt the woman's hands slacking a little bit.

"Hello?" Then a man came into view.

The woman's husband.

"Oh, Lord!" The woman grabbed her chest with one hand.

As she slunk away from Mother Eba back into the chair. The woman had let go of Mother Eba's hand.

Chapter 31

Stacey and Love was back at Stacey's apartment in PC, sitting on the platform. It was Friday and the afternoon sun felt good. Piedmont Courts was live. There were girls flirting with groups of boys as they walked down the sidewalk, people were out on their platforms smoking, drinking, talking or just sitting by themselves. There weren't any kids playing football in the street per usual because they were at the center that had recently opened back up.

"Love, you eva thought about having kids?"

"Yeah, one day. I ain't tryna have none by someone that's a dead beat."

"I hear that."

"When yo' baby daddy get out of prison?"

"Two thousand one."

"And what he in prison fo'?"

"Him and his homeboy robbed some white woman comin' from the ATM in ninety-three. When he got caught by da police, he had on a watch taken from a victim in another robbery. They hit his stupid ass. His codefendant got caught doin' some other shit and told on my baby daddy."

"Y'all was together?"

"No, he some bullshit. He was fuckin' around on me. Kacey beat 'em up."

"Whaattt!"

"That's when I found out he was a real coward."

"Why she beat 'em up?"

"Cause, he called himself tryna get loud wit' me one day in front of our niece, cussin', and shit. Kacey was like nigga you see my niece right here? He waved her off and she went straight to his ass and broke his jaw."

"Kacey, uh-uh."

"Twin is tough, man, I'm tellin' ya. She was already in military school. She was on a home pass, fucked his ass up. My twin is a beast. I ain't got the tolerance fo' that military shit. Twin got will."

Mother Eba's words suddenly came back to the woman when she realized she'd let go of Mother Eba's hand.

"Aaahhh!" She panicked, then tried to reach for those hands. Those hands were not there anymore, neither was Mother Eba. Nothing was there except darkness. "M—Mother Eba?" the woman cried out as she tried to feel her way around the darkness. She was trapped in this darkness which gave birth to death, sleep vexation and deceit. It was also associated with the Underworld. "Please, Mother Eba," the woman pleaded as she tried to feel her way around. There was nothing to feel for because nothing would fill this void.

The candle was still flickering in the darkness as Mother Eba sat at the small stable. The woman had been warned not to let go of Mother Eba hands.

Mother Eba blew the candle out and went downstairs to consult with Aunt Jean about what happened. Mother Eba could go after her though it was not obligatory. The woman had failed to make a contract that would bind another course of action in the event that something was to go wrong. Aunt Jean said no course of action would be taken for the woman. Mother Eba warned her three times. She would be crushed under the pressure of darkness until she ceased to exist. Total oblivion, the woman's soul would go to Ikedele.

Night had come in with the speed of a jaguar. Kasper, Tee, Koda, and Juicey were inside the van checking over their weapons. The AK-47, AR-15, a Glock .45 and a Glock 9mm. Kasper and Koda were kneeled in front of Tee and Juicey who was sitting in the rear bench seat. Like Kasper said, the middle bench seat had been taken out and ditched. The front passenger seat was gone as well.

"Ready to get this bread tonight," Kasper said as he racked the AK-47 and aimed it between Tee and Juicey.

"We ready wit' cha," Tee said. She was holding the Glock .45 and working the trigger mechanism before she slapped the clip in.

Juicey had the Glock .9mm on her lap, she said, "We ain't neva been outta town befo' have we, Koda?"

"Nope." Koda was smiling at her AR-15.

"We gon' get out," Kasper said.

Tee looked at her watch. "We need to get ready to roll. It's ten-fifteen."

The stolen van and truck pulled behind the Heads N Tails strip club. Big Bronze came out on time and met the 713.

"Okay, lil' cuz," he said. "I see you made it."

"That's cause you got my money."

Big Bronze gave that one cheek grin he always did. He ushered his patrons inside. The two *college chicks* wearing Gucci and open toe heels had his attention. Everyone could hear *Three 6 Mafia's Where Dem Dollaz* coming from the speakers, being played by the club's D.J.

"Welcome to Heads N Tails," Big Bronze said and opened the door.

The music came loudly. A bouncer was to the right, dressed in all black and an iced chain. He was a big man of about 6'6, 350 pounds. On the ceiling was the logo, Head N Tails with a woman standing, bent over grabbing her ankles. This logo danced with purple strobe lights that turned pink. An isle was straight ahead with stages to the left and right. On the left was a stage, where girls were on poles, being the nightly entertainment. The stage was littered with cash from both men and women that stood there with hands full of dollars.

There were bricks of dollars stacked on a counter that ran around the stage so that patrons could put their money there and drinks. Some people had bottles of liquor and some water. One of the naked strippers was on all fours dancing and a dyke chick pushed a pile of money toward her like casino winnings. To the left wasn't necessarily a stage but a trampoline, littered with money. The poles were hanging down from the ceilings as strippers, turned this way and that from up in the air naked. Then one would fall

down to the trampoline letting the recoil of it send them back into the air and onto their poles.

Then the isle opened taking you left or right or sending you straight in. The stages to the left and right were reversal of the first two stages. The 713 had passed. The music changed to *Sisqo's Thong Song*. Kasper smiled, they went down the aisle until it opened into an area with tables, chairs, and strippers giving lap dances. Big Bronze found Kasper, Tee, Koda and Juicey a spot in the back where they could sit, then took the *college girls* to the VIP.

Three Cadillac Escalades, one black, one white and the other grey parked behind the Head N Tails strip club. Two men got out, each wearing platinum chains that read: *Getty*.

The back door swung open and Big Bronze stepped out. "Fellas, come on in?" He dapped every man. "Yo' Magic I got bad news and good news."

"Talk to me."

Big Bronze went into his pocket. "Gotta give your money back," he said. Magic's expression was like an eight-year old's wondering what he'd done wrong. "The good news is some lil' college chicks bought choo spot."

"Bought me out?"

"They say y'all can chill wit them. Bottles paid fo', everything's available. Y'all still win—got sexy lil' bitches, too."

Magic shoved the money into his pocket and said, "A'ight."

Chapter 32

Anition was sitting in the living room, watching an episode of *Touched By An Angel*, when someone knocked on her door with hard bangs. She picked up her pistol and stormed over to check the peephole. It was Tron's sister and some of her homegirls. Anition unlocked and snatched the door open, with the gun concealed behind it.

"Y'all got a problem?"

"Bring yo' ass outside you devil-worshiping, bitch!" Tron's sister spat!" Some of the girls had knives.

"Y'all bitches come in." Anition opened the door wider and stepped back slightly.

When the first two females rushed the threshold, Anition revealed her gun and fired out shots. She killed one of the four girls and wounded Tron's sister and one of her friends. She would tell detectives that the girls came for retaliation and bombarded her home with weapons. That would be enough for self-defense.

"What are me and my cousin gon' get into tonight wit' choo and yo' homeboys?" Tia asked Magic.

"Shiid—you tell me. Y'all don' took our spot."

"I got a spot for you, it's a G-spot, you'll like it."

"Oh, yeah?"

"And it'll be all wet and shit."

Magic bit his bottom lip. '*Yeah, this a little nasty bitch,*' he thought. "You comin' back wit' us."

"Listen—we sluts. If you can't slut us out, then you'll do betta gettin' one of these strippers."

"Aye." Magic turned to holler at one of his boys. He motioned him over with a bottle of champagne in his hand.

"Yo."

"Dog, baby girl say she and her cousin tryna be sluts to some real niggas tonight."

"Yeah, I got that memo." Magic's homeboy motioned Felicia over with a finger.

"Yes?" She walked over to him.

"So, y'all gon' get wit' us?" he asked.

Tia jumped in saying, "I told 'em we ain't goin' nowhere if we can't slut."

Felicia said, "Yeah, that's what we like. We want everything X-rated."

Magic's homeboy looked at him saying, "Man, what tha fuck?" He looked at Felicia.

She said, "You gotta smack her in the face wit' it."

"Mmaannnn." He turned away and Magic laughed.

These girls were some real sluts. Magic's homeboy looked back to Felicia and said, "We taken y'all to our spot."

A stripper walked up to the table with her breasts out, dressed in a purple thong and six-inch heels. "Y'all need anythang?" she asked.

Kasper looked to his comrades who looked at him. He went into his pocket and gave the stripper a hundred, saying, "We good, we don't need nuttin'." He wanted to get some head but he was not here to entertain his personal pleasures. He was here for the business of his family.

"Good look." The stripper smiled and walked away.

Kasper watched that ass as it melted into the crowd. Then a thought occurred to him, he needed to step outside, so he could speak with Tee. He had Big Bronze let them out of the back and a bouncer would let them back in.

"Sup?" Tee asked.

"Man, forgot to look fo' some apartments to set the trap."

Tee only looked at Kasper and shrugged. She had no fucking clue. "So, what the fuck?"

Kasper looked off and said, "I hate that I forgot that part." He looked back at Tee.

She said, "So, you ain't got mo' plans?"

Kasper thought for a few moments. "Nah, dog, hell no."

Tee took a moment to think. "Well, it's only one thang to do."

"What?"

Tee leaned in and, in a hushed tone, gave him her plans.

Back in the club, Kasper paid a stripper to go up and signal the girl wearing the tube top to the bathroom.

Tee was waiting. "Hey, Tee."

"Tia, y'all gotta get them niggas to the hotel."

"But they say they gotta spot fo' us to go to. Y'all never got an apartment to take them to?"

Tee huffed. "No, Tia, you gotta get back to the room, man. Tell 'em y'all don't know them to go back to no spot with them."

"Damn, Tee."

"If they ain't tryna go back to the hotel tell 'em y'all good. This shit is dead. Bra just gon' have to be mad at me. Ain't no way we can let y'all get in their car goin' back to their spot. So, tell 'em that."

"Okay."

"Y'all good?"

"We fine, playin' our part." Tia looked down and said, "I don't think me and heels get along, my feet hurt."

Tee looked down at Tia's fat pink polished toes. "Okay, it won't be long." Then she looked back up. "They like y'all?"

"Who? Those niggaz, yeah." Tia laughed. "We told 'em we wanted them to slut us real bad."

Tee smiled. "Oh, yeah." Tia nodded as she laughed. "See if they ready to go now. If they ask about y'all ride say a car dropped y'all off."

"Okay."

"Tia, don't let them take y'all back to they spot."

"I won't, Tee."

Kasper and Tee had taken position along with Koda and Juicey. Kasper did not care who witnessed this. He was getting money.

Whatever parking space those mothafuckas took they were getting ran up on. Magic and his homeboy had no problem going back to the Marriott. What could go wrong? They figured.

Twenty minutes later, they arrived at the hotel.

"I think that's them in that white Escalade," Kasper said with his hand on the door handle as he watched the truck turn in. "I'm sure."

"Yeah, it's them. Let's go," Tee said.

"Kasper and Tee movin'! Juicey, com' on," said Koda. They were parked not far from their people.

Koda got out with her AR-15. Juicey held the Glock 9mm, smiling. They moved to Kasper and Tee's beat.

"You bet not move!" Kasper said menacing Magic's homeboy with his AK-47.

"Whoa!" His hands went up like a train robbery victim in a bad western.

Magic wanted to run when Tee came up. "Yeah, I wish you would," she dared indicating her weapons dramatically.

Magic sucked his teeth when Koda and Juicey came up. Koda was told to get the van, Tia and Felicia were instructed to go to their hotel rooms and wait. When Koda got the van, Kasper made both men get in on the floor, lying face down, as he and Juicey got in and sat on the rear bench seat. Tee had taken the space where the front passenger seat was missing and they were off.

"This was a setup?" Magic asked.

Kasper said, "Tha whole time."

The van was parked behind the abandoned house. Magic and his homeboy, Showboat, was in one of the rooms lying face-down beside each other.

"I applaud you lil' cuz," Magic said.

"Nigga shut the fuck up," Kasper said as he went to check out of the window. Koda and Juicey snickered. The streets were clear, Kasper turned back to the two men. "Big Bronze said y'all had it," Kasper lied. Holding the AK-47 by the neck.

"Shid he tha one got it. You see his club?" Magic said as he looked up at Kasper. "Come on, lil' homie, don't do it like this."

"Where tha money et?"

Magic said, "Y'all ain't got no mask on. Know y'all gon' kill somethin'." His boy Showboat just kept shaking his head in disbelief.

"We ain't got no masks on—" Kasper paused as he kicked Magic's shoe. "—cause we ain't from 'round here."

"I'm broke," Magic said.

Koda and Juicey laughed, Showboat looked up at them.

Kasper said, "You gon play games?"

"I ain't bullshittin'. Just spent all I had at tha club. Now I gotta find a lick, put me on one."

Kasper nodded. "Okay."

Kasper looked at Tee, pointed to Showboat and brought a hand across his neck. She went over pointing the Glock .45 and finally got to squeeze off one of its rounds. The sound of the gunshot bounced off the walls of the empty room. She had hit homeboy in the back.

"Aye yo!" Magic turned over and sat up.

Kasper pointed the AK-47 at him. "Lay yo' ass back down!"

Laying back down, Magic said, "That's my gotdamned cousin!" Then he heard Showboat gasping for air in deep droughts.

Kasper said, "Then we give you our kind regards. You gon' be next if you don't give up that money! We don't want no small shit either! We want them millions!"

"How you know he ain't have the money?"

"You the one that started doin' all the talkin'. If I gotta ask you again, I'ma say fuck that money and kill yo' ass, too. We need that now."

Magic sucked his teeth. "I got two point three million. You can have that shit."

"Well, make it ours."

Stilloan Robinson

Chapter 33

Lacey was sitting on the kitchen floor up against the cabinets drinking wine. Kasper had been the creation of her stress. He'd changed from the boy she first met in 1998. They had sex the night he'd gotten out of training school but he'd left shortly afterward.

"So, you a hit and run?" she asked, while tailing him to the door.

"I don't play baseball."

"I can't tell." Lacey huffed, sneering a nostril into a nasty snarl. *"Nigga, I can't stand yo' lil' punk ass!"*

"The feelin' is mutual," Kasper responded.

Lacey stressed over the young boy, he was just too adorable. She'd been calling him to inquire about Kanazi. When Lacey figured Kasper had no interest in her well-being, she hung up. Here she sat, with her face streaked with tears which caused her to call off her job today. She couldn't focus, Lacey took the glass of wine down, then poured another maximizing the glass, spilling it into her hand. She took a hard swig still thinking about the young boy that fathered her only child. There was no telling what her baby father was out there doing. But she knew he was doing what he wanted to do. Kasper was gonna be Kasper.

<div align="center">****</div>

Magic directed the 713 to a house in the outskirts of Houston that was isolated. The home looked as though it belonged to a klansman. Two redneck trucks that had confederate flags on them were parked on the gravel, a large confederate flag covered the front door and swastikas were posted on the windows. He'd created this look to keep away unwanted visitors. Magic led the way up to the door where they heard dogs barking.

"Call yo' mutts off," Kasper told Magic who did as he was told. He opened the door and the smell of those dogs rushed out.

"Mmm-hmmm!" Tee scrunched her nose. Three gold Bull Mastiffs were there growling.

Before he stepped inside, Kasper said, "Man, you need to tell yo' dogs to get the fuck on fo' I—"

"I got em! I got em!" Magic ordered the dogs to their rooms.

They only went in but kept their heads poked out, still growling. Magic had to get past that room to get to the room where he had the money. So, he made them get back in and closed the door. They whined, then barked as one of them began clawing at the door. Magic led his abductors to a back room that looked like it belonged to some spoiled white girl. There were dolls all over and stuffed animals over the bed and a large doll house.

"Nigga, where tha fuck the money et?" Tee asked.

"In the doll house," Magic said. "It's rigged wit' latches."

Kasper said, "Well, you need to unlatch it and get that money!"

Magic huffed, damn he had gotten jacked by some young ass mothafuckas who'd hemmed him up on a bullshit set-up he never saw coming. He began to unlatch the latch on the dollhouse so it could open in the middle. There sat a black double zipped duffel bag.

"Megabyte, we done wit' 'em," Kasper said.

Juicey occupied her weapon and pumped Magic with five slugs. He almost fell into the dollhouse but missed it. Then the dogs began barking violently.

The 713 decided not to go back to the room at the Marriott. Kasper chose a motel and paid some white prostitute to get two rooms with double beds. Koda and Juicey were in Kasper and Tee's room where the money was being split.

"Two-point-three million," Kasper said. "Half a million apiece. Y'all split the rest, I gotta make a phone call." He went over to the phone book on the nightstand, thumbed through it and called when he got the number.

Back at the Marriott.

"You think they got the money?" Felicia asked Tia. They sat on the same bed watching music videos.

"I wouldn't doubt it."

"If so, I wanna go shoppin' for some stuff," Felicia said. "You let Magic play in yo' pussy?"

Tia blushed. "Did you let Showboat play in yours?"

"Maybe, he had a big dick, too?" Felicia made Tia laugh. "Tia, that mothafucka was big!"

"You stupid."

"Was Magic's dick big?"

"I don't know I ain't feel it," Tia said then the phone rang. Tia jumped out of bed and answered it on the second ring. "Hello?"

"This Felicia?" It was Kasper

"No, Tia."

"It's Kasper, y'all straight?"

"Yeah, where y'all et?"

"Motel."

Felicia asked, "Who that?"

Kasper said, "We got y'all money."

After Tia mouthed who it was, she said, "How much?"

"Not over this phone, but more than enough."

"A'ight," Tia said.

"If y'all get hungry they got a sto' by the hotel y'all can go to."

"Okay."

"Love you, dog"

"Love you, too."

Kasper got off the phone saying, "Yeah, we got off tonight."

"Damn sho did," Tee replied. "Bra, with the money left ova it should go toward fucking trips and vacations."

Tapping his temple as he went and sat on the same bed as Juicey, Kasper said, "I like tha way you think. And I want y'all to get Nextel chirp phones so we can have communication." He laid back in the bed putting his hands behind his head. "Ain't none of y'all ever been to juvy?"

"I been," Tee replied from where she was sitting on the bed with Koda who was resting on the duffel bag of money. Tee was leaning toward the headboard as she said, "Police saw me put my pistol in a nigga's face. When I catch his ass, I'ma dirt his bitch ass."

"Sup, wit' y'all?" asked Kasper.

"Nigga used to say lil' fuck shit when he saw me and the girls. *You be eating they pussy. Do they pussy stank, Tee?* Lil' shit like that when he 'round his homeboys to get a laugh. I don't even look at the girls like that, we all just tight."

"Well, he on our list of pain," Kasper said. Koda and Juicey laughed. "Aye, what's so funny?" Kasper couldn't get an answer. "Y'all two ain't gotta rob. Y'all can go straight to Mental Health and get y'all a check." That made them laugh even more.

Tee was laughing her silent laugh. "Big check!" Kasper said.

Kasper smiled. "I don' got wit' some sillies." Then he turned serious. "Tomorrow we gon' be et Big Bronze back door fa bread. He's the next hostage." Koda and Juicey again became caught up in the elements of laughter. Kasper laid back once again saying, "Boy-boy-boy."

Chapter 34

Everyone went shopping for a few items the next day. Then Kasper went with Tee, Koda, and Juicey back to the strip club to get at Big Bronze, but he had gone out of town on short notice. When Sunday came Kasper hooked up with Melissa about the driver's license or ID. She charged Kasper $1,500 just to turn him on, which cost more than the fake license because he'd only paid $200 for that. Everyone packed their money into book bags so they could keep it on them when they got on the Greyhound.

It had gotten back to Kasper about the incident with Anition. He'd heard she was looking for another house. Kasper became furious. There was no way he could let his family get ran out of their own house. Anition was still his blood sister, so he made a phone call.

At 1:43 a.m. it was Anition who was riding around looking for a house. Her kids were at her mother's house. She couldn't sleep so she had nothing better to do but ride and look for 'For Sale' signs staked into lawns.

Anition turned down the radio because her phone rung.

"Yeah?" she answered.

"Anition?"

"Stacey, what's up?"

"Where you et?"

"Looking for a house," Anition said. "I'm straight, though."

"You lookin' fo a house at almost two in the morning?"

"Yep."

"Well—" Stacey sighed. "Phat Man called."

"And—"

"And he said stay yo ass where you et?"

"Stay where I'm et?"

"Yes."

"What he mean by that?"

"Phat Man said don't move nowhere. They on their way back from Texas and he gon' deal wit Tron's people when they get back."

"He don't even fuck wit' me, Stacey"

"Maybe he don't, Ann, but choo still his susta. That's prolly what he look et."

"A'ight then," Ambition conceded.

"I love ya."

"Love you, too."

By Monday the Greyhound had made it back to Charlotte with 713 on it. Later, they all went to Tron's mother's house so Kasper could speak to her. She let them all in and scowled at Kasper. He pulled her down into the garage.

"First of all," Tron's mother, Miss Rachel, said, "You have some nerve showing up at my house!"

Kasper said, "I'm apologizin' fo' everythang that's happened. So, I'm tryna settle this fo' it go too far," Kasper said. Shifting her weight Miss Rachel inhaled and exhaled loudly as she folded her arms across her breasts. Kasper continued, "All I'm askin' you to do is talk to yo people."

"My son didn't have to get shot like some—animal! My daughter got shot—" then she put her hand on her hips "Now if you'd excuse me, I have to get ready for bed."

"Just tell yo' people to leave Anition alone."

Miss Rachel looked at Kasper with a smile and sucked her teeth. Then she said, "Is this the same little brother that shot at his own sister, he's now taking up for?"

"You heard me."

Looking Kasper up and down, Miss Rachel said, "I don't have anything to do with *nothin'*." She emphasized the word nothin' as she slightly poked her head forward.

"Well, when yo' people get buried," Kasper said, "don't have nothin' to do wit' it."

Miss Rachel dropped her hands from her hips and snapped, "Are you threatening my family, boy?"

"Tell yo' people to leave it alone." Kasper turned to head out of the garage.

"Get the fuck outta my shit fo' I shoot choo dead!"

Heading through the door Kasper said, "You won't live past the last bullet you shoot."

"You just get cho ass outta my shit," Miss Rachel hissed as she followed Kasper through the door. "And take yo thugs' wit' cha."

Koda and Juicey chuckled as everyone stood to leave. Miss Rachel was still talkin' shit.

She said, "You and yo' whole family ain't nothin' but witches and devils."

Kasper stopped and turn around. "You heard what I said."

Miss Rachel drew back and slapped Kasper. *Whack!* Tee, Koda, Juicey, Tia, and Felicia charged the woman, but Kasper threw a hand up. "Nah, y'all." They froze in place. Then he said. "See you, Miss Rachel."

"You shoulda let them whoop her ass," Stacey said. She was on the platform with the 713.

Kasper stood up against the brick column opposite the one Stacey was sitting next to in chairs. Koda and Juicey sat on the ledge where Kasper usually sat.

"I deserve it," Kasper said. "And she had her rights."

"She'll be a'ight." Stacey looked down and saw Koda looking back grinning. She smiled back saying, "What choo smilin' fo'?"

"Lord," Kasper said. "She just silly as hell. Her and Juicey, and they argue all the time," Kasper said it as if he was tired of it. "They be in each other's faces daring the other to swing. But they say they don't fight cause they best friends."

"Then what tha hell they get in each other's face fo'?"

"Hell if I know. I wish they gon' slap the hell out each other and get it ova wit." Everyone else laughed. Kasper said, "They my people, tho'."

"Phat Man, you ain't brang me nuttin' back from yo' trip?" Stacey asked, changing the subject.

"I left it et the house, it's a necklace."

Tee said, "Oh, his nickname, Phat Man?"

"That's what I call my baby. He used to be a fat boy up until he was three. He ain't take y'all to meet Kandy and them?"

"Nah," Tee said. "Who that?"

"Our cousin, Phat Man's bully."

"She ain't my bully."

"Boy hush up, you know what it is wit' Kandy."

Kasper just shook his head as Stacey continued to tease him about Kandy.

Looking out the window that night Anition had her 9mm close. She noticed a black car that was parked on the curb. It looked like it was occupied. She got on the phone and called Stacey.

"Hello?"

"Stacey?"

"Yeah, what's up, Ann?"

Still watching out the blinds, Anition said, "It's a black Cherokee outside my house."

"You a'ight, Ann. Ain't nobody gon' fuck wit choo."

"It's people—"

"Don't worry 'bout that. It ain't nobody but choo lil' brotha and nem. You good, they gon watch yo' house."

Anition was silent, she knew then Kasper loved her.

"Hello?"

"Yeah?" Anition said. "Okay, Stacey"

"Okay, babes."

When Anition hung up her phone, it rang instantly. "Hello?"

"Anition?"

"Yeah, who this?"

"Tee, Kasper said go to sleep and quit lookin' out tha window."

Anition smiled a little, Kasper loved her after all. "Alright, thank you."

"Yeah," Tee said and hung up.

After school the next day the 713 went over to one of Kasper's aunt's house, who was really his mother's first cousin. The house was on the Westside in the Ashley Park neighborhood. Four of Kasper's second cousins and one first cousin was chillin' in a bowling ball green 1989 Caprice with gold spokes. They had the doors open and another cousin was leaning back against the car by the

driver's side rearview mirror, arms folded across small breasts and legs crossed at the ankles.

This was Kandy. "Sup, cuz?" Kasper said.

"Get et me. This tha folks?"

"Yeah."

Kandy popped her gum and said, "Well, introduce them fo' I smack the fuck outta you."

Koda and Juicey blurted out with laughter. Kasper smiled and said, "Kandy, man—"

"What? Don't make me raise up off this car."

"Go head, man, quit playin'."

"Well, make tha introduction then nigga."

Kasper introduced the 713. "And these tha no good cousins."

"Yeah, get cho ass whooped."

"Nigga, we'll beat choo the fuck up."

"You know not to play wit' us."

"Fuck a round and get lit."

Four of Kasper's cousins said in the ragged sequence of four separate threats all contained in the same second.

Kandy said, "You wanna get cho head popped?"

"Jus' playin', man. Y'all, this my second cousin, Kandy, and her susta is Sotra." They were all standing out of the car. Kasper pointed them out. "My otha second cousins, Antebella and Amber, and that's my first cousin, Pureka."

"Sup, y'all?" Kandy said.

The 713 spoke unitedly. Kasper said, "Kandy I need y'all to do me a favor?"

"What's that?"

"Anition needs somebody to stay et tha house till shit dies down." Kasper waved a hand at 713. "We gon' take care of any problems."

"Somebody shoulda been said somethin'," Sotra said.

She was tall, at about 6'3, twenty-years-old, with shoulder-length dreads and dark-skinned with grey eyes. Her voice was a deep baritone. Amber was a 5'6, redbone, with dark, wavy hair and

dark eyes. Boys called her Jello Jan because when she walked her ass would jiggle uncontrollably.

She said, "People still fuckin' wit' her?" She had the type of voice that made many phappy when they heard it.

"Not again but choo neva know."

"She et home now?" That was Pureka, who was dark-skinned, with a short Halle Berry cut and grey eyes. She was 5'6 and wore braces.

"I don't know, but do y'all have gunz?"

While going under the fender, Kandy said, "Nigga, do you think we—" She came up with a Mach-10 "—go without weapons in our possession?"

This made Tee smile, she was feeling Kandy who was a redbone, with grey, chinky eyes, 5'61/2 and thick at the age of twenty-one. Just like Kasper, she wore two long braids, a mouth full of gold teeth and a red bandana tied around her head thug lifestyle. She had a looped nose ring and a tattoo of a butterfly on each cheek.

"Choppa right here," Antebella said in her hoarse like voice as she held up an M-16. She had brown eyes and dreads that came to her shoulder, was 5'7 and brown-skinned.

"Big Thang." Amber cocked back what looked like a Tech-9.

Kasper said, "So, y'all got it?"

"We got it, dude," Kandy said.

Antebella said, "Fo' somebody that don't fuck wit' they susta, you sho' is goin' outta ya way."

"Make up wit' that girl, boy!" Kandy stated. "That's your susta."

"Man."

Amber shared her thoughts saying, "Cuz you lame as hell, word up man."

"You gotta straighten up, dog," Kandy said. "Y'all gotta problem wit' my lil' cousin get on over here so I can bust his head.

Chapter 35

"Lil bitch ass nigga went to my aunt's house wit' that bullshit!" One of Tron's cousins said. His name was Face, he was at Kah-Kah's dope spot sitting out on the front with the man. "If I catch his ass, it's on."

Being the man that he was Kah-Kah said, "Man, you wanna see, Kasper? I can call him." He showed his phone. "Or go da PC, I ain't tryna hear that shit. Go see him, nigga!"

"He ain't like that!" Face said.

"Tell you like I told Tron, Kasper's a gangsta," Kah-Kah stated.

"You on his set?"

"What?" Kah-Kah jumped up. "Nigga, get cho soft ass on from my spot, hoe! Yeah, you know how I get down. You gotta problem, what's up?"

"I'm gone." Face stood up to leave.

"Holla."

"Tell yo' punkass brotha-n-law show me he a G."

Somewhere around one in the morning Kasper, Tee, Koda, and Juicey were in a stolen truck. Attired in black pullover hoodies and black Nike gloves. Koda had said that she thought Ghosts wore white.

Kasper replied, "Yeah, but when Ghost Mob come, we bring the Grim Reaper wit' us. Nobody lives."

Koda turned into some Westside apartments called North Cross. "Go straight up," Kasper instructed.

Looking around Tee said, "Yeah, I licked this bitch they stayed ova here."

"Word up?"

"Almost got trapped, too."

"Where to now?" Koda asked because going straight up was about to go to the right. "Turn in a parkin' space, right here." Kasper pointed to the right and Koda whipped in there. "Cut tha car off." Kasper began to compass their surroundings. He was pleased that it was a dead night. "Come on y'all."

They jumped out in black masks that were plain and featureless made of mesh material. The mask was called a shun tut, the face of death. Everyone shun tut had 713 in red paint across it. Kasper got out of the truck with an AK-47 and everyone else followed the leader.

"Party time kick tha door in," Kasper said.

Tee took one step back as she leaned that way and with great force, booted the door causing it to swing back hitting the wall with a loud bang! Tee had the other AK-47 of Koda and Juicey's. Koda had the .45 Colt and Juicey had a Glock .49. They two would tag the apartment. Kasper and Tee would be the active gunmen.

The 713 was a spiritual essence of Kasper so if he tapped into his ability by the virtual essence of proximity contact, Tee, Koda, Juicey, Tia and Felicia would vanish as well just as Kasper's family could. Kasper tapped.

Face was naked in the bed, his wife Wanyika sat reverse cow-girl on his shaft. She brought her ass down in countless pounds crashing into Face's mid-section. Her hands gripped both of his legs. Wanyika had her head back and eyes closed, in sheer satisfaction. Face had his hands on his wife's waist, helping her retract as he responded with light raises. The climate surrounding the two was the essence of sweat, breath, and sex. Wanyika grinded in a back and forth, side to side motion with passionate effort.

A sonorous boom caused Face to catapult. His stomach and chest against, Wanyika's back as she paused and said, "What was that?"

Face moved all the ass his wife had and jumped out of the bed saying, "Somebody just kicked the door in!"

"How you know?" Wanyika began pulling the covers up on her body.

Face didn't reply, he replayed the earlier fallout with Kah-Kah about Kasper. That's when it hit him. He snatched up his .380 and went over to the door quietly and slowly. He pulled it open with the

gun pointing, ready. Face didn't hear anyone storm the steps, so he let his gun peek out before he did. Nothing. Nobody. All he heard was hissing. The shelves above his eyes came down indicating abashment. Face stepped further out of the room, slowly now, wanting to look around the corner down the steps.

"What's goin on?" Wanyika whispered behind him.

Face didn't answer, his gun slowly turned the corner pointing down the steps and then he looked. The front door stood open. Face moved down the steps slowly, his gun out in front of him. He wondered if that hissing was somebody spray painting?

"Somebody in here?" Wanyika asked.

Face looked back. "Go back in the room."

Wanyika's eyes grew wide with terror and she screamed. When Face turned his attention back, he saw two black, hooded figures. He could have taken a second to pop shots off, but he was too frightened. Anything beyond that second was too late. Bullets came flying at Face, proclaiming their destruction.

"What happened here?" Detective Shaw asked the officer that responded to the 187 in West Charlotte.

Face's body was riddled with bullets, he has tumbled down the stairs, his upper body had made it to the landing, but his lower body was still on the steps as he laid there on his side.

"Well—" the officer began. "The woman says, she and her husband were in the bed when they heard their door come flying open. Then check this out, she said when she peeled around the corner after her husband two people had—" The officer waved a hand to where the body laid. "—appeared out of nowhere wearing dark-colored hoods and a—"

"Appeared out of nowhere?" Shaw's eyebrows drew down.

"Yeah, she said they appeared out of nowhere. Like—taadaa."

"Are you kidding me?"

"Would I , Detective? Go look in the living room."

"What—the—hell is that?" Shaw asked as he looked at the tag that had been written twice on two walls.

"Seems like it says, Ghost Mob."

"Are they Satanists?"

"Don't know, Detective, couldn't tell ya."

"What do we have?" Detective Anderson came in.

Shaw only turned to see him then turned back to the graffiti, as crime scene techs snapped pictures all around. Cameras clicked like restless locusts. The responding officer filled Anderson in.

"Just appeared?"

The responding officer nodded. "That's right."

Anderson looked at the writing, then said, "I want to speak to the wife."

When the detectives spoke to Wanyika, she told them what happened and what she saw. She also gave them Miss Rachel's name and information because she'd told her about Kasper coming to her house.

Miss Rachel recounted details of Kasper's visit, giving his description and name but had no address. They ran his name through *Charlotte Mecklenburg Schools* and got a hit. He was picked up from West Mecklenburg and taken to headquarters.

Chapter 36

"Did you go over to Miss Rachel Locklear's home a day or two ago and threaten her about killing anyone?" Shaw asked.

"No." Kasper lied.

"Did you go over there at all?"

"No."

Detective Anderson asked, "Where were you last night?"

"Getting my dick sucked," Kasper responded

"This is really no time to be smart. You went over to this woman's house, threatened the lives of her and her family, and now—"

"You know that?"

"I know that you're lying."

"Psychic, you got talent don't cha?"

Squinting at the boy, Shaw said, "Aren't you the kid that shot the guy in the store last year?"

"No."

Shaw knew for a fact, Kasper was lying, it was just last year. The boy's description was unforgettable.

"I was the detective on that case—"

"And, so was I," Anderson stated.

"Kid—your face—your tattoos, the gold—"

"Cracka, fuck you! Take me da jail or take me back to school. Y'all up here bullshittin' and fuckin' wit' my grades, got me missing important classes."

"Tell us the truth," said Shaw.

"I was getting my dick sucked." Kasper's response was unbreakable.

Love turned into a corner store on Milton Road in Stacey's Seville as she was riding shotgun. Stacey gave Love a twenty saying, "Could you get me a box of Optimos, a big bag of Fritos and a twenty-ounce Mountain Dew?"

"Yeah, look—" She pointed to the store "They got cockroaches all out here on the wall and shit. Damn!"

"Nasty."

"Talk about it," Love said and got out.

Meanwhile...

"Why would you come back?"

"Bra—let me do what I do. Just pull into the gotdamn sto'."

"Nigga, you on a top ten *Most Wanted* list, Reese. You shoulda stayed yo' ass in Atlanta. It'll be just yo' luck that police run down on you."

"I'ma get some bread up and shoot back, Tank."

"Need to take yo' ass to Canada," Tank said. Then he looked to the passenger's window. "And roll yo' window up."

"I'm good."

"Okay, you good," Tank said pulling into KT Convenient store.

Stacey was feeling the candy, apple, red Impala that pulled into tha parking space next to her car, on the driver's side. The passenger sat up to fumble with the radio.

"Oh that's Reese," Stacey whispered. She reached for her gun and her cell phone rung.

"Yeah?"

"Stacey, it's Zya."

"Sup, babes?" Stacey was watching the car, wishing Love would come the fuck on, so she could handle this and be out. *The fuck was she in there doing? Giving the owner instructions on how to get rid of the cockroaches?*

Zya said, "I don't know, Stacey. I just have a hunch, so I wanted to tell you. You can't retaliate against your friend's baby father." Stacey's brows drew up. "To retaliate means to retaliate against the curse."

"I can't retaliate?"

"No, if you do, you'll only reactivate the curse. Then you'll curse the firstborn of your offspring. Your retaliation is empty. You'll do more harm than benefits. He was only used as a vessel— a tool. I know how you feel but you need to live and love life for Justice. You found a friend in Love, share your love with her."

Stacey began to weep, Reese was right there. Only a few feet away.

"I love you, sister," Zya said. "I'm here for you if you ever want to talk." Zya hung up because she could feel Stacey's hurt.

When Anition went on break she called Tron's mother who'd left a message on her voicemail.

"Hello?"

"You need to speak to me?"

"As a matter of fact, I do. First of all, I want to let to you know I could never forgive you for—"

"Look, Miss Rachel—"

"No-no-no, let me finish! Just hear me out. What happened— happened. I don't need anymore drama or bloodshed. So, I'm letting you know my family knows that I won't put up with it no more. So, you can tell your little bother to let it go. Please, this is getting waaayyy out of control. It's all in the dark and I want to leave it there. I want my family to move on."

"Okay, Miss Rachel."

"I would still love to be in my grandchildren's life."

"No problem."

"Okay, I'll talk to you later. Bye-bye."

Kasper walked up to Mario who stood by a locker talking to some girl. "Yo,' check this out," his lips were tight, "I let choo live, but don't run 'round here spreadin' my name! You, don't know me or—"

"Fuck You!" Mario bellowed.

It seems like the hallway had faded into dramatic silence. Kasper was considering whether or not he wanted to go to blows.

"You know what? I gotcha." Kasper turned to walk away.

"I gotcha momma," Mario said.

Kasper stopped and looked back. "Now, I really gotcha."

"New Orleans?" Tee asked.

Kasper had suggested that New Orleans would be the next spot to make a lick. The 713 was at Lacey's Eastside apartment, in the living room.

"Yeah," Kasper confirmed, brushing his thick hair.

Tee said, "I'm wit' it."

Kasper went upstairs to where Lacey was sitting on the bed playing Solitaire. She looked toward the door when her baby father came in. Lacey sucked her teeth and rolled her eyes.

"Aye, I might need you to get some bus tickets for me." Kasper playfully grabbed Lacey's foot as he jumped in the bed.

"Stop nigga!"

"You gon' get tha tickets?" Kasper laid back on the bed, putting his hands behind his head in relaxation. "You gon' get tha tickets?" He had to ask again.

"You *would* need somethin' from me, huh?"

"No," Kasper said. "Cause I gotta susta that neva tells me no."

"Well, why won't you ask her then?"

"The plan just came up, and don't act like I always want somethin' from you. I gave yo' ass fifty grand the otha day."

Lacey sucked her teeth. "Nigga, please! Where my baby?"

"Downstairs with her people. You gon' get tha damn tickets or what?"

"No, ask that '*Big Susta*' of yours."

"You know what—" Kasper got up. "That's what I'ma do. I'll holla et cha."

"If you leave don't come back."

"I wish I only had tha front parts of me so it wouldn't be a back," Kasper retorted.

Lacey twisted her face into a sour scowl, picked up the majority of the cards and threw them at Kasper who'd already turned out of the room.

She quickly got up saying, "Don't take Kanazi out of this apartment."

Stilloan Robinson

Chapter 37

"Let's go y'all," Kasper said to his family.

"Give me, my baby." Lacey went over and took Kanazi from Felicia with a little force.

Kasper sighed, Lacey was being a real bitch. He said, "I'll be out there y'all." When everyone left, Kasper said, "You been actin' like a bitch fo' a while! I swear I wanna knock yo' ass out!" He yelled. "But choo keep pushin' me I'ma get my cousin ova here to beat cho' ass."

Lacey began talking. "Whatever! You don't call me. And the only time you come over here is to pick up or drop off Kanazi!"

"That's cuz you're always on your bullshit. I don't owe you a goddam thing!" He spat.

"I know you don't! And I don't owe you shit either!"

"We even! Have my daughter et my old folks home tomorrow mornin'!"

"No."

Walking away Kasper said, "You can take her or I'll have my cousin come get her."

"When you leave—" Lacey followed Kasper to the door. "Don't come back, please! You want Kanazi don't you come get her. Send your mother or Stacey. I don't pack clothes, so you want the ones in my closet buy them again. I'ma burn them."

Kasper stopped at the door, his hand on the knob, and scowled back at her. "I must ain't want 'em cause I forgot all about 'em." He opened the door.

At that moment Lacey wished that she had a gun because she would have shot Kasper dead. "Get out!" she yelled.

Kasper was already headed toward his vehicle.

Thursday night the 713 was on the Greyhound to New Orleans. When they got there, they took two cabs to a motel and Tee got three rooms.

"We'll get suites when we on vacation," Kasper said. "We on high alert, so we don't need cameras in our faces."

Across the street was a Waffle House the family went to. "Y'all ready to get money?" Kasper asked while putting ketchup on hash browns.

Koda spoke up for everyone with a mouth full of Waffles. "Hell yeah."

"Look et the greedy in ya," Juicey said. Everyone laughed. Even Kasper couldn't help it.

Koda said, "And look et tha stupid in you!"

"Okay, y'all." Kasper chuckled.

"She started wit' me."

"Okay, Koda, Juicey leave her alone."

Tia said, "We gon' do the club thang again?"

"I don't know, dog. Shit don't work all tha time. But we gon' get money. New Orleans is a big drug state. So, it's money out here and we gon get some."

Tia and Felicia had to go back to the rooms just until their brother and sister prepared everything they needed. They went out and got a truck and a van. They took the van back to the hotel, Kasper and Koda got in the truck with Juicey at the wheel. They made it to a light in the Third Ward area and pulled beside a money green Jaguar. Two teenage boys were its occupants. They looked Kasper's age he saw that the driver wore a fade. The passenger had short cornrows and he was snorting something out of a sandwich bag. It made Kasper grimace. Both boys had on no shirts and wore big thick chains with a medallion from what Kasper could see that read: *CUT*—he couldn't see the other word. Their car was playing a *C-Murder* track.

"Juicey follow this Jaguar ova here when tha light turns green."

"Okay." Juicey followed the car to some project called Calliope.

Then it pulled into a parking space beside a red Excursion where a group of men and women were smoking, drinking and snorting.

"We out," Kasper said. "Time to find an abandoned house. They in there tonight." Koda and Juicey laughed.

"When you start selling weed?" Love asked Stacey.

They were out on the platform in PC. "My tenth-grade year in high school. I had it sold up, I had a white girl named Becky she will cop fo' ounces every Friday to be good fo' tha weekend. I even had a teacher copin'."

"A teacher?"

Stacey nodded and smiled. "Ole geeky ass cracka."

"How that happen?"

"Man, I don't know? He saw me, Love, I swear I thought I was bein' smooth. I had made a transaction durin' one of his classes, he was my science teacher. After class, he kept me back and said, *'Now, Stacey don't be selling your marijuana during my classes.'* Then he said, *'If your product is good I don't mind getting a nickel from you.'* But all he spent was five dollars a day."

"You get weed money and nothin' more?"

"Oh, I get that dope money, too. I want bricks if I can get it. I don't wanna sell ten and twenty dolla rocks from buyin' ounces. If I cop work it got to be a kilo or more."

"You don't know nobody?"

"Not that got it like that."

"What about somebody that may know somebody?"

"No, I don't do the middle-man shit. That puts people in yo' business. If I don't know tha big man already, I'll wait till opportunity presents itself. I need big dope."

Standing between the truck and the van that night, Kasper, Tee, Koda, and Juicey was ready for money. Tia and Felicia would not be needed but they would still get their fair share of the money.

Kasper held his .357 in hand. "Y'all know what it is. We catch 'em they ass is in that van."

"We ready," a smiling Koda said.

She and Juicey had the pumps and Tee had the Glock .45, Kasper gave her. She loved it.

Kasper said, "Let's ride."

He and Tee got in the truck, Koda and Juicey got in the van. Tee led the way back to Colliope projects and drove all around it but saw no money green Jaguar. Kasper called Koda and told her to stick around, while he and Tee went to ride around several blocks in radius to locate the car.

"Right there—right there!" Kasper pointed past Tee's face to a store.

The two boys were getting out of the Jaguar. Tee turned on the street, went down half the block and turned into that store. "Want me da tell Juicey and 'em to come to tha sto?"

"Tell 'em hurry up," said Kasper

As soon as Koda and Juicey pulled in, Kasper had a plan and fed it to the family. Kasper and Koda got out. The two boys came out and Kasper ran up on the driver when he got to the car.

"Yeah, you get on in there." The barrel was in the boy's side. He looked at Kasper coldly, but it wasn't as cold as Kasper's grey eyes. He said, "I'ma kill you if I gotta ask again."

Koda did not have the pump pointed at the passenger. She had it down and said to him, "You gon get in the car?" Both boys got in. Kasper sat behind the driver and Koda behind the passenger.

"Follow that truck," Kasper said. "Keep your hand on that wheel. And yo' boy betta keep his hands on the dash. Sweepstakes keep yo' eyes on the driver, I got the passenger."

When the 713 got the boys back to the abandoned house, they parked the truck and van around the back and put the Jaguar in the driveway. Inside the boys were put into one of the three bedrooms facedown. Kasper saw that their chain medallions said 'Cut Boys'. He remembered one of those rappers from No Limit representing the Cut Boys.

"Aye y'all can make this easy or hard," Kasper said. "I know y'all under somebody."

"Lil woadie, we got some money," the boy with the fade said.

"Nah, it's not gon' work like that." Holding the .357 with both hands, Kasper stepped over toward the boy with the short cornrows He pulled back the hammer and fired. Juicey had to hop to the side because skull fragments and brain matter splattered up. When the shot boomed, Tee had the face of a doctor's patient about to receive a shot as her shoulders came up. The gun was loud.

"Nah, dog!" The boy said as he slightly turned over holding up a merciful hand. "What choo doin'?"

Tee stepped towards him, threateningly, with her Glock .45. "Lay yo ass back down! We wanna know who you unda so we can get they money."

The terrified boy started talking...

Bloodhound and Blash were convening inside an Escalade listening to a *C Murder's* mixtape while looking out into the Calliope projects. The project was live, crackheads and heroin addicts were selling this and that. Some ran errands for the dealers. Females were yelling at their kids, who were out pass curfew.

Different stereo systems played various music. Someone was popping off firecrackers as young girls screamed playingly.

"Got my dick sucked by Michelle. Bitch had a nigga in the back of her salon sloppin' me, woadie," Bloodhound shared.

Blash smiled. "Ain't that ya boy Crisco's bitch, dog?"

Over a soft chuckle, Bloodhound said, "That bitch everybody hoe man. All den bitches in her salon sluts. Drina, Peaches—"

"Thought Crisco had Michelle on lock, woadie."

"That nigga a punk, she knows he soft. Crisco just pack lightweight. Sup wit dem boys Ball and Trap? Dem youngins get that money, dog, and they pay on time."

"That's why I got da chains fo da boys."

Bloodhound's phone rang.

Stilloan Robinson

Chapter 38

"Who det?" Stacey asked. "Anition?"

Ebony sucked her teeth as she approached the platform. "You know who it is."

"If you and Anition don't look like twins," Stacey said.

They did, Ebony was only but an inch shorter, fifteen pounds heavier, her breasts were big, and they had the same gap, but dark eyes. They both had neck length haircuts. Ebony was twenty years old and the fifth child born to Victoria.

She stopped in front of the platform. "And you and Kacey look alike."

"We're actually twins, smart ass," Stacey teased.

"That's what y'all call it? I thought choo was her replica. My bad." Love laughed.

"Hey love," Ebony greeted.

"Hey."

"Get choo a chair." Stacey went inside to get another chair.

She came back out and positioned it before the platform. It was not big enough for three people barely enough for two. "Where yo lil' boy et?"

"New Orleans."

"Doin' what?"

"I don't know. You got one mo year, huh?" Stacey said

"What college yo go to?" Love turned in her question.

"Syracuse, and yeah, one more to go. Really, Stacey, I wanna do another three and get my Masters. That's what I'm considering, but I'm ready to live my damn life."

"You should go for it, Ebony. If you got it in yo' mind to do that I really think you should." Ebony's only reply was a sign. Stacey continued, "Two years of school you'll have left."

"I know, that's a long time. I'ma just see what's up when I make it to that point."

Love said, "You gotta find yo' motivation to stay."

"Dead right," Stacey agreed.

"If I decide that's what I wanna do, I'ma transfer to UNC. So, I'll be closer to home."

"That'll work," Stacey said.

"That nigga Sleaze Ball just called, woadie. Say he and Trap gotta spot out 9th Ward," Bloodhound said while stuffing his money back into his pocket. "He got some bread fo' us."

"You ready?"

"We out."

"They comin' right?" Kasper asked as he used a thumb to pull back the hammer on his gun.

Sleaze Ball looked at Kasper. "Yeah, they comin', woadie."

"Okay." Kasper raised up that gun with both hands as Sleaze Ball started to speak and he blew the boy's face off.

This time Tee's look was as though she had a slushie brain freeze, stuck a finger in her ear and said, "That gun loud as hell."

Koda and Juicey were deep into the shadows when Bloodhound and Blash pulled up behind the Jaguar and got out. When they got up to the porch Koda and Juicey sprang from cover, brandishing pumps.

"Hold up, dog, don't shoot!" Blood Hound had sort of ducked and turned away as if he was going to try and run.

Juicey got up on him saying, "You run, I'ma blow yo' ass up!"

Blood Hound went into his pocket saying, "Here." He threw money to the ground. "That's about fo' grand, woadie."

Smiling, Koda said, "Get y'all punk asses in the house." The front door opened.

Kasper and Tee stepped out on the porch. "Get in here!" Kasper said holding his gun down by his side.

Both men were out in a room apart from Sleaze Ball and Trap, facedown. Blash sniffed at the air and said, "I smell death, woadie. Where Sleaze Ball and Trap?"

Looking down on both men, Kasper said, "They around. When we get what we want we gon let y'all go."

Blood Hound sucked his teeth. "You really think we believe that dog?"

"Believe it or not, but we need that bread."

"I dropped fo' grand outside."

"Nah," Kasper said shaking his head. "We want them millions."

"Shiiiddd," Bloodhound said. "I ain't got it."

Blash jumped in saying, "Man, where Sleaze Ball and Lil' Trap? The atmosphere don't feel right!"

Tee said, "Didn't we say they was around?"

"Let us see 'em," Blood Hound suggested.

Kasper was through playing. "We need those gotdamn millions! We ain't 'bout to play wit' y'all!"

Blash sucked his teeth and Bloodhound said, "Y'all gon' have to kill me, woadie! It's real!"

"Yeah?" Kasper nodded as he thought: *It is real, ain't it?*

"Man tell me about it." When Kasper moved to go through the man's pockets, he said, "You ain't gon' find no millions in my pocket, woadie. Sorry 'bout that." Blood Hound chuckled.

"'Bout to show you how real it is." Kasper snatched the man's cellphone. "Sweepstakes and Megabyte y'all watch these niggas. PartyTime step out wit' me."

Blood Hound said, "Sweepstakes, Megabyte, and Partytime? What they call you lil', woadie?" Blash chuckled.

Kasper ignored that and walked out into the hallway with Tee. She closed the door.

Kasper said, "They think this is a joke."

"They really do."

"We gon' get the last laugh." Kasper went through the phone and Tee said, "What choo 'bout to do?"

"When most people put they momma numba in the phone they usually put Momma or Momma Callin' shit like that so they know it's them callin'." Kasper found what he was looking for and showed the phone to Tee. "See?"

"You right." She saw the contact number that read: *Ma Dukes.*

225

Stilloan Robinson

Chapter 39

"This how y'all play it, woadie?" Blash asked Koda and Juicey. He was real black, with big lips, when he smiled, they seemed to somehow swell.

"Yeah, nigga," Koda said with a smile.

Blood Hound and Blash chuckled, then said, "Look at cha. Y'all 'bout tha silliest mufuckas, huh?"

Koda and Juicey laughed. Blood Hound was brown-skinned and had a scar that raged from his right cheek to his eye. He smiled at Koda and Juicey and said, "Y'all don't really wanna do this. C'mon, let me give y'all this extra stash in my back pocket? It's a chunk 'bout five grand, plus outside. That's bread!"

Blash said, "That's nine grand, not to mention seven I got on me. Get y'all some shit from the mall."

"Yeah," Blood Hound said "Y'all can split that, then merck them two mothafuckas and be straight. Let us go out tha window."

Smiling wildly, Koda pointed her shotgun at Blood Hound with one hand saying, "I'ma show you Solomon's path."

"Gon' take our offa and show yo' folks what choo just said."

Blash chuckled, then he pressed both of his hands to the carpet as if he was going to do a push-up and said, "What if I hop up?"

Juicey rushed over to him and stuck the barrel of the pump in his face. "You get up I'ma take yo head off." She had the face of a Nazi villain victimizing a pristine Jew. "So, go 'head."

Miss Brandy was just getting off work at the hospital and walking to her car when the phone rang. She stopped to answer it. "Yes?"

"Yes, I'm—Blood Hound just got locked up and—"

"Wh—what's goin' on?" Worry descended on Miss Brandy.

"He got caught wit' a pistol and some dope. I got his phone, his money, and his car if you can come get it. He told me da call you."

"Where you et?"

Kasper gave her the info. He hung up the phone and said to Tee, "The hell those silly ass girls, laughing et?" He frowned and Tee chuckled. "Look tha lady gon' come. If tha otha nigga bullshit afterward— we gon' call his people, too."

"A'ight." they both walked back into the room.

Blood Hound and Blash captured their entrance. Blash spoke, "Hey woadie, I got seven grand on me. Take that and we a'ight."

"And do what wit' that, wipe our ass and nose?" Kasper said as Koda and Juicey laughed.

Blood Hound commented, "You got some silly ass lil chicks on yo' team." Blash chuckled

"Shut cho hoe ass up," Kasper said looking out of the windows.

Blood Hound said, "Now you gon' piss me off."

Kasper turned his upper body to see Blood Hound. "You gon' really be pissed off in a minute." Maybe the rest of his body needed to see Blood Hound because he turned around and went to stand over the man. "Yo' bitch ass betta start prayin' for money."

Blood Hound closed his eyes and said, "Oh Heavenly Father hallowed be thy name—"

Koda smiled saying, "He think this game, I'ma send him down Solomon's path after we get tha money."

Blood Hound said, "I done walked down many paths. It ain't a path I can't walk."

"Okay," Kasper said.

"I gave y'all tha money I had, pimp. I got 'bout five grand in my back pocket and my homie say he had that generous offa."

"See if I can squeeze a lil mo' out cha. You said it was real so I'm 'bout to show you how real it is. Playtime is ova. You, act stupid somebody gon' get kilt. A bullet ain't got no name on it, so whoeva it kill that's who it was meant fo," Kasper said. "We ain't playin', you a see."

Blash said, "You gon' torture some real niggas?" Blood Hound chuckled.

"Y'all can laugh. You and yo' boy ain't got a clue. It's 'bout to get real! We don't torture nobody!"

"Y'all gon have to show us," Blood Hound said. "If you think I got some millions fo' you, you got it fucked up. I'ma real nigga, real niggas die every day."

"Well, prepare ya self, man," Kasper said.

It wasn't long when Miss Brandy showed up with another female. Tee met them at the door and welcomed them inside at gunpoint.

"What's goin' on in here?" Miss Brandy said.

Blood Hound saw the two women enter the room and said, "Hold up, woadie! How you get my momma and susta?"

"Didn't we discuss this? This is how real it is! Remember that conversation!" Kasper yelled.

"I tried to give you money!"

Kasper pulled the hammer back on his .357 saying, "Yeah, you did, huh?" He went over and with both hands he brought up that wonderful gun and shot Blash in the side of his head. His brain matter splashed all over Blood Hound's sister who was laying beside him. She and Miss Brandy began yelling and screaming. Tee made that face again and shrugged her shoulders at the boom of the gunshot blast.

"Why you shoot my homie!" Blood Hound hollered.

Kasper hollered back saying, "Cause real niggas die every day! So, he gone. Where tha money et? And you know how much we want!"

Miss Brandy said, "Hound, just give it to him please!"

"I got what choo want et my momma house!"

"How much?"

"Nigga, one and a half million!"

"My people gon take her. Party Time and Mega Byte go get that money," Kasper instructed.

Kasper watched out the window as Tee and Juicey left with Miss Brandy in her car. He turned to Blood Hound whose sister was still crying. "Let me tell you somethin', dog. Turn ova."

Blood Hound turned over with a huff and mugged Kasper. "Yeah, what's up?"

"Dog, I don't play wit' nobody when it's time to get money. Shit is not sweet, homeboy. Yo' boy got popped cause you wanted to play. If I want it, I get it. And if I gotta kill whoeva to get to it, it's murda."

"To be honest dog—it ain't nuttin' else to talk about."

"You was laughin', and playin' earlier. Now I don' showed you how real you said it was, you through talkin'. But choo right, tho, turn yo' bitch ass back ova. You walkin' in Solomon's Path tonight." Kasper stepped back over to the window.

Miss Brandy had gotten to the money that was in the floorboards under her bed in a satchel. As soon as she gave it to Juicey, Tee shot her in one ear and blew out the other one. After keeping up with directions they helped each other get back to the abandoned house.

Kasper said to Blood Hound, "Told you we was gon' get that bread."

Tee went over and shot his sister in the head.

"So, y'all gon' kill us anyway!" Blood Hound shouted.

Koda went over quickly to Blood Hound with her thumb and middle finger pressed tighter as if ready to snap them and put those fingers between his eyes. She said, "Sūcof!" Which meant pay attention in the Krepesk language.

That instantly got Blood Hound's attention staring cross-eyed at those fingers. Hypnotized, Koda chanted the phrase taught to her by her Black Face, which was Kasper.

"See his eyes, see his face, ask for Mercy or his grace. If you run across his path, you better have his staff." Koda snapped her fingers with a loud pop.

Blood Hound's face bumped the floor with a violent thud. He was out cold, to Solomon's path. But Kasper had forgot something...

Chapter 40

Blood Hound suddenly awoke, he got up from where he laid on the ground squinting in confusion as he looked around. He was on a subway, was he dreaming or was he really here? This was Solomon's path in the Book of Dookari. It's only recognized as the Lupscis *pronounced Loopsis*. A stage between dreams and being fully awake. After King Solomon had been buried, Lord Enki resurrected him because he needed a King to rule the Lupsics. He liked King Solomon's rebelliousness toward Lord God or Yahweh of whom was Lord Enkis' rival and gave the Lupscis to King Solomon. This was also where black people came that were trapped in comas or that had died while in them.

As he looked around there were people about the subway in leisure; kids on the platform, girls playing double-dutch cheered and boys played cops and robbers. Other people were huddled in groups, talking, shooting dice, or listening to music. Guys were kissing girlfriends and girls were gossiping and laughing. Down where the tracks should have been was nothing, just a dark space. There was no way to get to the other side of the platform where other people were, and it was best not to fall down there.

A group of boys walked by BloodHound. Like everyone else they looked like they came from different eras, people from the 1940s, 50s, 60s and so on were here.

Blood Hound grabbed one guy and asked, "woadie, where I'm et?"

The boy snatched away saying, "Nigga, don't choo fuckin' grab me! You crazy? And my name ain't no goddamned, Woadie, mothafucka." This guy looked like he was from the 80s era.

A boy that looked like he was from the 70s era whipped a butterfly knife open while saying, "Bruce, you wanna slice this boy to pieces?"

Blood Hound said, "I don't know where I am, I'm just askin' ya."

Bruce pulled out a switchblade and said, "Nigga, you don't touch me."

Four other boys whipped out their knives. Blood Hound turned and took off down the platform that was never-ending. The group of boys ran after him. Blood Hound was looking for an exit as he ran steps that maybe led up out the subway tunnel but there was none. This tunnel was all there was. Then he felt a foot clip him and he fell in a hard impact on his stomach. The boys took ahold of him and started stabbing.

Blood Hound was crying, "I only wanted to know where I was." Then his crying turned to screaming as he looked up and saw a girl seated on the bench two-feet away, with her legs crossed, watching. He knew the girl, it was his fourteen-year-old cousin who'd gotten into a car accident in 1984 that left her in a coma until she died. She knew who he was, but it was nothing that she could do but watch as her cousin get chopped up. She watched like it was nothing new to her. This was everyday life on Solomon's path.

Kasper, Tee, Koda, and Juicey were in the truck going down the street when something felt too far out to the boy. He looked back out of the window. Somebody or something was following them. The feeling was in Kasper's soul.

He looked upfront and said, "Aye, Tee, turn on the next street." Kasper looked back out the window as Tee made the requested turn. A grey Lincoln Town Car matched that turn and he said, "That Grey Lincoln followin' us."

From the front seat, Juicey looked out the sideview mirror, Tee looked out the rearview mirror and Koda looked back with Kasper.

Tee said, "How you wanna—" Her words ceased when passengers of the Lincoln issued gunfire.

"Tee go!" Kasper shouted as bullets slammed into the truck.

Koda tried hanging out the window with the pump to fire back but the position was way too awkward and her shots went wild and it would definitely be hard to launch another round into the chamber. At her position, she couldn't do anything but take Tee's gun and fire back with it. Kasper only had one round left in his gun. He

aimed it out the window with both hands trying to get a good target, so he could take out the engine, but it was hard to do with Tee swerving and all. When he fired off the bullets went wild.

When Kasper saw the face of one of the assailants, he noticed how mute it looked and said to himself, "Them Daimons, damn they got out."

Daimons or rather demons where Devine or God-like beings with their own special powers. These Daimons are the souls of the dead that had been trapped in the intermediaries between the Lupscis and the Poviks. Kasper had forgotten to close the microcosm of the Lupscis when he allowed Koda to open it sending Blood Hound there, which allowed some of the Daimons to get out where they would become enemies of the natural world and opponents to whoever opened the Lupscis without closing it. They were after Koda.

"It's live out here," Love said to Stacey.

Everybody was in the parking lot smoking, drinking and listening to car stereos. Out in the streets, boys and girls ran races to see who was the fastest of them all.

"I got that weed if anybody want some. And I look out, I take food stamps, quarters, dimes, and pennies. That's what they make cent rolls fo'. I'll take ten dollas in pennies. I'll pick up a penny off the ground if I see one."Stacey was dead serious

"Damn." Love chuckled.

"That's money, Charlotte is a big city and I guarantee you it's about—" Stacey thought then said, "—maybe twelve million pennies out around here cause people don't want 'em. That's one hunnid twenty-thousand dollas just out there." Stacey took an elegant sip of her alcohol. "Eighty-five percent of Americans come out tha sto' wit they change, it could be three dollas and one cent, we'll drop tha receipt and the pennies then pocket the bills."

Love laughed, because it had rung true, she'd done that. Leaving pennies in the green Newport, taking a penny, leave a penny bowl.

Stacey said, "I got plenty of pennies, Love." Then one of the guys she knew walked up. "Sup, Rico?" Stacey picked up her glass of drink.

"What choo know, Stacey?"

"I know the streets is talkin'."

"They definitely doin' that. Got the police listenin' and shit," Rico said, and Stacey laughed. Rico nodded at Love and said, "How you?"

"Fine." Love smiled and half waved.

"Stacey, you got that haze?"

"Yep," Stacey said with a pop of her lips.

Rico looked down and counted out some money, saying, "Stacey, you know I need one of yo' most famous ounces." He handed Stacey the money.

Using her left hand she took it as her right hand went down into the pocketbook, Stacey said, "Look alive cause it's—" She was handing him the product. "—comin' right at cha."

"You don't neva run out, do you? Been slanging this weed since ninety-five and you ain't neva not one time say you was waiting to reup."

"To run out and wait for a reup means to delay my bread. If I'm waiting to reup I still got some, playa."

"I 'preciate it, Stacey. Stay up!"

"You too." Stacey and Love watched Rico walk off and Stacey said, "He reminds me of this nigga named Jermain that use to get weed from me all tha time. He got kilt."

"By who?"

"I don't know fa show but it's a nigga name Rocko sittin' in county jail fo' his murda now. They found his body up here." Stacey pointed back. "On the train tracks by da soup kitchen. Say his face and all was sliced up." She cringed and Love grimaced, Stacey continued, "He was cool. When I first moved down here, I met two

boys my age, KC and, did I eva tell you about, KC and his homeboy Hollywood, the Rock dude I mentioned?"

"Yeah," Love said. She had to wait a second to get the rest of the story because Stacey picked up her glass and sipped some more liquor. Love noticed she didn't even wince when she drank.

"Anyway, he jumped out on Hollywood the same day we was comin' back from, Miss Boonie's apartment from buying a cigar cause tha sto had closed. They snatched him up in a car and found his remains a month later"

"Damn," Love said. "What about KC?"

Stacey sighed deeply. "He was my dog. My smokin' buddy. We always walked to the store. One day he walked by himself—" A tear dropped from her eyes. Stacey wiped it away, sniffled and said, "He neva came back." A soft wail came out of her.

Love said, "What happened to him?"

Stacey took a second to say, "Got hit by a truck." She cried.

Love regretted asking that last question. Stacey was hurt, KC was like a brother to her. They had become close in a short period of time. Stacey welcomed KC to anything she had. If he wanted to stay over, he could. He stayed two rows up with his grandmother. Stacey did not want KC running around Piedmont Courts getting into trouble, so she took him in.

Love said, "I don't want choo to talk about it." *Especially while you're drunk,* she thought.

Stilloan Robinson

Chapter 41

It was like the fire coming from the Lincoln had no close, as the Daimons fired rounds from handguns and from a 9mm assault rifle. The shots came in rapid addition, the 713 was not prepared for this. Kasper's gun was already jaded, so was Tee's. Juicey had been firing and the pump was useless as long as Tee was ahead of the Lincoln.

"Pull ova somewhere, Tee, so we can jump out!" Kasper said.

Tee came to an intersection and stopped. Everyone left the pumps and got out running. Kasper led the way around a rundown gas station. Behind it was a ten-foot fence. Tee tossed the satchel over, everyone climbed and fell over but Koda. She couldn't seem to get up and over it.

"Come on, Koda!" Kasper urged as the Lincoln was getting through the intersection running a red light and getting clipped in the back causing it to fishtail.

"I'm—" Koda was trying her best but she couldn't climb it.

Come on, Koda, please! That was Juicey pleading silently for her best friend.

Kasper was on the fence as if he was going back over it cursing himself for not closing the Lupscis by reciting a prayer from the book of Dookari.

"You can do it, Koda," he said.

"They comin!" Tee shouted.

That must have been all it took because Koda climbed that fence with all effort applied, losing a shoe in the process. Soon as she got to the top to go over, the Lincoln rammed the fence sending Koda toppling over. Kasper tried as best he could to catch her, softening her fall. He helped her up and the 713 ran. When Kasper looked back, he saw Daimons climbing the fence with one hand holding their guns with the other. He led his sisters around a church and into some woods. The 713 conquered his ability and they all stopped. They turned to watch. In this cloaked state, they were able to see thermal energy.

The Daimons rushed around the church and stopped just before the woods with their eyes hard and searching. They knew the group was there. They also knew they were parting with the unseen. The Daimons were propelled by the promise of action. Shooting accuracy was no longer an issue, from here on out everything would be point blank but the Daimons had to find their enemy first.

They stood looking around allures. The Daimons were in the form of humans because they had possessed the bodies of human civilians and were using them as vessels. Their only thing was a sign of possession. Kasper knew these Daimons would not leave. It was only one thing he could do. He held out an invisible hand.

"Ripē," he said telepathically.

The purple glowing celeprque grain appeared. Gun barrels became attracted to this glowing piece. -Meküt em Jorko- the Povik Valkejnx appeared. The Daimons saw this strange creature and their guns were ready to counter him if he became the enemy.

Jorko could see Kasper and his comrades.

Kasper said, "Tsak ewā eth nemeds."

Jorko turned his head towards the Daimons and bent an arm over his shoulder as he slowly pulled up a dwarf, it didn't ring against its sheath, it hissed. The sword was long sharp and glistened dramatically.

One Daimon popped off a bullet built by mankind but did not have enough power to stop Jorko. Jorko was extremely fast. He went about slanging that amazing sword this way and that, spinning around the enemies chopping here, cutting there, stabbing and slicing. When Jorko was finished the Daimons lay about the ground destroyed. Jorko turned his head to look at Kasper as he slowly sheathed his weapon of destruction. "Done."

"Knathe uh rof et boij lewned," Kasper was thanking Jorko for a job well done. Jorko nodded. "Zelp Zola wth Lupscis?" he asked Jorko to close the Lupscis.

Jorko vanished. -ewa- The cleprque grain disappeared.

"What was that thang, bra?" Tee asked. The family was walking down the street.

"Yeah," Juicey wanted to know, too. Kasper told them. Juicey said, "Is he part of tha faith?"

"No," Kasper said as light rain began to fall, pelting their faces.

"Koda, you straight?" Kasper asked while putting an arm around her neck.

"Un-huh," Koda said. She had half her thumb in her mouth.

Kasper said, "I ain't know you suck your thumb?"

Juicey spoke up saying, "She only do that when it rains."

Three squad cars rode past them. Tee said, "This shit was crazy."

"Yeah, it was." Then he stopped. "Here, Koda." He took off his right shoe so that Koda could put it on.

She looked at it and said, "What, yo' shoe?"

"Man—what the hell else I'm givin' you?"

"Oh." Koda chuckled as she put the shoe on.

"You gotdamned crazy," Kasper said. Koda laughed and they all continued on down the street. Kasper spoke, "I'll neva leave y'all, man. Neva, I love y'all."

Adjusting the satchel on her shoulder for a more comfortable position, Tee said, "I love you, too"

Koda and Juicey returned their love in unison.

Kasper said, "Best believe I'ma be there fo' y'all."

"What choo woulda did if them thangz woulda got me?" Koda asked.

"I wouldn't let 'em get close to you. I woulda been ova that fence." He pulled Koda close.

She smiled at his affection. Koda loved Kasper.

A car got been hotwired and the 713 made it back to the motel. There was a knock on Tia and Felicia's door. Tia opened it and Kasper, Tee, Koda, and Juicey entered the room. Kasper put his arm around Tia in a playful headlock and walked with her over to one of the beds as she punched playfully at his stomach.

"This tha money?" Felicia picked up the satchel Tee had put on the bed as she laid back.

"One and a half million," Kasper said plopping down on the bed beside Tia.

Felicia poured the money out and smiled at the thick stacks. "Y'all don't play, do ya?"

"We don't play," Kasper corrected. "When we get money y'all get it, too."

Koda sat beside Tia and said, "We told 'em we wasn't playin'."

Felicia was putting the money back up.

Juicey was sitting on the floor with her back up against the bed. "They prolly didn't take us serious because me and Koda was laughin'."

Kasper said, "Y'all can laugh all tha fuck y'all want. Niggas gon' take us serious cause we gon' show 'em how serious it is."

"What happened to yo' shoe?" Tia asked.

"It's right here." Koda showed her foot and took the shoe off. "I lost *my* shoe."

"How?" Tia asked and Kasper told her the whole story starting with Sleaze Ball and Trap.

"Damn," Felicia said. "Demons?"

"Yep," Kasper said. He got up. "Niggas gotta undastand." he looked to his family. "We comin' fo' that cash. We gon' get mo' money and that's fo real. The Ghost Mob is comin'. This is just tha beginnin' , mothafuckas is gon' see tha family."

Monday afternoon Kacey stepped into pod 6300 in the Mecklenburg County jail to kick it with her sister Anition. "That shit between you and brother dead?"

"I told you to tell him I was willing to forgive and forget, squash everythang."

"They just came back from New Orleans, so I'ma get SP to get on him."

"Houston last week New Orleans this week. What he got goin' on?"

"Hell, I don't know, but like I said I'ma holla et SP."

240

"Yeah, okay sound good," Anition said.

"My word, susta, you know if I tell Stacey to do somethin' and it's regardin' her Phat Man, she'll do it."

Anition waved the possibility off and said, "Whateva, Kacey. Don't bus' yo ass tryna do it. Kasper do what he wanna do."

Loud verbal aggression in Spanish resonated through the dayroom and everyone got quiet. Kacey and Anition looked up towards the top of the steps where a group of Mexicans were confronting one of their own. The two sisters knew the Spanish vernacular.

One of the Mexicans said in Espanol, "Why did you fucking tell?"

Anition had found her way to the man down device clipped on her uniform, in case she had to press the red button. The Mexican was trying to explain that he did not tell anything. One of his nationalities came with a soap in a Cisco and whipped it down on that Mexican's head.

Anition hit the button and Kacey yelled, "Lock it down, fellas! Let's go—lock it down!"

The Mexican took the steps in great galloping bounds as his nationalities rushed after him. He got caught before he could finalize the steps. The other Mexicans had him bent over the steps pummeling him. Anition and Kacey were spraying mace but it wasn't helping, it seemed like it was giving them fuel because they kept beating their victim.

"Y'all stop it gotdamn it!" Kacey shouted as other deputy's ran in for assistance.

Stilloan Robinson

Chapter 42

After school, the 713 made it to Stacey's apartment where she was sitting on her platform.

"Damn, do you eva sleep?" Kasper asked.

Stacey chuckled. "Can't, you know I got insomnia. Had it for years."

"Sheba told yo' ass to see a doctor."

"So they can give me sleeping pills? I'm cool, I need to holla et cha, too." Stacey stood up with her pillow and gun and used her gun hand to reach down for her pocketbook. "All y'all come on in I got food to eat up."

Koda said, "That was good news, Juicey." She chuckled. Everyone was following Stacey inside.

"Shut tha fuck up stupid mufucka!" Juicey snapped.

Kasper huffed.

Koda said "You stupid! I was only showing how you appreciate free food." She smiled.

Kasper stopped in the living room looking back to Koda and Juicey saying, "Man please shut up! Koda quit starting shit, dog, both of y'all." Stacey chuckled. "Silly ass girls!" Kasper said.

Everyone but Koda and Juicey laughed. Stacey took her young brother out on the back stoop.

"Phat Man, talk to yo susta, baby."

"Who?"

"You know who. Who do you think?" Kasper looked off. Stacey put an arm around the boy's neck and said, "Come on, dog, that's yo susta, Phat Man." She shook him softly. "She okay to iron out tha wrinkles, son. Don't do her like that. What if she don't wake up tomorrow mornin' or you don't wake up tomorrow morning and you neva gave a chance? You, her lil' brotha, her only brotha." Stacey kissed Kasper's forehead.

He said while putting an arm around her waist, "I ain't tryna talk to her."

"Please, Phat Man," Stacey pleaded and kissed the side of Kasper's eye twice. Her baby brother was so near and dear to her.

He had keys to her place and his own room. *"You can come live wit'
me anytime." she had once told him. "Just like you got cho own
place in Big Susta heart you got one in any place I get."*

"I ain't got nuttin' to say to her," Kasper said.

"Nigga—" Stacey moved away from Kasper like he had passed
gas. "You bein' plain hateful to yo' own blood! I should knock the
damn shit outta you! That's yo' susta! She ain't got no pride to keep,
boy! Anition wanna make it right between y'all! Meet that girl halfway, Phat Man. She yo' whole flesh and blood! Came out the same
dick and damn pussy!" Stacey punched Kasper softly.

A robbin flew down and landed just before the stoop. It cocked
its eyes at Kasper maybe sizing him up and classifying his hateful-
ness. A person that only communicates to the world with guns and
violence living out his brutal dreams of a terrorized world. The bird
may have hated Kasper presences because it flew off.

Kasper said, "I don' took up for her."

"So, make up."

"There y'all go." Kandy stepped out on the stoops. She had a
white bandana tied on her head a white top on that said, *2 Real For
Y'all*! When Kasper looked at her, she said, "Tha fuck yo' ass
lookin' et?" Only she was teasing.

"Kandy, gon' head man." Kasper smiled.

Stacey was serious when she said, "Get in his ass."

"She ain't gon' bully me."

"What's up, babe?" Barsuesha said, stepping out.

She was Kasper and Stacey's second cousin. Twenty years old,
dark eyes and 5'5. Brown-skinned with dreads that flowed down to
her back.

By this time Kandy had jumped off the stoop and said, "Brang
yo' ass off tha porch then."

"Oh shit," Barsuesha said while pulling on her hair.

Kasper said, "Kandy, quit playin' man damn."

"That's what I thought." She leaped back onto the porch.

Stacey said, "Tryna get this King to talk to Ann."

"He still ain't talkin' to her?" Barsuesha frowned.

"No, man."

"Come on, cuz." Kandy snatched Kasper into an embrace hugging an arm around his neck. "Enough is enough, dog. Talk to that girl. Quit actin' fuckin' stupid and get wit' that girl, nigga. We love you, boy. You the only male relative we got. You know that, fuck wit' cho susta."

"Nah, man."

"You bein' a real dickhead," Kandy said.

Barsuesha pushed Kasper's head.

Stacey moved to say to Kasper more seriously while pointing a finger at him, "You need to choose to make it right wit' cho susta." Then Stacey directed that finger downward. "You get cho' ass ova there tonight and do it," she finished.

Kandy said, "We came to get some green."

Anition was just closing her room blinds that night when she saw a sliver 96 Cadillac Fleetwood pulled up alongside the house. She crinkled her brows and went downstairs to look out of the peephole.

Kasper sat reclined in his Cadillac with Koda at the wheel smiling. They had just pulled up.

"You goin' in there?" asked Koda.

"Yeah, dog. Gotta set it straight wit' Ann," Kasper said, hand on the door handle. "We kinda been beefin' fo' a long while. So, I'ma go in here and get et her, I ain't gon' be long."

"A'ight." Koda was cheesing.

Looking at her curiously, Kasper said, "You and Juicey won't no perfect match fo' anybody else comin' up as friends." He chuckled and got out, Koda laughed.

The boy walked slowly to the house. It was time to set aside the bullshit and be family. By the time he got to the porch the door opened and out came Anition.

"Hey," she said to her baby brother.

"Anybody been messing wit' my susta?" Kasper stopped.

"Nope, I think they had enough of my lil' brother fo a time."

"Good."

"Are we family or what?"

"Yep, and I love you!"

"I love you, too, come here." Anition held out her arms for a big hug and Kasper filled them.

It was real early in the AM, about 2:20 when Juicey dropped Kasper, Tee, and Koda off behind Harding high school. Back in the back of it was a path that led into Koda and Juicey's neighborhood.

"You know what room this bitch ass nigga sleep in?" Kasper asked Juicey.

She said, "No, I don't know."

"We'll find it," Kasper said.

Dressed in their night attire they vanished. The plan had already been worked out. Koda led Kasper and Tee through backyards leading up to where Mario stayed. Kasper knocked on the back door.

Miss Tonya had just gone to sleep when she heard the knock on her back door. A huff escaped her lips. *'Why the hell is anybody knocking on my back door?'* she thought.

Miss Tonya wasn't going to get up, but she wanted to know who was knocking on her back door this late at night and why? She moved through the kitchen with the stealth worthy of a burglar and peered out the peephole saying, "Who the hell is it?"

"Me," a voice replied.

"Me who?" Miss Tonya said. "I can't see nobody."

"I'm right here," the voice tried to convince her.

"Where?"

Silence.

Miss Tonya sucked her teeth and unlocked the door. Then she opened the screen and peaked out her scarfed head, scanning left, then right like a mechanical clown at a carnival that scares children. *Nothing.* She stepped out onto her porch and the scary clown scanned left, then right. Something she didn't know of moved past her into the house.

"Ooh, that was prob'ly a ghos'." Her pun was the fortell of the existence. Miss Tonya moved back inside, locked her screen door, then her big door and headed back to the bed. She didn't know that it was a ghost, but it opened her doors to let in its confederates.

Miss Tonya laid on her side, facing the wall, hand under her ear, ready to rest. Weight made the floors creak, and Miss Tonya popped her eyes open, her eyebrows knitted, and she cocked her head like an animal hearing something strange. When the sound of hard air resonated, that forced Miss Tonya to turn and look toward the door. Outside a few dogs started barking, big dogs, then smaller dogs. After hearing a room door open, Miss Tonya threw the covers off, swung her legs out of the bed and sat up to listen closely.

Her head bowed like she was about to say grace at the dinner table. Something funny was going on in her house. A light came on in a room, the shine spilled under the door. After a few hot seconds, the light went back out. The door closed quietly, and creeping became revived. Miss Tonya jolted up from the bed and moved to her room door with quick, light steps. She twisted the doorknob slowly and peaked, frightened. When she saw what it was her face became like a Halloween fright mask, aghast.

She closed her door and tiptoed to her cordless phone over on the nightstand, then called the police.

"911 what's your emergency?" The dispatcher asked.

"Yes, two people wearing some—kind of masks and black hoodies are—" Miss Tonya paused when she heard yelling.

"Nigga get cho bitch ass up! You thought it was a game!"

"Lawd have mercy!" Miss Tonya ran to her door and looked out.

"Hello, Ma'am?"

"My God, Jesus!" Miss Tonya whispered in a hard cry, seeing her son being snatched out of his room in a tank top, boxers and his feet bare.

"Ma'am?"

"These people just came into my house and took my son! Oh, Lawd help me, Jesus." Miss Tonya ran up the hallway saying, "They taking my son outta tha house!" Miss Tonya saw three black-

hooded figures moving across the lawn with her son going toward a waiting van.

"What's your address, ma'am? Tell me everything that's going on."

When her son started putting up a fight one of the suspects shot him twice in the side of the head by the temple.

"Whooo!" Miss Tonya jumped up and down like a church votary catching the Holy Ghost. "They don' shot my son! They don' shot my son!" she screamed.

"Ma'am, you need to talk to me so I can help you."

"The people got in a red van minivan! I'm in Wonderwood Acres on Allegheny! Please—please—please!"

"Can you see the tags, ma'am?"

"No-no-no, please help me!"

Chapter 43

Juicey was speeding up Alleghaney, came to Freedom Drive and made a right. A square car was turning into the gas station not concerned about the van until it screeched loudly. That's when a BOLO: *Be on lookout* went out about a red minivan. The sirens rendered to life.

Kasper looked back, then upfront saying "Juicey, let's go."

Juicey stormed the van down Freedom Drive with a confident smile and checked the rearview. Blue lights rotating with white light threw back its reflection. The police tried to weave around a truck that couldn't quite pull over. Juicey hung a right on Camp Green and shot up around the curve.

"Shit!" she cursed the all-white police car that was waiting to come out of the middle school on the right with its bold blue stripe running the length of the Ford.

It was ready to take Pershing action. But the first car was coming so fast it had to wait. Juicey went up through Ashley Park. Sirens blared behind the 713 and lights flickered uncontrollably. Juicey pressed the emergency brake as she made a hard right out onto the main drag Wilkinson Boulevard causing a screech as the back tired smoked. Kasper was holding on to the back of the seat, praying Juicey didn't flip the van. Tee's facial expression was a person at a theme park experimenting on a ride that takes a three-hundred-foot plunge. Koda was up there with Juicey enjoying the thrill with a smile.

"Mmmhh," Juicey said as she pulled the brake lever to bring life back to the rear tires. Then she put her foot on the gas and belled down Wilkinson. Two more police cars were racing up behind them.

"Get th—" Juicey blared the horn at a Toyota that was not moving fast enough before going around it out of the lane.

She made a left into Remount road in time before an Escalade could hit her. The van went back to full speed passing cars had the sounds of rushing wind. The light was green where Remount crossed over onto West Boulevard. Juicey shot right through it.

Kasper looked back to see where the police were. They were fifty yards back and gaining.

"They comin' boy," he said to himself. He turned out the window saying, "Fuck all this shit." Then he said to Juicey, "Go, dog!"

"I'm tryna, bra. I'm tryna." Juicey swerved in and out of lanes around cars to gain length.

South Treon was at the next intersection. Juicey slowed up to make the right because mashing the emergency brake became less attractive due to traffic. The van was back at the red line swerving around cars and blowing at them. In the rearview mirror blue lights were trying to defeat the night. Juicey took South Treon to Nations Ford Road. The helicopter was making its appearance by then. Koda and Juicey were so silly they were smiling the whole while.

This was how they got their thrill taking the police on high-speed chases. Kasper was worried about his life. High-speed chases turned deadly and he was not with this type of action, playing daredevil with cars, jumping around traffic. Tee was worried about getting away period.

"Stop at that light," Kasper said. "We ghost."

Three of the van doors stood wide open when officers surrounded it with their guns drawn, the helicopter spotlight shinned down on it from above like a miniature sun.

"Where the fuck did they go?" one officer asked.

"The doors came open, but I never saw anyone get out," A second officer said. His gun was still pointed at the van like the suspects would jump out at them.

"So, where the fuck are they?" A third officer asked.

The first officer said, "I don't know but somehow they're gone."

The young teenage girl stood approximately 5'8, with long hair twisted and dark.skin. The meeting she held was clandestine in the meadows out past some woods. Hundreds of black males and females ranging from ages fourteen to twenty-four attended as they stood in rows of fifteen, it was dark, and a large fire blazed behind

the young girl as she stood on a platform overlooking the crowd. She wore a black cloak with a black ribbon tied around her waist which represented knowledge acquired from the underworld.

This was the emblem she wore which was an Ekquinede. To possess this em Elia was to possess supreme knowledge from the Poviks. It was Lord Enkis evil brother Enlil that designed this symbol when he partnered with the devil. Not anyone who was of a God Goddess or a Sovakites of the Poviks had no knowledge of this symbol or had no order to possess the symbol for wear.

"I am your leader," the young girl spoke to the crowd. "Your Lord, your God. You will serve me and for me. You will submit your mind to me and your souls to will be sacrificed. Your relentless loyalty will suffice to my device. The mind and body you will devote to me for my benefit. My supreme cause I shall not be denied. I will not be denied. For my powers will overwhelm every the most, stern supreme being. So, I say to you I am the abundant God. Now bring up your weapons." And in an abrupt movement everyone brought their handguns up to the temple.

"I bought my knowledge and powers you will be resurrected. Now execute," the young girl demanded, and gunfire erupted in one harmony.

Zya turned over out of her sleep and threw up yellow bile then coughed violently. She swung out of bed and trudged to the bathroom to rinse her mouth and splash water on her face. She rested on the sink as she looked in the mirror breathing heavily. That dreamed scared her. The medallion the young girl wore was trouble and far too evil. Zya did not even know the girl or how she came to possess that medallion in a dream. It only meant that a storm was brewing. It was something to worry about.

To Be Continued...
Ghost Mob 2
Coming Soon

Submission Guideline

Submit the first three chapters of your completed manuscript to ldpsubmissions@gmail.com, subject line: Your book's title. The manuscript must be in a .doc file and sent as an attachment. Document should be in Times New Roman, double spaced and in size 12 font. Also, provide your synopsis and full contact information. If sending multiple submissions, they must each be in a separate email.

Have a story but no way to send it electronically? You can still submit to LDP/Ca$h Presents. Send in the first three chapters, written or typed, of your completed manuscript to:

**LDP: Submissions Dept
Po Box 944
Stockbridge, Ga 30281**

DO NOT send original manuscript. Must be a duplicate.

Provide your synopsis and a cover letter containing your full contact information.

Thanks for considering LDP and Ca$h Presents.

Ghost Mob

COKE KINGS V

KING OF THE TRAP II

By **T.J. Edwards**

GORILLAZ IN THE BAY V

3X KRAZY II

De'Kari

THE STREETS ARE CALLING II

Duquie Wilson

KINGPIN KILLAZ IV

STREET KINGS III

PAID IN BLOOD III

CARTEL KILLAZ IV

DOPE GODS III

Hood Rich

SINS OF A HUSTLA II

ASAD

KINGZ OF THE GAME VI

Playa Ray

SLAUGHTER GANG IV

RUTHLESS HEART IV

By Willie Slaughter

THE HEART OF A SAVAGE III

By Jibril Williams

FUK SHYT II

By Blakk Diamond

TRAP QUEEN

By Troublesome

YAYO V

GHOST MOB II

Stilloan Robinson

KINGPIN DREAMS III

By Paper Boi Rari

CREAM II

By Yolanda Moore

SON OF A DOPE FIEND III

By Renta

FOREVER GANGSTA II

GLOCKS ON SATIN SHEETS III

By Adrian Dulan

LOYALTY AIN'T PROMISED III

By Keith Williams

THE PRICE YOU PAY FOR LOVE II

By Destiny Skai

CONFESSIONS OF A GANGSTA III

By Nicholas Lock

I'M NOTHING WITHOUT HIS LOVE II

SINS OF A THUG II

By Monet Dragun

LIFE OF A SAVAGE IV

MURDA SEASON IV

GANGLAND CARTEL III

CHI'RAQ GANGSTAS II

By **Romell Tukes**

QUIET MONEY IV

THUG LIFE II

EXTENDED CLIP II

By **Trai'Quan**

THE STREETS MADE ME III

By **Larry D. Wright**

IF YOU CROSS ME ONCE II

ANGEL III

By **Anthony Fields**

FRIEND OR FOE III

By **Mimi**

SAVAGE STORMS II

By **Meesha**

BLOOD ON THE MONEY III

By J-Blunt

THE STREETS WILL NEVER CLOSE II

By K'ajji

NIGHTMARES OF A HUSTLA III

By King Dream

THE WIFEY I USED TO BE II

By Nicole Goosby

IN THE ARM OF HIS BOSS

By Jamila

MONEY, MURDER & MEMORIES II

Malik D. Rice

CONCRETE KILLAZ II

By Kingpen

HARD AND RUTHLESS II

By Von Wiley Hall

Available Now

RESTRAINING ORDER **I & II**

By **CA$H & Coffee**

LOVE KNOWS NO BOUNDARIES **I II & III**

By **Coffee**

Ghost Mob

RAISED AS A GOON I, II, III & IV
BRED BY THE SLUMS I, II, III
BLAST FOR ME I & II
ROTTEN TO THE CORE I II III
A BRONX TALE I, II, III
DUFFLE BAG CARTEL I II III IV V
HEARTLESS GOON I II III IV
A SAVAGE DOPEBOY I II
HEARTLESS GOON I II III
DRUG LORDS I II III
CUTTHROAT MAFIA I II
By **Ghost**
LAY IT DOWN **I & II**
LAST OF A DYING BREED I II
BLOOD STAINS OF A SHOTTA I & II III
By **Jamaica**
LOYAL TO THE GAME I II III
LIFE OF SIN I, II III
By **TJ & Jelissa**
BLOODY COMMAS I & II
SKI MASK CARTEL I II & III
KING OF NEW YORK I II,III IV V
RISE TO POWER I II III
COKE KINGS I II III IV
BORN HEARTLESS I II III IV
KING OF THE TRAP
By **T.J. Edwards**
IF LOVING HIM IS WRONG…I & II
LOVE ME EVEN WHEN IT HURTS I II III
By **Jelissa**

Stilloan Robinson

WHEN THE STREETS CLAP BACK I & II III
THE HEART OF A SAVAGE I II
By **Jibril Williams**
A DISTINGUISHED THUG STOLE MY HEART I II & III
LOVE SHOULDN'T HURT I II III IV
RENEGADE BOYS I II III IV
PAID IN KARMA I II III
SAVAGE STORMS
By **Meesha**
A GANGSTER'S CODE I &, II III
A GANGSTER'S SYN I II III
THE SAVAGE LIFE I II III
CHAINED TO THE STREETS I II III
BLOOD ON THE MONEY I II
By J-Blunt
PUSH IT TO THE LIMIT
By **Bre' Hayes**
BLOOD OF A BOSS **I, II, III, IV, V**
SHADOWS OF THE GAME
By **Askari**
THE STREETS BLEED MURDER **I, II & III**
THE HEART OF A GANGSTA I II& III
By **Jerry Jackson**
CUM FOR ME I II III IV V VI
An **LDP Erotica Collaboration**
BRIDE OF A HUSTLA **I II & II**
THE FETTI GIRLS **I, II& III**
CORRUPTED BY A GANGSTA I, II III, IV
BLINDED BY HIS LOVE
THE PRICE YOU PAY FOR LOVE

258

Ghost Mob

DOPE GIRL MAGIC I II III
By **Destiny Skai**
WHEN A GOOD GIRL GOES BAD
By **Adrienne**
THE COST OF LOYALTY I II III
By Kweli
A GANGSTER'S REVENGE **I II III & IV**
THE BOSS MAN'S DAUGHTERS I II III IV V
A SAVAGE LOVE **I & II**
BAE BELONGS TO ME I II
A HUSTLER'S DECEIT I, II, III
WHAT BAD BITCHES DO I, II, III
SOUL OF A MONSTER I II III
KILL ZONE
A DOPE BOY'S QUEEN I II
By **Aryanna**
A KINGPIN'S AMBITON
A KINGPIN'S AMBITION **II**
I MURDER FOR THE DOUGH
By **Ambitious**
TRUE SAVAGE I II III IV V VI VII
DOPE BOY MAGIC I, II, III
MIDNIGHT CARTEL I II
CITY OF KINGZ
By **Chris Green**
A DOPEBOY'S PRAYER
By **Eddie "Wolf" Lee**
THE KING CARTEL **I, II & III**
By **Frank Gresham**
THESE NIGGAS AIN'T LOYAL **I, II & III**

Stilloan Robinson

By **Nikki Tee**
GANGSTA SHYT **I II &III**
By **CATO**
THE ULTIMATE BETRAYAL
By **Phoenix**
BOSS'N UP **I , II & III**
By **Royal Nicole**
I LOVE YOU TO DEATH
By Destiny J
I RIDE FOR MY HITTA
I STILL RIDE FOR MY HITTA
By **Misty Holt**
LOVE & CHASIN' PAPER
By **Qay Crockett**
TO DIE IN VAIN
SINS OF A HUSTLA
By **ASAD**
BROOKLYN HUSTLAZ
By **Boogsy Morina**
BROOKLYN ON LOCK I & II
By **Sonovia**
GANGSTA CITY
By **Teddy Duke**
A DRUG KING AND HIS DIAMOND I & II III
A DOPEMAN'S RICHES
HER MAN, MINE'S TOO I, II
CASH MONEY HO'S
THE WIFEY I USED TO BE
By Nicole Goosby
TRAPHOUSE KING **I II & III**

Ghost Mob

KINGPIN KILLAZ I II III

STREET KINGS I II

PAID IN BLOOD **I II**

CARTEL KILLAZ I II III

DOPE GODS I II

By **Hood Rich**

LIPSTICK KILLAH **I, II, III**

CRIME OF PASSION I II & III

FRIEND OR FOE I II

By **Mimi**

STEADY MOBBN' **I, II, III**

THE STREETS STAINED MY SOUL

By **Marcellus Allen**

WHO SHOT YA **I, II, III**

SON OF A DOPE FIEND I II

Renta

GORILLAZ IN THE BAY **I II III IV**

TEARS OF A GANGSTA I II

3X KRAZY

DE'KARI

TRIGGADALE I II III

Elijah R. Freeman

GOD BLESS THE TRAPPERS I, II, III

THESE SCANDALOUS STREETS I, II, III

FEAR MY GANGSTA I, II, III IV, V

THESE STREETS DON'T LOVE NOBODY I, II

BURY ME A G I, II, III, IV, V

A GANGSTA'S EMPIRE I, II, III, IV

THE DOPEMAN'S BODYGAURD I II

THE REALEST KILLAZ I II III

261

Stilloan Robinson

Tranay Adams
THE STREETS ARE CALLING
Duquie Wilson
MARRIED TO A BOSS... I II III
By Destiny Skai & Chris Green
KINGZ OF THE GAME I II III IV V
Playa Ray
SLAUGHTER GANG I II III
RUTHLESS HEART I II III
By Willie Slaughter
FUK SHYT
By Blakk Diamond
DON'T F#CK WITH MY HEART I II
By Linnea
ADDICTED TO THE DRAMA I II III
IN THE ARM OF HIS BOSS II
By Jamila
YAYO I II III IV
A SHOOTER'S AMBITION I II
By S. Allen
TRAP GOD I II III
By Troublesome
FOREVER GANGSTA
GLOCKS ON SATIN SHEETS I II
By Adrian Dulan
TOE TAGZ I II III
By Ah'Million
KINGPIN DREAMS I II
By Paper Boi Rari
CONFESSIONS OF A GANGSTA I II

262

Ghost Mob

By Nicholas Lock

I'M NOTHING WITHOUT HIS LOVE

SINS OF A THUG

By Monet Dragun

CAUGHT UP IN THE LIFE I II III

By Robert Baptiste

NEW TO MONEY, MURDER & MEMORIES

THE GAME I II III

By **Malik D. Rice**

LIFE OF A SAVAGE I II III

A GANGSTA'S QUR'AN I II III

MURDA SEASON I II III

GANGLAND CARTEL I II

CHI'RAQ GANGSTAS

By **Romell Tukes**

LOYALTY AIN'T PROMISED I II

By Keith Williams

QUIET MONEY I II III

THUG LIFE

EXTENDED CLIP

By **Trai'Quan**

THE STREETS MADE ME I II

By **Larry D. Wright**

THE ULTIMATE SACRIFICE I, II, III, IV, V, VI

KHADIFI

IF YOU CROSS ME ONCE

ANGEL I II

By **Anthony Fields**

THE LIFE OF A HOOD STAR

By Ca$h & Rashia Wilson

THE STREETS WILL NEVER CLOSE
By K'ajji
CREAM
By Yolanda Moore
NIGHTMARES OF A HUSTLA I II
By King Dream
CONCRETE KILLAZ
By Kingpen
HARD AND RUTHLESS
By Von Wiley Hall
GHOST MOB II
Stilloan Robinson

BOOKS BY LDP'S CEO, CA$H

TRUST IN NO MAN

TRUST IN NO MAN 2

TRUST IN NO MAN 3

BONDED BY BLOOD

SHORTY GOT A THUG

THUGS CRY

THUGS CRY 2

THUGS CRY 3

TRUST NO BITCH

TRUST NO BITCH 2

TRUST NO BITCH 3

TIL MY CASKET DROPS

RESTRAINING ORDER

RESTRAINING ORDER 2

IN LOVE WITH A CONVICT

LIFE OF A HOOD STAR

Stilloan Robinson

CPSIA information can be obtained
at www.ICGtesting.com
Printed in the USA
LVHW050037090321
680891LV00017B/728